VECTOR

VECTOR

Dear Elizabeth,
Pleasure to meat you today!
Don't underestimate the
power or the danger of the
printed words.

Thanks for Reading,

Richard Zanetti

A THRILLER

RICHARD ZANETTI

ARCHWAY
PUBLISHING

Archway Publishing books may be ordered through booksellers or by contacting:

Archway Publishing
1663 Liberty Drive
Bloomington, IN 47403
www.archwaypublishing.com
844-669-3957

ISBN: 978-1-6657-6068-3 (sc)
ISBN: 978-1-6657-6070-6 (hc)
ISBN: 978-1-6657-6069-0 (e)

Library of Congress Control Number: 2024910476

Print information available on the last page.

Archway Publishing rev. date: 08/28/2024

There is no genius free from some tincture of madness.
—Seneca the Younger

one

MEMORIAL DAY, MAY 27TH, SPRINGVALE, CONNECTICUT

The grand marshal, veterans, fire engines, and marching bands commemorated the national holiday in this small coastal town. First Avenue buzzed with activity as residents and visitors gathered on blankets and beach chairs, waving flags and cheering the parade. Music, enthusiasm, and the enticing scent of the pancake breakfast at St. John Church filled the air.

Emma Burr had not missed a Memorial Day parade since she moved to Springvale some twenty years ago. She and best friend, Jackie, arrived early to stake out a shady spot under the century-old maple trees in front of the old courthouse. They always sat on a giant blanket near the curb, so no one could block their views. After the parade, they treated themselves to two blueberry pancakes drowned in maple syrup.

They watched as the First Selectwoman raised the American flag in front of the Wall of Honor, honoring veterans who had made the ultimate sacrifice. As the colors went up, the town's chief administrator let go of the halyard and fell into the arms of the police officer standing by her side. He helped her to a chair, as an assistant and two paramedics from a nearby ambulance rushed over to assist her.

The high school band marched by, performing a well-rehearsed John Philip Sousa piece. The trombone player dropped his instrument, resounding when it hit the street.

The noise brought Emma to her feet. She saw the player sink to his knees, coughing and holding his head. Two onlookers helped him up as the band marched on and didn't miss a beat.

Overcome by dizziness, Emma steadied herself against a tree, thinking she got up too fast. Her mind raced back to what she had eaten the night before—nothing out of the ordinary.

"Oh, no!" she said, as the day went dark, and the ground rushed up to meet her thin, frail body.

Shouting Emma's name, Jackie rushed over and tried to revive her, to no avail. Panic-stricken, Jackie waved for the paramedics. One ran across the street to help.

A drummer collapsed near to where the trombone player had fallen. The bass drum boomed and rolled against the curb.

A family of four, carrying a blanket and lunch basket, hastened across the street, avoiding marchers as they fled. Three frightened onlookers followed in their wake.

A woman behind Jackie and Emma cried out as her husband crumpled to his knees. A man pulled his wife away from them.

The Memorial Day Parade in Springvale, Connecticut came to a sudden halt. Joy and celebration veered towards anxiety and fear. Worried parade goers collected their things and scrambled off in disarray. A few stood up, debating what to do.

Megaphone in hand, the chief of police stood on stage and calmly explained why he was canceling the event. He issued exit instructions and urged people to go home in a peaceful and orderly way.

Paramedics carried Emma to an ambulance. She died on her way to the hospital.

RICHARD ZANETTI

two

MEMORIAL DAY, MAY 27TH, PARK RIDGE, PENNSYLVANIA

K alyan Chatha, Director of Emergency Medicine at Mercy Hospital, found the ER inundated with ailing people. Some occupied the floor, while others, with desperation-etched faces, stood awaiting help that never seemed to come. The crowded space made movement nearly impossible. Outside, those ailing in cars or seated on the sidewalk were equally desperate to get in.

"This is worse than COVID," Chatha said to David Whitcher, observing the bedlam enfolding around them. "Six have died and three are in trauma resuscitation."

"I'll make some calls," replied the newly appointed Park Ridge Health Director. Whitcher hurried to his office, locked the door, and dialed Pennsylvania's Health Deputy in Harrisburg.

An answering service forwarded the call to Chief Administrator Adam Parker. Whitcher identified himself and nervously described the ER situation. "We're not sure, but we think it's, um, a bug, with flu-like symptoms: headaches, fever, and nausea. Six people. Six have died from this thing, Mr. Parker. We need your help as soon as possible."

"No other towns have reported anything like it," Parker said, with studied calmness and control. "Call Smythe in Allentown. They can take the overflow. I'll alert the CDC and HHS to determine if this is a health emergency and get back to you."

"Okay," said Whitcher doubtfully. "I, I just don't know—"

"Call me in an hour with an update." Parker disconnected.

Chatha knocked on Whitcher's door, then tried to open it. He knocked again, louder this time. "We need you, Dave! We just lost another patient!"

RICHARD ZANETTI

three

MEMORIAL DAY, MAY 27ᵀᴴ, BAY CITY, TEXAS

The mayor's emergency message was sent by text, email, phone, and fax to all Bay City residents and to local radio and TV stations:

"Because of the sudden and severe illness that has struck our town, I have canceled the Memorial Day Parade today. We will provide updates as we have them. In the meantime, we urge all residents to stay home and only go out as needed. Next year, we look forward to paying tribute to the men and women who died for our country."

Steve Rolandi, medical director of Bay City Hospital, had seen a lot on his watch: typhoid, gunshots, cholera, and bodies so badly broken from auto accidents that it took a minor miracle to save them. He wasn't sure how to proceed this time, but knew he had to remain calm.

Solemnly, he responded to the reassuring voice on the other end of the phone. "Seems like the flu, not COVID. One third of the town is sick. Two have died and—" Rolandi paused. "Yes, sir, yes, sir." He hung up and rubbed his eyes, burning from twenty hours of no sleep.

four

BIOLOGICAL WEAPONS GROUP HEADQUARTERS, ATLANTA, GEORGIA

Marv Brockman found the fluorescent light, antiseptic smell, and unnatural silence of the third floor conference room unpleasant today as he gathered his dedicated team of managers there so early. But the order came from the President, and as usual, he obeyed.

Brockman glanced at Joe Dunphy and Roy Atkinson seated at the table across from him. Since the recent unexpected downsizing order from the House and Senate Appropriations Committee, they had been toiling tirelessly on a sarin project and were nearing exhaustion, working sixteen-hour days. "Warriors," he proudly dubbed them. "Dedicated."

Dunphy glanced up at the clock. "What happened to Imelda? She knows it's 0500." Manager of the Counterintelligence Group of agents, scientists and technicians, Dunphy was best at addressing oblique problems that often escaped logical solutions. While he occasionally went off rails, he had moments of brilliance that made him a valuable asset and leader of the team.

Atkinson yawned and stretched his tall frame. The bearded manager of the Cyber Emergency Division got high on fixing bugs and quickly solving complex problems. His ability elevated him to the rank of BWG's "cringineer." Other hackers winced as he effortlessly eliminated the baffling software glitches they couldn't resolve. He looked up when the door clicked open.

Imelda Burke entered, holding a container of black coffee, a lightly toasted bagel, and a cell phone. As she turned, the bagel slipped off the coffee container. She deftly caught and balanced it on her phone before it hit the floor.

Dunphy grinned and clapped his hands.

"No bite for you." Imelda turned to Brockman. "Sorry, Marv. I'm still practicing for these late-night sessions. No more, right?"

People often cited Imelda's skillful management of the Scientific and Technological Components Division, coupled with her perseverance and biological expertise, as reasons she became one of the youngest managers at BWG.

But more cynical observers attributed her lofty status to physical attraction—a knockout with captivating green eyes, straight nose, and firm jawline—and they considered her totally unapproachable, even when wearing jeans, a Caribbean blue lab shirt, orange socks, and matching sneakers, if not for her scruffy ponytail.

She placed her breakfast and phone on the table and took the chair next to Dunphy, who broke off a piece of bagel, and popped it into his mouth.

Imelda smiled, used to his antics.

Brockman looked up from his laptop and grimly addressed his colleagues. "Sorry, guys. I got the urgent call late last night, so here we are. As you can guess, it's about the three flu outbreaks."

"Yeah," said Dunphy, shifting in his chair. "What happened there?"

"We don't know yet. But we do know this. Vector, a terrorist, or terrorist organization, predicted the outbreaks in those three towns."

"Predicted?" said Dunphy.

"That's right." Brockman smirked. "Everyone at the White House and the National Security Council thought it was a hoax and didn't want to risk embarrassing themselves. Some lunatic wanting to vent or something. So, mum was the word for a while."

"They should have told us sooner," said Atkinson.

"No kidding," Brockman sighed. "Yesterday, the President received a second email from Vector. It threatens the release of a deadly agent in three large cities. Vector claims it will kill millions if we don't pay a ransom by Thursday, July 18th—one billion in gold bullion."

Dunphy blew out air and typed some numbers on his phone. "That's like twelve and a half tons, isn't it? Good luck carrying it."

"What does he think?" said Atkinson. "He's Goldfinger?"

"A biological threat to extort an untraceable fortune," said Brockman. "*That* got everyone's attention."

Imelda tapped her fingers on the table and said sourly, "It happened on our watch."

"NSA urged the President to go full force on this," said Brockman. "All the agencies are involved. Jim Malone, the new secretary of DHS, will oversee the operation."

Atkinson said, "They proved what they could do, didn't they?"

Imelda got up and slowly paced the room. "How did they do it? Infect three towns in different states all on the same day, all perfectly synchronized." She returned to her chair.

"What's easier," asked Dunphy, "infecting a small town or a large city?"

Imelda gazed at him. "Depends on the method, right?"

"The threat is real." Brockman glanced dolefully from one manager to another to emphasize the point. "Bottom line: we have less than two months to determine how Vector did it and neutralize the threat."

"What about the sarin project?" responded Atkinson. He and Dunphy had spent a month on it and were close to completion. "We have only a week before—"

"Table it," blurted Brockman. "I'll inform Malone. He knows what's involved here since the downsizing. We focus on Vector and stop this thing."

Brockman paused. "I want an action plan from each of you by 0900 tomorrow, three pages. Tactical procedures, resources, and goals should be included along with timeline, risk, and probability assessments. Describe and assign priorities to your teams and how you'd involve support services and the operational divisions. I've ordered all the associates to support you. Fact-check and verify your plans . . . One more thing. If we can't find Vector, I think the President will pay, as sad as that may seem."

Imelda's eyes rolled. "Do that and we'll be paying extortionists forever."

The action plans were in Brockman's inbox when he arrived early the next day. He had just finished reading them when Imelda stuck her head in his office door.

"Good morning." A smile flickered on her lips. She knew her plan was solid and eager for his reaction, while aware he didn't like to rank the people on his team.

He logged off, removed his glasses, and rubbed his eyes, the lack of sleep apparent in his bearing. "You know, if it weren't for the politics, this job would be a lot easier and a lot more fun. They cut our staff by half, reduced our funding, and still expect us to come through when it counts." He sighed. "Don't mind me, just grousing."

Imelda studied his lined face with apprehension, and cared about Brockman like the father she hardly knew. "Take it easy, Marv. Get some rest. We have the team. We're on it."

"Under a microscope, Imelda. Money's tight. The Finance Committee thinks we need to be cut further. I even heard rumors about folding us into the CDC." Leaning forward on his elbows, he stared at her. "About this Vector thing. We can't afford—"

"—more bad press?" she said.

Brockman nodded, for it seemed like yesterday when the denunciations started. CIA director Lou Sanford had set them off, criticizing BWG for not processing samples fast enough after Ebola killed five Americans and made others sick. The media quickly picked up on Sanford's accusations that made the matter worse: BWG had yet to fully recover.

Imelda took the chair across from him. "I've been waiting for this, Marv, a real challenge. Let me lead it. You said I'm ready."

He sighed again. "Our reputation depends on what we do. And there's more here than meets the eye. I'm sure Washington knows more than they want to admit—a potential nightmare."

"I can do it," she insisted. "Did you read my action plan?"

He nodded. An awkward calm followed until she broke the silence. "Well, what do you think?"

He took a deep breath. "I'm happy you want the job, Imelda. It shows initiative. But you've only been here two years and lack the experience."

"Hold on." She raised her hand. "Since I started, I worked hard to prove myself. Paid my dues, team player. But you gave the big jobs to the others."

Brockman shook his head. "Imelda, I—"

"I never groused about it, especially the Ebola case, but it hurt being passed over, not once, but twice. I know I can handle this. I earned it. And I'll do my best to make you proud."

"You have a brilliant future in front of you and lots of time

RICHARD ZANETTI

to make your mark. Why rush it with something like this? It's an enormous risk."

"For me?" she scoffed. "How can I prove myself if I don't take risks?" She rose from the chair and placed her hands on his desk, leaning toward him. "Nothing can substitute for experience. Cases like this don't come around every day. I won't disappoint you, Marv. Please, I deserve it."

"Let me sleep on it," he said.

five

WASHINGTON HEIGHTS, NEW YORK CITY

When their car screeched to the curb in front of a convenience store, Police Sergeant Alex West, flush with adrenaline, let his door fly open and was out before it stopped. Someone had called in a robbery in progress. Alex checked the street: deserted except for a young man peering through the convenience store window.

Inside, a masked man waved his gun menacingly at the desk clerk, whose hand shook so much he could hardly get the bills out of the register. The clerk handed him what cash he had, then raised his trembling hands, showing he had no more to give. Several bills floated to the floor as the robber jammed the rest into his jacket pockets. Heading out the door, he glimpsed the cruiser idling near the curb and froze when he saw the sergeant.

"Drop it!" Alex shouted, glancing back for his partner, who hadn't moved from the car.

The perp pointed his weapon at Alex. "Don't!" Alex shouted.

The gun exploded. Alex felt the painful impact from his vest as he drew his weapon and fired. The bullet missed the robber, accidentally striking Danny Taylor standing near the window.

The burglar escaped as Taylor fell onto the sidewalk, clutching his bleeding chest. Alex hurried to the young man and peered into his frightened face. The bullet had struck just below his heart. Alex kneeled beside him and told him to hold on as he called for help. Danny's face slowly dissolved into the face of the young man's mother, sobbing uncontrollably.

Drenched in sweat, sheets knotted around his waist and legs, Alex lay there, heart pounding from the terrifying dream that haunted him. He sat up, trembling and nauseous, and held his head in his hands as he tried to recover.

Showering quickly, Alex toweled off, lathered his face and methodically shaved, a routine that never failed to improve his frame of mind. He broke out a new white shirt and red-striped tie. His old gray suit would have to do for the Kartan interview today. Quickly dressing, he headed out onto 181st Street, crowded with morning commuters slogging up the hill to catch the downtown A Train.

Parked in front, his Trailblazer needed a wash. No time for it now. He got in, made a U-turn, turned right on St. Nicholas Avenue and headed west across the George Washington Bridge. Bathed in morning sun, the Palisades glittered from the dew, and a tugboat plowed its way up the Hudson River.

Alex turned on the radio as a newscaster recapped today's top stories. ". . . hundreds of people in Springvale, Connecticut, Bay City, Texas, and Park Ridge, Pennsylvania have gotten sick from a flu-like virus. Several have reportedly died from complications. Authorities at the Centers for Disease Control haven't been able to identify the cause of breakout or explain why it struck only three towns and how it spread so quickly. In other news . . ." Alex flicked off the radio and took Route 80 West to Nutley, New Jersey.

Surrounded by an eight-foot-high barbed-wire security fence, the pharmaceutical company's twenty-story, glass-and-steel headquarters occupied a park-like setting amid tall trees, colorful flower beds, and sculptured shrubs. Alex checked in at the gate and parked in the last visitor's space.

He entered the building through the marble proscenium and presented his card to the receptionist. "We're expecting you, Mr. West." She summoned a stone-faced guard, who escorted Alex to an executive conference room on the third floor. The door was open and Alex walked right in.

Martin Haley, a stocky man in a gray tweed suit, seated at the executive table with three company officials, looked up when Alex entered.

"Good morning," Alex said with a smile, hoping to make a good impression. His friendly nature, athletic build, and six-foot height typically won people over.

Haley rose slowly, as if it were a great effort to lift his unwieldy torso, and shook the outstretched hand. "Welcome, Mr. West. Thanks for coming."

"My pleasure, Mr. Haley."

Haley might have been handsome in his youth, but the years hadn't been kind to him; his round face was puffy, and frown lines crossed his forehead. "Joining us today are CFO Kevin Baines, corporate attorney Mike Slade, and Nicky Belle, VP in charge of contracts."

Alex shook their hands and took a seat, excited about bidding on a corporate project, a first for his struggling private detective agency. Leaning back, he focused on what he planned to say. It wasn't often he pitched to a CEO.

Haley adjusted his rimless glasses. "Coffee? Water?"

"No, thanks, I'm fine."

"Good. Let's get started then." The CEO placed his hands on the table. "I'll be brief, Mr. West. Two years ago, we signed a contract with Professor Gerfried Enslein. Heard of him?"

Alex shook his head.

"A distinguished molecular biologist and expert in gene splicing. He agreed to supply us with cultured living cells to develop a cure for autoimmune diseases. We paid him handsomely: two million upfront, to be exact. Unknown to us, the IRS was investigating Enslein for tax evasion." Haley glanced at Belle. "Our vetting process has a lot to be desired, I'm afraid."

Belle averted her gaze; Haley's sarcasm wasn't new to her.

"Enslein worked with us for only three months before they indicted him for tax evasion," Haley continued, passing a hand through his thinning, gray hair. "They found him guilty and sentenced him to six months in jail. When he got out, he disappeared with all our money. Vanished. We don't know where he is."

Baines raised a cautious hand. "Some companies will let white-collar criminals go free if they can collect the insurance, Mr. West. But it's not our style."

Haley nodded. "We worked with Enslein before. Knew him, trusted him, and convinced our board to invest in him. Well, he lied to us, cheated us. We want him to pay for what he did. It's the principle, you see." He glanced at Alex. "I'd guess he shouldn't be too hard to find."

It amused Alex when clients made light of finding people, especially a wealthy, intelligent fugitive who could be anywhere on the planet—a common negotiating ploy to gain a lower fee. Alex was eager for the deal, but wouldn't lie to get it. "It'll take some time."

Slade stared at his phone. "How long, exactly?"

"Six months if we're lucky. Maybe a year."

"As I recall, your reputation in Pinewood for finding people was pretty good, Mr. West." Slade leaned back and rubbed his chin. "One of the best locate cops in New York State, I believe."

"Yes."

"Do you work alone at Inteletech?" resumed Slade.

"My partner's a retired cop and we have an assistant."

"I read about the Danny Taylor incident," said Belle. "Would the social stigma from that event impede your search for Enslein?"

The question didn't surprise Alex. The incident was the first to appear on social media searches, with over a thousand comments, mostly critical. "A grand jury acquitted me of all charges. A tragic accident that happened years ago and will have no effect on our work."

"Are you licensed to carry, Mr. West?" continued Belle.

Haley's face twisted into a grimace. "We aren't asking Mr. West to find a murderer or armed robber, Nicky. Just a common swindler."

"That's okay," said Alex calmly. "Yes, I'm licensed to carry."

"Would you use your weapon?" Slade asked.

Alex smiled at their persistence. "Yes, in a life-threatening situation." He turned to Haley. "Finding people is our specialty, Mr. Haley, and if you hire us, we'll find Enslein."

Haley removed his glasses and rubbed his eyes. "How's business, Mr. West?"

"Good. But we're not too busy to devote the time and resources to finding this guy," stated with firm conviction.

Haley nodded. "I'd like to point out that analytically you don't measure up to the competition. But we made our decision based on a high recommendations and thorough reference checks. People say nice things about you. We think you're the right man for the job."

"Thank you."

"Can you find Enslein in sixty days or less?"

"We'll do our best."

"If you do, we'll pay you twenty-five grand plus your normal fees and expenses. If you don't, we'll pay your fees and expenses and find someone else." Haley waited for a beat. "Well, what do you think?"

"Sounds good," said Alex. "But I have to confer with my colleagues first."

"Nicky will draft a contract for your approval and—"

"Excuse me, Martin." Slade leaned forward. "I'd like to emphasize the importance of confidentiality."

"Absolutely," said Alex, turning to Slade. "Whatever ground rules you'd like."

Slade continued, his voice quavering slightly. "Some board members are willing to—"

Haley moaned, silencing his attorney. "I repeat, Mr. West, it's the principle. We trusted Enslein, and he stabbed us in the back."

A darkening sky matched Alex's frame of mind, driving back to the city, mulling over the job offer. Inteletech was barely surviving on smaller jobs that the big firms normally wouldn't touch. The Kartan contract was exactly what they needed to break out of the bush league and prove to prospective clients that they could handle almost anything.

Still, the deal troubled him, as if it were too good to be true. The same feeling Alex had years ago when he joined the Savage Colts, a street gang in Troy, New York.

He was thirteen when the Colts promised the world to him—girls, cash, self-confidence, and chill. But he quickly learned it wasn't something he wanted in his life.

Alex drove out of the Lincoln Tunnel, navigating through heavy crosstown traffic, and parked on East 41st Street as thunder rumbled in the distance.

He paused on the sidewalk to admire the gargoyles and glittering spire on the Chrysler Building. Alex chose the iconic skyscraper for Inteletech's office, hoping its history and class would rub off on his fledgling detective business. So far, that hadn't happened.

Connie was on the phone and hung up as Alex entered. At fifty-two, she looked much younger than her age. Her class and professionalism opened doors for them. She looked up and raised an eyebrow. "Well, what happened? Did you get it?"

"We did! Got the Kartan job!"

She high-fived him. "What about that raise you promised?"

Alex laughed. "Yeah, after *we* get paid." He looked around. "Where's George?"

She tilted her head at his closed office door.

George partnered with Alex at the Pinewood Police Department and left with his buddy to start Inteletech, trusting Alex's business skills and unwavering integrity. Not as hard now as in his precinct days, but George was still imposing at six feet two and two hundred pounds.

Alex startled him when he barged through the door without knocking.

"Damn it, Alex! Don't do that!"

"We got it!"

George sat back and folded his arms. "I knew you could do it."

Alex took a chair and filled him in on the offer.

George rarely smiled, but the thought of that bonus put a huge grin on his face. It faded when he noticed Alex's troubled expression. "What?"

"I don't know. Haley decided on the spot. No consultation. No negotiation. Just okay, here's the offer, you got the job. Like he took us for granted. Everything happened a little too fast. I had the feeling I wasn't getting the complete story."

"Why?"

Alex shook his head. "A hidden agenda? Something about Enslein he's not telling us? I'm not sure."

"Nobody's gonna tell you everything, Alex. Politics. Corporate bullshit. He must like you."

"He may have liked me, but I don't think he had the full support of his board. Like finding Enslein was Haley's baby, despite what the members thought. Haley seemed a little shifty, too. Maybe that's it."

George raised his hand. "But is that a valid reason to reject the offer?"

"No."

George got up and looked out at the rain splashing on the windowsill. "He's the boss. Wants to hire us. Pay us big bucks. Picked us over the competition." He turned and stared at Alex. "So, what's the problem?"

"It's the same feeling you get when you stop a perp and look him in the eye, if he's gonna be a problem or not."

"Enslein or Haley?"

"Maybe both."

"So what are you sayin'?" George blew out some air and sat down. "This isn't Danny Taylor, is it?"

It wasn't the first time George had brought up that fateful incident. But Alex wasn't pissed. George was the only cop who supported him after the shooting. The loyal friend who never wavered. "Gimme a break, George."

"You told me when we started this company, we'd take cases as they came. Now that we got a chance for a real job, you're getting antsy?"

"No. No. The pros outweigh the cons. We take it and find this creep in sixty days or less."

six

ZAFAR NATIONAL BANK, BEIRUT, LEBANON

Hunched over his desk, Ahmad ran the numbers. According to his calculations, the bank would clear one hundred million dollars if the deal went through. The finder's fee would make him a millionaire.

Ahmad hoped for the best, acutely aware that fifty percent of foreign gold transfers failed from financial collapse, fraud, theft, or negligence. He dialed the client's access number and waited.

"Yes," answered the client.

"Ahmad."

"I was wondering what happened to you, Ahmad." Spoken with a Swiss-German accent. "You should not keep me waiting."

"The bank agrees to receive the gold shipment, handle custom regulations, provide documentation, and insure against theft. We will ship the gold to the Malvabi Refinery in Switzerland, where they will launder it. The declaration label will claim the gold came from a Brazilian mine."

"I expected that," said the client. "What else?"

"You agree to the following conditions."

"Go on."

"We will deduct from the transfer a ten percent processing

charge, million-dollar finder's fee, and five percent personal security expense."

"Personal security expense?"

"Risk assessment rate based on the gold's origin," said Ahmad.

"Outrageous," scoffed the client. "American gold is more reliable than any other."

"Problems have occurred in the past. I apologize, but we cannot change that."

"What else?" demanded the client, displeasure in his voice.

"We ensure Swiss Customs and Border Security will not reveal the origin of the gold."

"The Americans will try to track the shipments and the payment," said the client.

"Zafar National Bank will circumvent restrictions set by the U.S. Office of Foreign Assets Control. We have done it before."

"What guarantees do I have?"

"None."

"You drive a hard bargain," sneered the client.

"You can always try another bank."

"I accept the conditions."

"Your code number is six-two-four-six. When can we expect delivery?"

"By July 18th."

"Pleasure doing business with you, six-two-four-six."

seven

BIOLOGICAL WEAPONS GROUP
HEADQUARTERS, ATLANTA, GEORGIA

Imelda and Brockman jogged side-by-side on treadmills in BWG's health facility—a daily routine for them.

Before hiring Imelda, Brockman rarely exercised, claiming he didn't have the time. Only her nagging and browbeating got him to join her in treadmill training. He eventually liked it and slowly got in shape.

He glanced at Imelda's reflection in the overhead mirror. "I received some pushback from picking you to head this Vector thing."

She turned off her treadmill and waited until it stopped. Brockman did the same.

"Who?" she asked.

"Sanford thinks you're inexperienced."

"Ha! He doesn't even know me. Blaming me for the Ebola delay? What's he trying to do? Get rid of us?"

"The order for our involvement came directly from the Attorney General's office. Sanford will have to deal with us like it or not."

"It's a chance to prove ourselves." She restarted the treadmill. "Could help with funding, too."

Brockman frowned. "Don't count on it."

"They wouldn't cut us off in the middle of a project, would they?"

"No. But it may be our last chance."

RICHARD ZANETTI

eight

INTELETECH, MANHATTAN, NEW YORK CITY

S pread out on Alex's desk were Gerfried Enslein's résumé, school and college records, research files at Kartan, comments from Enslein's colleagues and students, and Haley's scribbled notes.

Alex paraphrased the resume and records for George, sitting across from him, as he read them: "Gerfried Jacob Enslein was born in Nidwalden, Switzerland, where he went to elementary and secondary schools. He graduated from high school at fifteen, top of his class. Attended the University of Basel's Biozentrum and earned a Ph.D. in biochemistry, making him one of the youngest students to do so."

George gazed at Enslein's high school graduation picture of a sad, anemic-looking youth with dark, close-set eyes, a curved-down mouth, and straight black hair parted in the middle. "Not a happy camper."

Alex nodded. "Maybe they bullied him because they were jealous of his grades."

"You sound like you know about this."

"Yeah. I saw it and never liked it . . . After graduation, Enslein got a two-year visiting professorship in genomics at Princeton, where he studied genetic variants linked to contagious diseases, a topic rarely studied by his peers."

"Eccentric, too," muttered George.

"This is interesting," said Alex, reading from Haley's notes. "Teaching gave Enslein heartburn and vision syndrome, and he couldn't wait for his professorship to end."

George laughed. "A friggin' prima donna."

"Enslein dated his lab assistant, Marsha Farmer. They married after he left teaching."

"I'm surprised he found someone," said George, gazing at Enslein's face."

"After Princeton, he landed a research position at the U.S. Army Medical Research Institute of Infectious Diseases. The Army fired him after two years for 'procedural violations,' but wouldn't reveal what they were."

George leaned back in his chair. "Think it's political?"

Alex shrugged. "You never know with the government. Anyway, Enslein became a private consultant to pharma and biotech companies, traveling extensively. And Enslein and Farmer divorced."

"Why?" asked George.

Alex shook his head. "A year later, Enslein, Haley, and Gerald Durning, a well-known microbiologist, launched Pharmacap, a small biotech company." Alex sipped some coffee. "Pharmacap specialized in drug encapsulation and declared bankruptcy when the FDA rejected its patent. After that, Enslein disappeared for two years. Nobody knew where he went."

George folded his arms. "Did Haley mention Pharmacap?"

"No."

"What's he hiding?"

"Exactly," said Alex, as he continued to read. "Enslein reappeared two years later at a Biotech Conference in Philly. Haley, then CEO of Kartan, contacted his former partner and offered him a high-paying consultancy job, which Enslein accepted. Three months later, Enslein was arrested for tax evasion, fined a hundred thousand, and sentenced to six months at Durham Correctional in North Carolina. After serving his time, Enslein disappeared again—this time with Kartan's two million."

Alex dropped the file on his desk and stretched his arms. "The data's sketchy and filled with holes, but a lot better than starting cold."

George straightened up. "What do you think?"

"He's a genius, flush with cash, and could be anywhere. It won't be easy."

"Traveled a lot."

"Right. See if you can get his travel schedule from Customs and Border Protection and contact the Army for his work at Fort Detrick. I have a date with his ex tomorrow."

nine

FIVE STAR APARTMENT COMPLEX, PRINCETON, NEW JERSEY

Marsha Farmer lived in a two-bedroom flat on Moran Street. She hadn't moved since the divorce, but recently started looking for another place. Before Alex could knock, the door swung open to reveal a short, rather plain woman with straight dark hair framing a pale, angular face. She was wearing leather sandals and a dress with horizontal stripes that didn't flatter her at all.

"Alex West," she said, extending her hand. "Right on time."

Alex shook her hand and followed her into the living room, that had an unobstructed view of St. Paul's Cemetery across the street. Alex glanced out at several people standing around a newly dug grave site.

"I buried my dog there," said Farmer, following his gaze. She gestured to the couch. "Please."

Alex sat down and smiled. "I appreciate your taking the time to meet with me, Ms. Farmer. As I mentioned when we spoke, a company hired me to locate Professor Enslein, and I thought you might help."

She raised an eyebrow. "Why are they looking for him?"

"He disappeared with two million of their money."

Her face soured as she moved into a club chair and crossed her legs. "As I mentioned on the phone, I don't know where he is. I haven't heard from Gerfried since the divorce." She gazed past him, as if she had second thoughts about agreeing to this interview.

Alex sensed he might be moving too fast. "It's nice here." Gesturing to the window. "You like living in a college town?"

"It was convenient when we were both working at the university, but it can get a little boring unless you're into college sports and university theater.

He smiled. "You mentioned your divorce. Do you mind talking about it?"

"The legal reason was 'irretrievable breakdown.' But the real reason was cruel and inhuman treatment, although he was psychologically cruel as well."

"Oh?"

"Looking back, I made a mistake marrying him. My mother told me not to do it. Her first husband was a bastard, so she knew the type. But I was a know-it-all back then and didn't listen. I knew Gerfried was a little off, but not that far off."

"Like what?" said Alex.

"Sometimes mean and had a bad temper . . . I thought he'd become more normal with time. And maybe I could change him. I was wrong and wound up in living hell."

She gazed dolefully at the ceiling and didn't speak. An uncomfortable silence followed. Alex was about to ask another question, but she beat him to it.

"When I first met Gerfried, he was strange, antisocial actually, but he awed me with his brilliance. We often had coffee together in the cafeteria. He was the only man who really paid any attention to me. I liked him and knew his eccentricities and faults, but I thought . . . you know, that maybe I could help him get over them."

Alex sat back. "How was he strange?"

"Impulsive. Had an attitude. He threw things when he got mad, and he insulted people when they made mistakes. They disliked him at Princeton. There were rumors the other professors thought he had lied about his credentials and that he stole the professorship. Gerfried thought it was his youth they resented. I don't know." She looked away. "Maybe because he was a foreigner. Whatever it was, they snubbed and maligned him."

"How did he react?"

"He didn't complain to anybody but me, and he endured it. His professorship ended without a going away party. A disrespectful insult. No goodbyes or farewells. Just take your stuff and go. So, after two years of teaching, he rejected academic life, and shopped around for something better. Then he heard about a job at the Army Medical Research Institute in Frederick, Maryland. It paid well and he wouldn't be teaching. He took the job and wanted to move there.

"I didn't want to give up this apartment, so he got a room in Frederick, and came home on weekends. It stressed our marriage, but the money was good. Two years later, the Army fired him without warning."

"Why? What happened?"

"He never spoke about it, and the Army didn't publicize it. I don't know what happened, but he was furious. He smashed some dishes. 'Ruined my reputation,' he said. He got distant and mean spirited. Hit me once during an argument."

"What did you do?"

"I took it," she admitted. "He was depressed and angry and I forgave him. I loved the man. But I knew then that I could never change him.

"When companies found out he was available, they hired him for research and consulting. They never asked about the Army job. Just happy to get him." She leaned back and uncrossed her legs.

"So, that's what he did: traveled for months at a time—Greece, Russia, Japan, Switzerland, Florida—you name it. Oh, he'd email or text me and call once a week, but that was it. And when he returned, it was for a week, and then he'd be off again, flying to who knows where."

"Who did he visit?"

"Pharmaceutical companies. At least, that's what he told me. He said they wanted advice or proprietary work."

Alex leaned forward. "Do you remember the companies? Where they were located?"

"He didn't talk about his travels. Rarely mentioned. But I remember some cities he went to because he asked me to book his flights: LA, Chicago, St. Petersburg, Florida, Athens, Zurich, Moscow, too. He wasn't fond of the Russians—gave him a hard time with his visa."

"If you had to guess, where do you think he is right now?"

"No idea." She got up and headed for the kitchen. "Something to drink?"

"Water's fine."

She returned with his water and went back to her chair.

He took a sip. "No idea where he is?"

She shrugged. "He liked it warm." Then she pointed to a framed photograph of a castle on a cliff. "He took that when he was in Rhodes, Greece."

Alex got up and studied the picture. "Cool castle. What did he say about it?"

"Nothing. Nothing at all. Just hung it there. Everything was a mystery with him."

Alex returned to the couch. "Do you know any of his friends or acquaintances who could help?"

She paused, as if searching for the right words. "Gerfried was a habitual loner, Mr. West, who avoided interaction with others. He liked to be alone. He'd sit, oh, he'd sit for hours, preoccupied with his thoughts. Gazing at his feet most of the time. Nobody could compete with them, I guess."

He smiled.

"And then." She made a sour face as if it pained her to continue. "He scared the hell out of me."

"How is that?"

"Killed my dog."

Alex sat up, horrified. "Your dog? Why?"

"Lucky never liked him. My English Setter. After the Army job, Gerfried got mean, would kick him if he didn't obey and put him outside in the cold or rain. He said he was afraid of getting sick from fleas and ticks that carried the plague."

She shook her head. "Hypochondriac. Worried about catching some deadly disease. Lucky didn't have any fleas or ticks. Inside most of the time. I argued with him, but he insisted. 'It's the dog or me,' he warned. So, reluctantly, I agreed to give Lucky away and started looking for a family that would care for him."

"That must've been hard to do," said Alex. "Giving up your dog."

"Well, I must admit I didn't look very hard, thinking Gerfried would get to like him and we could keep him. But nothing changed. After being constantly mistreated, Lucky growled at Gerfried and fought back. He nipped him on the leg once. I was out shopping. When I came home, I found Lucky on the kitchen floor. Dead. Gerfried had poisoned him."

Alex gasped in shock. "That's horrible."

"He left him there for me to see," said Farmer, trembling, with tears in her eyes. "I cried and screamed, slapped and punched him, completely lost it. I was sobbing, and he walked out, muttering that the dog reminded him of his heartless father. Gerfried hated him, too.

"That was the end. One moment of fear . . . It turned my love to hate. Terrified I'd be next, I immediately filed for a protective order to keep him away while I got a divorce."

She trembled and looked down. "People who commit violence against animals often commit violence against humans. I was afraid to be next." She folded her hands and leaned forward. "Jeffrey Dahmer tortured and killed animals when he was a kid. Maybe Gerfried did, too."

She got up and looked at her phone. "I have a doctor's appointment in half an hour, Mr. West. I have to get ready."

Alex rose to his feet. "Of course. Thanks for the time, Ms. Farmer."

She went to the door and opened it. "I'm an excellent cook. Let me know when you're in town again and I'll give you a home-cooked dinner. You'll like it. I'm sure."

"I'll do that." He shook her hand and walked out.

ten

DELTA FLIGHT 17 TO ST. PETERSBURG-CLEARWATER AIRPORT, FLORIDA

Alex lowered the tray table and opened his laptop to review George's notes on Enslein, pausing on the professor's mugshot, taken when he was arrested for tax evasion. Scary dude, he thought.

Court records of the tax evasion case were missing, but George had a copy of Enslein's prison report. The professor had been a model inmate at Durham Correctional Center in Durham, North Carolina, keeping to himself and rarely talking with others. His sole visitor was M. Kavi, a woman. Alex made a mental note to ask Marsha Farmer about her.

Tom Baker, a staff sergeant from Fort Detrick, recalled sending Enslein's lab supplies and files to 51 Commercial Drive in Palm Grove, Florida, a shrimp plant. The sergeant told George he got the address from a leftover shipping label because the original manifest was missing. Marsha Farmer had mentioned the professor's trips to St. Petersburg. It was close to Palm Grove, which led Alex to book the flight.

The pilot announced they were about fifteen minutes from arrival. Alex leaned back, closed his eyes, and wondered if he should've carried his Glock today. The 9 mm lay buried in his sock drawer with twenty rounds of ammunition. Ever since the convenience store tragedy, he'd been worried about making another mistake.

The PA crackled as the flight attendant announced their approach. Alex raised his chair back and stowed the laptop. The professor's sinister face was stuck in his mind.

Alex cranked up the AC on the Dodge rental as he crossed the Howard Franklin Bridge over Tampa Bay. A gray mist obscured the coastline and all but the tops of the city's tallest buildings. He exited on Route 41, known as the Tamiami Trail—a combination of the city names of Tampa and Miami. In modest traffic, he headed south, wondering why Enslein would ship his laboratory equipment and files to a shrimp plant. That strange request was further motivation to go there. He puzzled over why the plant address didn't register on his GPS, but figured he could find it just the same.

Palm Grove was in Hillsborough County, a few miles south of a place called Bullfrog Creek. A dark thunderhead threatening rain appeared in the distance as Alex took the exit for Shore Road. The two-lane blacktop snaked along the coast of Hillsborough Bay past stucco houses, gas stations, and shopping centers. Farther south it passed shallow inlets, ponds, and acres of swamp grass. Occasional billboards, used car lots, and vegetable stands broke the monotony.

He bore right on Commercial Drive, which looped along the bay and rejoined Shore Road about five miles later. The sky continued to darken, and a few drops of brown rain streaked the windshield as the area became more industrialized.

Rusty pipes and broken windows in shuttered factories served as ghostly remnants of more prosperous times. The few addresses he saw were in the hundreds and descending. He reduced speed and drove on, stopping now and then to search for an address.

When he saw a sign for 44 Commercial Drive, he turned around and headed back. Mounted on a wooden post at the end of a dirt driveway was a rusty mailbox with a faded 51 on its side, invisible when going the other way.

Alex rode the dusty drive a quarter mile toward the bay, passing two bullet-ridden NO TRESPASSING signs.

He slowed down when he saw a weathered two-story building that looked like a metal prefab abutting Hillsborough Bay. A faded TALAS sign sat obliquely on the roof.

A new chain-link fence encircled the plant, topped with two strands of razor wire. Such pricey security for an eroded plant raised a red flag for him. In front, a shiny red Firebird convertible showcased the otherwise empty parking lot. Alex stopped at the gate and lowered the window.

A muscular man of medium height, wearing a faded blue shirt, overalls, and red bandana around his forehead, approached the car with an awkward gait. He stopped and waited for Alex to speak.

"Hi," said Alex, stepping out of the car in a friendly manner. "I'm opening a diner in Palm Grove and looking for a good shrimp supplier. Heard Talas was the best."

"We're closed." The man hawked up a ball of phlegm that landed a few inches from Alex's shoe. Alex stepped back and smiled.

A door on the front of the building swung open and a boy in his late teens stepped out. "What's up, Benson?"

The muscular man held his gaze on Alex. "I can handle this."

"No problemo." The boy disappeared.

"When do you open?" Alex glimpsed a dark-haired man emerging from behind the building.

"No idea." Benson glared at the man, and he hurried away.

"I heard Talas has new owners." Alex waited a beat. "My friend told me to ask for Gerfried Enslein. Is he here today?"

Benson's eyes narrowed. "We're closed." He took a bold step forward.

Alex had met a dozen guys like Benson when he wore a Pinewood badge, angry men with bloated egos always trying to prove how tough they were while hiding their insecurities. "Just tryin' to be friendly." He took one last look at the plant, got back in the car, and drove away.

Unlike many coastal towns, Palm Grove failed to attract many tourists, turned off by the strip clubs, bars, and pawnshops that helped to breed one of the highest crime rates in Hillsborough County. Disgruntled out of towners, termed it "Harm Grove."

Alex parked the Dodge in front of a drugstore on Myrtle Street and walked one block to City Hall on Cedar. The two-story white-brick building had a wooden porch with four fluted columns supporting a shingled overhang. A tricolor flag draped over the revolving door led to a hallway.

The door to the Town Clerk's office was on the right. Alex opened it and walked right in.

A middle-aged woman with steel-gray hair glanced up from her computer and furrowed her brows. She was alone in there.

"Hi," said Alex. "I was wondering if you could help me."

"You could knock," snapped the woman with a sneer. "This *is* an office, you know."

"Sorry, I didn't want to startle you." He smiled and looked around. "Slow today?"

She puffed her lips and exhaled. "Who *are* you?"

"A real estate agent looking for bargains. I bet you'd know a bargain when you saw one."

She eyed him up and down as though he were a Martian. "Too pricey for me."

He extended his arms and smiled. "Yeah, but I'm on sale today."

"I'll pass." She focused on the monitor. "Who do you work for?"

"Bogard Realty." He had seen the realtor's sign when he drove in and was happy to remember it. "I'd like to see the property assessment and last transfer for the Talas Shrimp Plant."

"Talas, you said?"

"Right."

She pushed the mouse around and typed in the name. After a moment, she clicked her tongue. "Baxter Holding owns it. Bought it seven years ago after Pat Butler died. Nobody paid the taxes. The bank foreclosed on the property and sold it to Baxter for $285,000."

"What's Baxter Holding?"

The woman shrugged. "No idea. Cyprus company. Cyprus registry."

"Cypress, Florida?"

"Nope. Cyprus, the country."

"Any address?"

"P.O. box."

Alex leaned over and tried to read the monitor. She clicked off the property certificate and looked up at him with a querulous expression.

"Know anything about that place?" he asked, hoping to squeeze a little more out of her.

"People talk. Late with their taxes. And what's his name?" She clenched her teeth. "Tomek. William Tomek. He signs the checks and gives everybody a hard time."

"T-o-m-e-k?"

"Yeah."

Alex showed her Enslein's picture. "Ever seen him around?"

She frowned. "Looks like that villain in the old Bond movies. Who is he?"

"A professor."

She gestured toward the door. "Knock next time."

Her sudden dismissal surprised him, but he had learned something, and thanked her with a smile. He walked out, pushed through the revolving door, and paused on the porch to text George to run a search on Baxter Holding in Cyprus, *the country*, and William Tomek, who might live in or near Palm Grove, Florida.

Heat radiating from the buildings was like the inside of a pizza oven as Alex walked to Cedar, wiping sweat from his brow.

He stopped in front of a pawnshop. The door was open, and three spheres hanging over the door reminded him that two to one, you won't get your stuff back.

He walked in and inquired about Enslein. The clerk said he had never heard of the man and flipped a CLOSED sign on the door after Alex had departed.

Alex crossed the street to a hardware store and bought bolt cutters and work gloves. On his way out, he saw a mailman wearily trudging his route. Alex waited for him to come out of the corner coffee shop and asked about Talas.

The mailman knew of the shrimp plant, but little else. He said Alex could probably find fishermen who used to work there at Mr. P's, a "seedy" bar on Bay Road.

A rumbling in Alex's stomach reminded him he was hungry and feeling hollow inside. All he had eaten was a blueberry muffin and coffee on the plane.

At the local diner, he got the meatloaf special. Then he drove back to the motel for a cold shower and a change of clothes. It was shortly after 10:00 p.m. when he headed to Mr. P's.

Bay Road, a dusty, two-lane strip lined with motels, diners, and convenience stores, traced the contour of the coast south, weaving in and out from the water. After about two miles, Alex spotted Mr. P's, the only bar around. Pickup trucks, Harleys, and muscle cars almost filled the lot. Alex parked in front of a bait-and-tackle shop across the street—his ride didn't qualify.

Mr. P's was seedy, all right: fishnets and sea shells hanging from the ceiling, chicken wire on the windows, faded pine paneling on the walls, and a massive bar and gilded mirror that looked like they came from Hearst's castle.

It was noisy and crowded for a Thursday night—anglers in work clothes and deck boots; locals in jeans, shorts, and T-shirts; biker dudes and chicks in black sleeveless shirts, baggy pants, and duty boots; and a few tourists trying to look cool and own the scene. Above the din, he recognized Brad Paisley's, "Playing with Fire."

Alex found the last vacant barstool and ordered a bottle of Iron Rat Stout, a local beer. Nobody but the bouncer paid him any notice. He nursed the beer and asked the pretty lady behind the bar to point out some fishermen for him.

"Try Corrales." She gestured to a man at the end of the bar, whose weathered face bore a deep gaff scar on the right cheek. He was speaking Spanish with a young woman who slipped into the crowd when she saw Alex approaching.

Alex apologized to Corrales for intruding and waited for a break in the music before he spoke again. "I'm a private detective working on a missing person's case and looking for this man." He produced Enslein's picture. "I think he works around here."

Corrales studied the picture, drained a bottle of Corona, and didn't speak.

"Let me get the next round." Alex signaled the bargirl.

Corrales removed a cigarette from a soft pack in his shirt pocket and lit it with a match. He took a long drag, exhaling toward the ceiling.

The bargirl served two sweating bottles wrapped in paper napkins. Alex tipped his bottle toward the fisherman and took a swig. "Where're you from?"

"Honduras."

Alex shook his head. "Don't know."

"*Bonita*." Corrales gazed down at his calloused hands. "They try to kill me. That's why I left."

"Who's they?"

Corrales looked up, took a long swallow, and blotted his mouth on a sleeve. "Shrimp companies. Stop us from fishing. Everything was okay before they came. Then they shot at us and people started dying."

Alex leaned closer. The Honduran accent and surrounding noise made him difficult to understand. "Why?"

"Protect the ponds from bandidos." He exhaled. "A lie. They don't want the competition." Corrales pressed a thick brown finger into Alex's chest. "I tell you, my friend, it is dangerous to steal. Enough shrimp in the Gulf, so we don't have to steal." He flicked ashes on the floor. "Bad business now. Plants are closing."

"You know Talas?"

"Out of business, long time ago."

Alex stared at him. "How's that?"

"We used to sell to them, maybe a hundred pounds a week." He shook his head. "No more."

"Who runs the place?"

"Tomek. *Cabrón*. See him around with three men. They worked for me before. *Bobos*." He sipped his beer. "Don't know what they do. Don't want our shrimp." Corrales shrugged his muscular shoulders.

"They have money. *Un gran yate en Punta Negra*." He pointed to Enslein's picture and nodded. "Maybe I saw him there."

A sudden disturbance erupted behind Alex. A biker had a young woman by the arm, and she was struggling to get free. She slapped him across the face and screamed as he shoved her down on a table.

When the biker raised his fist to hit her, Alex seized his arm. The biker spun and swung a left at Alex, who ducked and deftly sidestepped while twisting the biker's right arm into a hammerlock. The man screamed in pain; two more inches and the arm would dislocate. The bouncer tapped Alex on the shoulder and whisked the biker out the door. The girl wiped tears from her eyes and thanked Alex. A few people clapped.

Corrales nodded when Alex returned. "*Bien hecho.*"

"*Gracias.*" Alex took a swig of beer. "Can you email me the name and registry of that yacht?"

"I call you," said Corrales.

"Five hundred if you do. And five hundred more if you get me the names and addresses of the three guys who worked for you." He handed Corrales his card.

They shook hands, and Alex slipped out the door into the hot, muggy darkness.

Shore Road was ominous at night: overhanging branches like witch's claws; skulking green and yellow eyes prowling the sewers and gullies; and abandoned buildings—grave markers of better days.

The moon sat low in the night sky—a thin, silver crescent barely visible through the yellowish haze. Fine with Alex. The darker the better for what he had to do.

Night cloaked the windshield, and the road glimmered beneath a thin layer of ground fog that carried with it a faint scent of the sea.

No traffic, so the going was easy, as he drove back to the Talas plant, wondering if anyone was there this time of night.

He killed the headlights on the dirt road and parked near the gate in a thicket of thorny shrubs that barely hid his rental. The Firebird was gone. He turned off the engine and sat listening to the staccato clicking of crickets and cicadas among a troupe of covert night creatures. No sound or light came from the shrimp plant.

Alex pulled on the work gloves, took the bolt cutters, and got out of the car. The hardened steel chain with hexagonal links securing the gate was impossible to cut; he couldn't get a grip. So he snipped a hole in the chain-link big enough to crawl through.

After pausing for a moment to listen to the insects, he ran in a crouch towards a bank of metal casement windows and felt something brush against his leg. Rat? Snake?

At the far corner of the building, he found a broken window and climbed through onto what resembled a loading dock.

One could barely see in there. He flicked on his penlight, revealing several crates and pallets, and a card table and four chairs against the wall. To his left, a rear door promised access to the plant. He doused the penlight, approached the door, and turned the knob. It opened with a click.

A metal staircase leading to an upper floor ended at a small office dimly lit by a pale green light coming through an interior window. A laptop, monitor, and printer occupied the top of a locked government desk against the wall. Tacked above the desk, a three-by-five-foot U.S. map.

Searching for a tool to jimmy the drawer, Alex froze when he heard a sound coming from the window. He looked down at a guard walking through what appeared to be a science laboratory. On his hip, a .38 Special. The guard rapped his truncheon on the wall to the beat of the tune he was humming and disappeared, followed by the thud of a door opening and closing.

Alex waited a minute and then quietly descended the stairs and cracked open the loading dock door. The guard wasn't there.

A compressor sprang to life, covering the sound of Alex's feet running across the loading dock. Soaked in sweat, he climbed out the window and returned to the car.

On the drive back to the motel, he tried to make sense of what he saw. The lab equipment seemed much too complex for breeding shrimp, reminding Alex of a crystal meth bust at Pinewood. Was Enslein dealing drugs?

eleven

INDEPENDENCE HALL, SPRINGVALE, CONNECTICUT

Paul Stewart greeted Dr. Imelda Burke warmly, extending a handshake as she entered his office. Gesturing towards a seat, he invited her to sit down. Dressed in a sharp blue suit, the health director exuded courtesy, calmness, and professionalism. "Welcome to Springvale, Dr. Burke."

"Thank you." Imelda sat on the edge of a chair and opened the laptop on her knees. She was wearing a dark gray jacket, matching skirt, and black leather flats. "I appreciate your taking the time to see me on such short notice." She smiled to put Stewart at ease, aware that visits by government agents often intimidated local town officials. But, she was quick to realize, Stewart wasn't the intimidated type.

"Happy to be of service," he replied. "We'd also like to learn more about the flu outbreak."

Imelda typed Stewart's name, title, and contact information into her database. "For starters, I'd like the names, health records, and addresses of all those infected."

"Of course." Stewart opened his desk drawer and handed her a flash drive. "We prepared this when we got your call. About half the health records are confidential. And there may have been a few who never reported they were ill. But I think the count is pretty accurate." He pointed to a wall map of the town, where flags marked reported cases. "As far as we could tell, there's no pattern, no explanation why some people got it and others didn't. We checked just about everything."

Imelda smiled again. "I'm sure you did, Mr. Stewart. My being here doesn't question your procedures."

Stewart nodded. "You know, the suddenness of this illness stirred up a hornet's nest. The media was all over town. We're not used to that level of publicity."

"Anything unusual occur before the outbreak?"

"No," he recollected. "Wait." He held up an index finger. "Big fire at the lumberyard. And a pileup on Route 25. The local paper didn't report the accident until a couple of days ago. Most of their staff was sick, too."

"The virus is very aggressive," she said, "and has a short incubation period. What was the weather like?"

"Some rain. That's about it." He handed Imelda a copy of the *Citizen*, Springvale's weekly newspaper. "You might find something on the calendar inside."

Then he removed a three-ring binder from a cabinet and opened it. "Our report to the Board of Selectmen. The letter I sent to the Public Health Department in Hartford. Medical reports from local doctors and a water quality analysis from Springvale Hydraulic." He closed the binder and gave it to her.

"Thank you." Imelda placed the binder, flash drive, and newspaper in her briefcase. "I'd like to set up meetings with directors of the town's health department, human resources, and chief of police. I also want to test the reservoir."

"Sure. I'll be happy to escort you around while you're here."

"I appreciate that." She closed her laptop. "If you don't mind, I'd like to start now."

Stewart rose from his chair and gestured to the door. "I notified Cal Cronin you were coming. Chief of police. We can use my car."

The hours flew by and by six o'clock Imelda had taken over fifty photographs, several pages of notes, and had met with three town officials.

As they drove back to town, Stewart pointed out Joe's Bar & Grill. "Great place to eat. And they have a good wine list."

Imelda nodded, but didn't reply.

"You know if you're free for dinner . . ."

"Thanks," she replied, "but I have a lot to do. I'll call tomorrow and give you my schedule."

He dropped her in front of the Springvale Inn, where she changed into jeans and a sweatshirt, and ordered a pepperoni pizza and iced tea from room service. After checking in at the office, she spent the evening studying his report, which was thorough, but contained no clues regarding the sudden outbreak.

The next day, Imelda conducted etiological tests, examining air, water, soil, and food. She also interviewed several flu patients who didn't know how they got sick.

One thing popped out at her, however. The illness was not airborne, as she had suspected. The vast majority of Springvale's population didn't get secondary infections.

Aside from that, all other tests proved negative. Whatever caused the epidemic was no longer there or so well concealed as to elude her investigation. She expected to have some answers by now and wondered if her eagerness to head up this case had been a big mistake.

twelve

AMTRAK STATION, SPRINGVALE, CONNECTICUT

As Imelda waited for the train to Philadelphia, she phoned Brockman to review her Springvale visit.

"The outbreak had no particular pattern," she explained, "except it infected more adults than children. And transmissions weren't airborne."

"Strange," said Brockman. "You'd expect it with the flu."

"Cases were scattered, just a few in bordering towns. You know, I thought I'd find something, anything." She sighed. "It's like this thing fell out of the sky. Sorry, Marv."

"Don't be silly," said Brockman. "If anyone could've found the source, it would be you. Remember the sarin attacks in Japan? The top guy was the director of Japan's Ministry of Science & Technology before he became a terrorist. He had a ranch in Nepal, where they tested sarin on livestock."

"Tested it?" said Imelda. "Like Vector tested the flu in these towns?"

"Could be," Brockman said. "Joe discovered the virus was like the one that broke out on that cruise ship three years ago. They dubbed it the Norwalk Agent. Joe has the names of researchers who worked with Norwalk-like viruses. Most of them should be

RICHARD ZANETTI

familiar to you—Durning, Grajewski, Enslein, Britton, Palmer, and Abramson."

Imelda moved away from a group of noisy commuters. "When I was at Hopkins, my professor had us review papers from the Gordon Conference. I remember how brilliant Enslein's was."

"Any of them could be involved," said Brockman, "or somebody could've gotten hold of their research. Anyway, it's a lead. Listen, check in when you get to Park Ridge. Maybe we'll get lucky."

Brockman disconnected as the Acela rolled into the station. Imelda boarded, feeling better than she did before the call. She took a quiet seat in the car's rear, preferring the sleek, silver train to flying— plenty of room to sprawl out and do her work.

The familiar sound of the rails reminded her of when she was a little girl living with her Uncle Ted and Aunt Casey outside Doles, Georgia. She could often hear trains passing their farm at night. For a lonely child living on a rural farm, those sounds were an inspiration to travel.

Ted and Casey adopted Imelda when she was five years old, after her father had died. Her mother passed away the year after she was born. They raised Imelda like one of their own, with lots of love and understanding. She attended the finest schools that could barely provide for her insatiable appetite for learning.

Imelda prided herself on remembering things. What she saw and heard made a corresponding impression in her brain. These impressions were always there when she wished to recall them. With a mind like that, she impressed her teachers and cruised through high school with straight A's, graduating summa cum laude. At Stanford, she excelled at almost everything, earning honors in chemistry and English. She set school records in freestyle swimming and track. While very popular, she rarely went out on a date, focusing instead on academics.

Her commitment paid off. Accepted at three prestigious medical schools, she chose Johns Hopkins because of its research program. And set her sights on a joint M.D./Ph.D. program, graduating in seven years with honors.

Her research won her one of the school's respected Investigator Awards, written up in the *New England Journal of Medicine*. It caught Marv Brockman's attention. One month later, she became BWG's youngest member.

thirteen

FORT DETRICK, MARYLAND

S taff sergeant Tom Baker agreed to meet Alex off base at the Swordfish Grill in Frederick, a fifteen-minute ride from Fort Detrick. Alex was on his second beer when a muscular black man in a white T-shirt, combat pants and boots walked in, stopped, and looked around. Alex stood up. Baker smiled and headed for him. They shook hands and Baker sat down.

"You look combat-ready," said Alex. "Not a lab rat." He raised two fingers to the server while pointing at the beer.

"I caught some shrapnel in Afghanistan and got reassigned here when I recovered," said Baker. "I miss my team and the action. But I can't move like I used to." He picked up the menu. "I only got an hour, Alex, and could eat a horse."

"Sure." When the server delivered the beers. Baker ordered a salad and 14-ounce filet and Alex got the salmon.

"Did you find him?" said Baker, sipping his beer. "Was Enslein eating shrimp?"

Alex laughed. "The professor wasn't there. But the plant was dirty and looked like a meth lab to me."

Baker cut a piece of steak. "So, how can I help?"

"The Army won't tell me why the Professor was canned. I was hoping you could fill me in."

"For your ears only?"

Alex drained his beer. "Me and my partner."

"I can tell you what I know, as long as you forget me."

Alex nodded.

"Enslein was fuckin' weird and a loner. He didn't eat or talk with us. Usually stayed in the lab and munched a sandwich. Cursed at people if they screwed up." Baker chewed some steak and cut another piece. "Most of us didn't give a shit. We knew these guys were geniuses, and some were crazy like a loon. We gave them that."

"What did he do?"

Baker smiled. "Could've killed somebody. That's what. He infected fleas with paratyphoid, bubonic plague, and cholera. Then he planted the little blood suckers on clothing, which he dropped inside the rabbit and monkey pens. He said he was testing for the most efficient killer. But he was careless and allowed some fleas to get away. They infected a lab assistant who almost died. The brass started an inquiry. All of us testified. A jury said Enslein ignored a regulation. If he were on staff, they'd dishonorably discharge him and lock him up for two years. In his case, they fired him and let him walk."

"How did he react?"

"He blew his fuckin' stack. Said the Army set him up, that they knew what he was doing, and knew the risks. Enslein smashed things when he left. His lab looked like a cyclone hit it."

"Did you ever hear from him again?"

"Nope. Everything was confidential, like he was never there."

fourteen

PARK RIDGE, PENNSYLVANIA

I melda drove her rental car into the sleepy little town and cruised slowly down the main drag, passing aging wood-frame buildings, small shops, and converted factories. High-top sneakers swung from a power line crossing the road.

The old mining hub hadn't completely recovered from mill closings two decades earlier. A new computer assembly plant helped to stave off wide-scale unemployment.

She was ten minutes early for her five o'clock meeting at Town Hall with David Whitcher, health and safety director. Whitcher was waiting at the door when she arrived. They shook hands, and he led her to his office.

Imelda took the chair next to Whitcher's desk as he sat back and nervously shuffled some papers. She could detect from his darting eyes and guarded actions he was uncomfortable.

"We didn't track the flu cases," he said in a thin, raspy voice. "The epidemic, you know, it caught us, caught us off guard, Dr. Burke."

She placed her laptop on the floor and smiled to put him at ease. "It caught everybody off guard, Mr. Whitcher."

Whitcher frowned and studied his hands. "Well, I haven't, um, been trained to handle, um, epidemics. I was . . ." He looked up furtively, then stared at his desk. "Am I in trouble over this?"

Imelda waited until he looked up at her. "I'm here to help you, Mr. Whitcher, not to cast blame on what you did or didn't do. Look, no one expected this epidemic. And no one could have predicted it, including us. So I'd like you to help me shed light on what happened."

"People died on my watch." Whitcher's eyes filled with tears. "*Six people.*" He blotted his eyes on the sleeve of his jacket. "How do I live with that, Dr. Burke? *My fault.* I didn't know what to do. I could've done something. Something to save them. But I, I . . ."

"Are you a doctor?"

He shook his head.

"Then what *could* you have done? It wasn't your fault, Mr. Whitcher."

Whitcher leaned forward and covered his face with his hands to hide his tears. Imelda got up and put her hand on his shoulder. "You didn't kill those people, Mr. Whitcher. The virus did."

Park Ridge General Hospital was a forty-year-old building in the worst part of town. If the neighborhood reflected the healthcare, no one would want treatment there.

Whitcher introduced Imelda to Dr. Chatha, who was eager to supply her with medical reports of those admitted during the epidemic. He offered her a temporary office and the use of the hospital's analytical lab.

She spent the evening sorting through poorly prepared records, often missing vital information. They revealed, however, a demographic pattern similar to the Connecticut cases: about the same percentage of men, women, and children infected in a twenty-mile radius of the town center and an average patient age of forty-eight.

Unlike Springvale, Park Ridge didn't track the flu cases, much less determine their cause. The town simply couldn't afford it.

Imelda stayed the course and performed the required tests.

But she came to realize the cause of the mysterious flu epidemic wouldn't be determined in Springvale, Park Ridge, or Bay City, Texas. Whatever had triggered these outbreaks was no longer there, or, if it was, she couldn't find it. She emailed Brockman a thousand word summary report that revealed more about what didn't cause the outbreaks than what did.

fifteen

MONOLITHOS CASTLE, RHODES, GREECE

Perched on a cliff, the massive structure cast a foreboding presence over the Mediterranean Sea. A drawbridge crossed the empty moat that led to an iron portcullis and a small gatehouse. On opposite ends of the wall were identical towers, decorated with ornate coats of arms, serving as lookouts or gun emplacements.

A tourist might suspect the Knights of Templar built the castle. But they'd be wrong. Yiannis Karras designed and constructed it, modeling it after a 12th Century Crusader fortress.

When Karras died, it remained in his family for a century until his heirs could no longer afford the exorbitant taxes and upkeep. They reluctantly turned it over to the Greek government, which converted it into a museum and opened it to the public.

But tourists preferred the beautiful beaches on St. Paul's Bay, Ladiko, and Kallithea, to the ancient structure, armor, and weaponry. Some people claimed the place was haunted and produced strange sounds, like the mournful moaning of a dying animal. The castle became an embarrassing liability.

In 1999, the Greek government sold it for the bargain price of € 950,000 to an unidentified person, who later transferred ownership to M. Kavi, owner of the Havasi Nightclub.

At a candlelit table in the castle's lavishly appointed study, Majreen Kavi, Gerfried Enslein, and Gant, his loyal bodyguard, had just finished a sumptuous dinner of a roasted rack of lamb.

Enslein watched as Kavi withdrew an unfiltered Gauloises from a hard pack and bent to light it with a candle.

Tall for a dancer, she had full breasts, a small waist, and wide hips. Long, black, luminescent hair highlighted her oval face, dark piercing eyes, and brows curved like Turkish swords. Olive skin, ruby lips, and a regal nose further enhanced her aura.

She stood up—the very essence of sexual allure, mystery and danger—and held Enslein's stare. He went to her and placed his arms around her waist. Kavi kissed him on the cheek.

Enslein smiled. "My mother kissed me like that whenever I showed her my report card. Straight A's in every subject and accolades from my teachers. She loved what I had done, *but not him*. I could never please the high and mighty one."

"Your father?" she asked.

"'Perhaps this is the wrong school for Gerfried,' my father would say. 'Glockhausen is not so easy.' He would drop my report card on the table, as if it were unworthy of his interest."

"How cruel," said Kavi. "For a man to treat his only son like that."

Enslein smirked. "According to him, I would never amount to anything. But I showed him."

Kavi took a deep drag and exhaled at the ceiling. "Yes, Gerfried. You are a genius."

"That is why I adore you, my dear. You appreciate me, and what I can do for you. So does Gant." He joined Gant at the window, staring out, as the deep-red sun dipped into the Aegean. His tall, muscular defender was loyal as the day was long, strong as an ox, and possessed a heart of stone.

Enslein lay face down on a padded table as Kavi rubbed almond oil into his pale, flaccid shoulders. She worked her fingers into the space between the right humerus and clavicle, searching for pinched nerves. "You should exercise more," she said, applying pressure. "Getting flabby."

"Ow!" Enslein winced and opened his eyes. "I feel anger in your hands, Kavi."

She kneaded the bundles of nerve tissue between each pair of vertebrae, digging her knuckles into the spinal column. "The trunk of life. We must respect it."

Enslein rolled over and pushed her away from the table. "That hurts!" He sat up and faced her, a defiant look on his face.

"I'm sorry," she said. "It's because I care for you and want you to be healthy. I have so much to be thankful for."

He reached for his robe. "Remember when we met?"

"The day I lost my dancing job and could barely pay the rent. You saved me, darling." She smiled. "Now I have everything a woman can desire: nightclub, yacht, villa."

Enslein waved his arm in a sweeping throwaway gesture. "And title to this castle, my dear." He tightened the belt on his robe. "You save me from the predators."

"Sometimes I worry they will find you."

"Nobody knows where I am. Never doubt me, Kavi. My plan is foolproof."

"When will you tell me about it? You are so secretive, my darling. You trusted me when we worked with the Russians. What changed?"

"It is unnecessary for you to know."

She frowned and turned her back on him. "Why not?"

"If my plan succeeds, you will be rich beyond your wildest dreams."

"We already are rich, aren't we?"

"This is nothing."

Kavi removed her diary from under the mattress. The leather-covered journal was her sanctuary—a place to express her innermost thoughts and plans, and a secret vault of dreams and dark desires.

She wrote, "You think you are so smart you pompous ass—that my job is merely to enhance your sexual pleasure. I allow it, but it will not last forever. What are you up to? What are you hiding from me? I will be your devoted lover for now, but I, not you, will decide my destiny."

sixteen

TALAS SHRIMP PLANT, PALM RIVER, FLORIDA

For Enslein's men, the poker game was a welcome break from tedious maintenance jobs, chronic boredom, and endless waiting. It filled their time, and the stakes were manageable.

William Tomek placed his cards face down and waited for the others to decide. The Kid, aka Joseph Walsh, and Mario Cosenza folded. Michael Benson, who had confronted Alex at the Talas gate, angrily tossed three sevens into the middle of the table. Tomek laughed and raked in the pot.

Benson glanced at his dwindling cash. "You didn't make it, did you?"

Tomek smiled. "Ante up."

Benson turned over Tomek's pair of queens, violating a cardinal rule in poker. "I knew you were bluffing."

Tomek ignored him.

Everyone dropped ten bucks into the pot. Mario shuffled and pushed the deck to the Kid, who knocked. Mario dealt five cards to everyone. Tomek stacked his hand, lifted it inches from his face, and squeezed out pairs of jacks and nines. "I'm good."

The Kid took three cards. Mario opted for one. Benson took one card and bet twenty. The Kid and Mario dropped out. Tomek covered Benson's bet and raised ten. Benson saw the ten and raised another twenty.

Tomek shook his head and dropped twenty. "Okay. Waddya got?"

Benson proudly spread pairs of sevens and threes on the table.

Tomek held up his winning hand.

Benson angrily swept the pot onto the floor.

For a moment, nobody moved, as Tomek stared at Benson with a face of stone. "That was stupid, asshole. Pick it up."

"Fuck you!"

"Pick it up," quietly said, but with conviction.

Benson stood and tossed his chair into the corner of the loading dock. It clattered against the wall and came to rest on its back. Tomek stood and punched Benson in the face. A short left jab that packed a lot of power. Benson staggered backward and crumpled to the floor, blood spurting from his nostrils.

"Pick it up."

Benson moaned and licked his blood.

"I said, pick it up!"

With bloody hands, Benson raked coins and bills into a pile and then pushed them toward Tomek.

"I'm in charge," said Tomek. "If you don't like it, you can leave."

Tomek removed a pint of scotch from his desk drawer, unscrewed the cap, and took a swig. He often thought about his crew, worried they'd screw up, or if he had to kill someone and find a suitable replacement.

In some ways, they were like the two ex-cons and drifter he had hired for the flu job. He killed all three of them as Enslein ordered.

Tomek knew Mario from Palm River. The stocky, thick-necked street fighter ejected wise guys and cheaters at a local strip club. He could bring down an opponent with his fists and knee strikes to the groin and thighs. His solid build, cauliflower ears, and arm muscles were enough to intimidate most customers. If he had a weakness, it was women, especially redheads.

The Kid lived in the fast lane, laughed a lot, and got high on coke and angel dust. A high school dropout, he almost died when he climbed a TV tower during a thunderstorm. Lightning struck the tower five minutes after he climbed down. His friends knew him as a reckless thrill seeker who played Russian roulette with the Suicide Special, an old revolver his dad had given him.

But the Kid showed up on time, and could dismantle a diesel engine with his eyes closed. If he had a weakness, it was his mouth. He rarely kept it shut.

Benson was the wild card: unpredictable temper and snarky attitude. He knifed a drunk during a barroom brawl and got away with it. The drunk had called Benson a gimp. Since he was a kid, Benson limped from what doctors said was a "structural abnormality." A year later, he served three years on Rikers Island for beating up his girlfriend. She never completely recovered.

But Benson was the smartest of the three, a skillful driver, dependable, and Tomek could control him. Weakness? A sore loser.

Tomek glanced at his watch: 5:45 p.m. He expected Enslein's call in fifteen minutes. He met the professor at Durham Correctional Center. Among the inmates, Tomek was one of the few who could understand the mystery man's theories and "remarkable" achievements. Tomek had a semester of chemistry at college before they expelled him for cheating, so he knew the lingo.

Tomek figured Enslein for a genius, sitting for hours as the professor postulated about a genetic fountain of youth, cloning, and miracle cures for cancer and AIDs. He also hinted about a grand "stratagem" that would "set him up for life."

The day before Enslein got out, he told Tomek he needed a manager for his shrimp plant in Palm River, Florida. The idea of trading crowded city streets for palmy beaches appealed to the ex-con. When paroled, he bought a one-way ticket for the eleven-hour bus ride from Durham to his new home in the Sunshine State.

At 6:00 p.m. sharp, the phone rang. Tomek answered on the second ring.

"How is the weather, my friend?" Enslein's coded question.

"Hot and humid." Tomek's "all's good," reply.

"Is she seaworthy?"

"The bilge pump needed repair, and we cleaned the hull."

"Crew?"

"Fine."

"Get it to Rhodes as quickly as you can."

"Will do."

"Security?"

"A guy from town wanted to buy some shrimp. That's about it."

"Your men?"

"Benson acted up today. He'll be no trouble now."

"Did you get the vaccine?"

"Yup. Injected myself. What's it for?"

"To keep you healthy."

"What about the others?" Tomek asked.

"No. I depend on you."

"Don't worry."

Tomek heard a click, and the phone went dead. He was relieved at not being ordered to kill his men after the job was done, assuming Enslein would do that for him.

seventeen

NATIONAL COUNTERTERRORISM CENTER, WASHINGTON, DC

Prodded by the President for an update on Vector, Jim Malone ordered the mini-summit in the fifth-floor conference room.

Seated around the table: CIA Director, Lou Sanford; NSA Director, Jack Illonardo; FBI Director, David Boyce; Deputy Director of the Terrorist Threat Integration Center, Jeremy Ryno; and BWG's Marv Brockman and Imelda Burke. Also, in attendance: Susan Comisky, U.S. Attorney General, and Jack Rentz, Secretary to the President.

"Good morning, everyone!" The director of the Department of Homeland Security stood and scanned the room, assuming everyone there knew the purpose of the meeting. His only regret . . . it was late in coming.

Conversations quickly ended as the attendees focused on the speaker. One could tell from their expressions how much they respected Malone for his smarts and for many years of government service.

Malone flagged his assistant at the door. "They said they'd have coffee. But I don't see it." His assistant disappeared to find the missing cart.

"Sorry for the short notice," Malone continued, "but the boss wants to move fast on this." His expression was rueful, but determined.

"We've gone ten years without a terrorist attack. Not bad, considering the risks. Much of that credit lies with our intelligence community represented by all of us around this table. So, I'm confident that by working together we can stop this threat before the deadline."

A long silence filled the room.

"We haven't faced a menace like this before," Malone continued. "And what makes this threat so dangerous is that it defies normal investigative procedures. A demonic plot aimed at killing millions of innocent people in three unidentified cities. And even if we pay the ransom, there's no guarantee it won't happen. The President has ordered us to withhold from the media any mention of Vector and the extortion plot. Information or material disclosed without authorization could cause panic and grave damage to the nation and jeopardize our ability to hunt down this terrorist. Ensure there are no leaks, or there will be fury at the Oval Office."

He turned to Sanford and sat down. "Lou will bring us up to speed on the CIA's progress."

Sanford stood and took a moment to observe the others. "We ran Vector through the Terrorist Information System. It contains the names of known or suspected members of terrorist groups. So far, we found nothing that links Vector to any of these people or groups. So, we can assume Vector is a new terrorist, and probably a loner. We also used the A & C algorithm. We call it acey-deucey."

The others chuckled.

"It identifies bio-terrorists and predicts future terrorist hotspots."

Comisky sat up in her chair. "What's the source code?"

"Anthropological and criminological behavior research," said Sanford. "It combines historic and daily crime information and produces real-time predictions."

Malone furrowed his brows. "Is it accurate? Worked in the past?"

"Twice the accuracy of human practices," stated Sanford in an expository tone. "It eliminates biases and supplements intuition. It identified a recent Iranian plot to bomb the Port of Beirut."

Malone nodded his approval.

"We also searched the Global Terrorism Database," continued Sanford. "An open-source tool based on over 200,000 cases. Each incident details weapons used, target type, casualties, and those responsible. We merged and crosschecked the two databases and narrowed our search to forty-four suspects in seventeen countries. Any could be Vector. Our Rapid Response Team, NSA, and the FBI are tracking them down."

"What about Interpol? asked Malone. "It has an antiterrorist branch."

"I wouldn't count on them," said Sanford. "Lebanon is a member. And a Lebanese bank agreed to take the gold. For all we know, the Lebanese are part of this, but they claim ignorance of future bullion deposits."

Malone's eyes flared with impatience, and his voice took on an edge. "What are we doing about it?"

"Contacting authorities and expats who might've had dealings with the bank," said Sanford. "We have nothing to report."

Malone frowned. "Make use of every tool, including Interpol. Three weeks isn't a lot of time."

"We'll look into it," said Sanford. "China, too. It's hosting bioweapon labs on every continent with laundered cash."

Boyce raised his hand. "The synchronized nature of the Vector attacks requires high-level, onsite intel. I don't think China's involved."

"I think you're underestimating them," said Malone. "Anything else, Lou?"

Sanford shook his head and sat down.

Illonardo stood and addressed the table. "We've committed three thousand agents to data collection, screening, and surveillance.

Based on human and signal intel, we narrowed down the number of U.S. terrorist subjects to twenty-three."

"On what grounds?" asked Malone.

"Many subjects aren't capable of carrying out such an attack."

Malone sighed. "Intelligence has been wrong before."

Illonardo reviewed his notes. "We're confident in our decisions, Jim. A few suspects are in jail. And many terrorist organizations capable of such an attack are out of business or neutralized."

"Okay. But that's forty-four from the CIA plus your twenty-three," said Malone. "Sixty-seven suspects. A big job in three weeks." He turned to Boyce. "What's going on, Dave?"

"We have field agents striking every key terrorist cell in the country, chasing leads. So far, we came up with twenty-nine suspects. All are among the sixty-seven previously mentioned."

Malone waited for a beat, then pointed at Brockman. "Your turn, Marv."

"I'll defer to Dr. Burke. She's spearheading the investigation."

Imelda noted Sanford's smirk as she rose to her feet and flashed a virus schematic on the overhead screen. "The Norwalk Agent that caused the three flu epidemics." She directed the laser to the bottom of the molecule. "Notice the orthomyxovirus group. It gives the virus its character. Here it's common influenza. We believe Vector may have been involved in its research. So, we went through CDC records and found six molecular biologists who fit the bill: Gerald Durning, Samuel Grajewski, Kensey Britton, Seth Palmer, Gerfried Enslein, and Bobi Abramson."

"On what basis?" said Rentz, looking like he just woke up.

"They researched the Norwalk Agent using molecular assays, RT-PCR, reverse transcription polymerase chain reactions, and antigen detection tests," said Imelda. "They all perfectly duplicated the Norwalk virus."

"Are they the sole researchers with this ability?" Sanford looked around the table, as if he had just asked the perfect question.

"No. But their familiarity with the Norwalk virus suggests one of them or someone else may have used or altered one of their duplicates to infect the three towns. One more thing," said Imelda, "we define a vector as an engineered molecule capable of carrying a biological agent or infectious pathogen to a host. A rogue molecular biologist might use that name to show how confident he is about getting away with this. They are all prime suspects. Last night, we sent each of you their names and contact information."

Sanford scanned his email. "Nope. Don't have them."

"Me neither," said Boyce.

Illonardo shook his head.

"I have them," said Comisky.

"Me, too," said Rentz.

"Ditto," echoed Ryno.

Imelda frowned in disbelief. "We'll resend them today."

Malone stared at Imelda. "Is that all you have, Dr. Burke—six suspects? Nothing on the outbreaks in those three towns? How it happened? Delivery method?"

Illonardo casually waved his hand. "How was the virus spread?"

"We're not sure," Imelda replied. "It's a common flu virus, but not airborne."

"So what?" said Sanford.

"It's spread some other way," Imelda said.

"And you can't find it?" said Malone with a grim expression.

Imelda sat down. "Not yet. But we will."

"What's taking so long?" asked Illonardo.

"It took you seventeen years to find Kaczynski," snapped Brockman. "Or was that a fluke?"

Illonardo rolled his eyes.

Malone stood and addressed the group. "BWG will handle all testing, screening, and analysis of potential bioweapons and suspect materials."

Cursing under his breath, Brockman jumped up, drawing the attention of the others. "That's a big job, considering our recent downsizing. The other agencies have labs. They should help carry the load."

"You have the best people and best equipment for the job," countered Malone. "We all have to pull together if we want to get this done in twenty-four days."

"It reduces us to specimen collection and accessioning," argued Brockman. "This is bullshit."

"But it enables others," ordered Malone with an implacable expression. "Just do it!" He glanced from Brockman to Imelda. "I'm not impressed by your reports today. Sixty-seven suspects need to be screened in three weeks."

"Seventy-three, including the six researchers!" corrected Brockman, still seething from the testing order.

"Yes," said Malone. "Seventy-three. Possible? *Maybe.* But I'm not sure you can do it effectively." He took a deep breath. "We must have full cooperation between our organizations or we'll never get it done. I'll share what you said with the President today. But the clock is ticking. Find Vector fast or there may be bodies in the street and hell to pay." He walked out and didn't look back.

Brockman followed Imelda into the foyer and pulled her out of hearing range of the others. "There's no way Sanford will help us," he hissed. "He'd refuse to make us look good. We can lean on Boyce and Illonardo, but I think Sanford persuaded them to dismiss us, as well. We're on our own with this."

eighteen

PHILADELPHIA INTERNATIONAL AIRPORT

"Thought you might want to know what Joe and I dug up on the researchers." It was Atkinson on the phone with Imelda, standing in line at the car rental office.

"That was fast," she said.

"We found Britton at MIT," Atkinson continued, "working on intracellular transport. He doesn't believe someone got hold of his research and he didn't know it. And he thought it was highly unlikely, considering the time factor and how careful he is."

"Do you believe him?" asked Imelda.

"Yes. Britton's academic history and research are squeaky clean. So is Abramson's. He's an administrator at Merck and well respected by his peers."

"Abramson graduated from Stanford," said Imelda, "and often comes back to visit. I agree. He's a Boy Scout, not a terrorist."

"He's also convinced that nobody has his research, which, he says, is only in his possession. Joe and I believe neither of them is involved."

"I wouldn't write Britton off so fast," cautioned Imelda.

"Okay. We can dig some more. Meanwhile, Grajewski died last year of lung cancer at eighty-one. And Palmer passed away from

COVID the same year. Palmer was ninety-three. Their employers will send us what research they have on those guys. Durning's dead, too. Murdered during a home invasion. The Philadelphia police blame it on a burglar."

"So, that narrows it down to Enslein," said Imelda, "the last researcher standing."

"Enslein taught at Princeton for two years and then moved on to Chief of Bacteriology at USAMRIID," said Atkinson. "The Army fired him but wouldn't reveal why. We filed a FOIA request for the case files. It usually takes eight-to-ten weeks, but Malone thinks he can get the files in a week. Enslein worked as a consultant after leaving the Army, then partnered with Martin Haley and Gerald Durning at a company called Pharmacap."

"What do you know about Pharmacap?" said Imelda.

"Specialized in vaccine encapsulation. After the FDA turned down its patent application, the company filed for bankruptcy."

"Who's Martin Haley?"

"CEO of Kartan Pharmaceutical. Two years after Pharmacap went down, Haley hired Enslein as a consultant at Kartan."

"Where was Enslein during those two years?" she asked.

"That's the question. No records anywhere. Three months after working at Kartan, the authorities arrested him for tax evasion, and sent him to Durham Correctional Center. Nobody has heard from him since."

Imelda sighed. "That's a bummer."

"You're talking to Durning's widow today?"

"On my way."

"She may know what happened to Enslein. Safe trip." Atkinson disconnected.

nineteen

FIVE YEARS EARLIER
65 ARTHUR AVENUE, PHILADELPHIA, PENNSYLVANIA

Gerfried Enslein and Gerald Durning entered Durning's apartment for a nightcap before calling it a day. They had been working late at Pharmacap and were looking forward to relaxing.

Durning turned on the lights and closed the door. "Anna's staying with my daughter tonight so we don't have to whisper. I have a bottle of Macallan I've been dying to try." He went to the kitchen and returned with the bottle of scotch and two glasses. "Ice?"

Enslein shook his head. Durning pulled the cork, poured two drinks, and raised his glass in a toast. "To success!"

"Success," echoed Enslein, sipping his drink. "Excellent!" He licked his lips and smiled, and then his face fell. "What worries me is how long they are taking to decide."

"Why wouldn't they approve?" Durning said. "It's revolutionary and saves lives."

"Because they are stupid and corrupt."

Durning settled back in the recliner and nursed his drink. "We should publish our research."

Enslein shuddered. "No. Absolutely not. It's proprietary."

"It can be profitable if the FDA doesn't approve. I have Haley's permission to do so."

"Well, you don't have mine," said Enslein with a scowl. "Forget it."

"The vote is two to one, Gerfried." Durning smiled.

Enslein sat on the rocking chair across from Durning and pitched back and forth. "Have you ever heard of the rocking chair test?"

"No."

"It is used to make big decisions in your life."

"Like what?"

"Well, it could be anything. To invent a special product that does not need FDA approval. To move somewhere warm and sunny. To make life and death decisions."

Durning laughed. "To make a ton of money?"

"Yes! And to remove all obstacles." Enslein pulled off his tie and put it in his pocket. Then he stopped rocking and got up to look at Durning's wedding picture on the wall. "Anna looks beautiful, and, except for the gray hair, you have not changed a bit."

"Gray when I was thirty," Durning chuckled.

Enslein moved behind the recliner, withdrew the tie and deftly slipped it around Durning's neck. His partner tried to speak, but Enslein jerked hard, choking off his words. Durning reached back and tried to break Enslein's hold, but his pull was tenacious. Durning thrashed and twisted and fought desperately until the lack of oxygen gradually took its toll. He grew weaker and two minutes later he was dead.

"My research, my decision." Enslein pocketed Durning's wallet and gold watch, washed and dried his empty glass, and returned it to the cabinet. He entered Durning's office, removed the computer hard drive, wiped his prints off everything he touched, and walked out.

twenty

65 ARTHUR AVENUE, PHILADELPHIA, PENNSYLVANIA

Imelda parked her rental in front of the three-story apartment building in Hunting Park. Not the most dangerous neighborhood in the city, but not the safest either. She gathered her briefcase, locked the car, and climbed the stairs. A gust of wind blew dust into her face. Shielding her eyes, she opened the outer door, entered the foyer, and rang the bell to apartment 3A. After a moment, she rang again. A minute went by and Imelda wondered if Mrs. Durning had forgotten about their appointment.

A short, gray-haired woman wearing bunny slippers and a red bathrobe, frayed at the sleeves and collar, opened the inner door.

"I saw you from the window or I don't come down," said Mrs. Durning. "You never know who's at the door these days. Are you the government lady?"

"Yes." Imelda presented her ID. "Thank you for meeting with me."

They climbed stairs to the third floor and proceeded down the hall to a two-bedroom apartment, cluttered with knickknacks, books, and magazines. A TV news show was playing in the kitchen. The apartment had the musty odor of stale air.

Imelda had a soft spot in her heart for old people and couldn't help wondering if Mrs. Durning could care for herself living alone like this. Many people her age were struggling to survive on small pensions and Social Security.

Mrs. Durning joined her guest in the living room and cleared the recliner of laundry. Her hands were thin and wrinkled with protruding veins. A gold wedding ring seemed too large for her ring finger. "Please sit, child. Sorry 'bout the mess." She placed the laundry on an end table. "Now you said you want to talk to me about Gerald."

"Yes." Imelda sat on the recliner. "I'm sorry about your loss."

"That's all right. I'm over it."

"We're interested in his work."

Mrs. Durning frowned and took the couch across from her. "I didn't pay attention, to be honest. He'd tell me about it, but I didn't understand. Scientific gobbledygook."

"Did he keep records?"

"On the computer in his office." She pointed over her shoulder to a closed door.

Imelda rose to her feet. "May I?"

"Well, the police said the burglar took the hard drive whatever that is. Maybe they thought they could sell it."

Imelda's brows shot up. "They took his research?"

"Yes."

"Was it ever recovered?"

"No."

"Where is his computer?"

"I threw it out. Didn't work anymore." She shrugged. "Good riddance."

"Do the police have any suspects?"

Mrs. Durning straightened up and smiled. "To be honest, I don't think they're very good around here. Not like Chestnut Hill, you know. Muggers don't even hide when they drive by," she tittered. "That's a joke."

Imelda returned to her chair and looked into the woman's eyes. "Do you mind if we talk about the murder?"

"No." Mrs. Durning looked out the window with a blank expression. "I was staying at my daughter's house. She wasn't feeling well. Gerald came home late that night. He often worked late. The police say the burglar must've followed him in when he opened the door. No sign of a break in or struggle." She turned and gazed at Imelda. "I found him the next day, lying on his back right here." She pointed to a spot on the living room floor. "I'll never forget how he looked—surprised, eyes wide open. Strangled, you know."

"Terrible."

Mrs. Durning's expression was calm and stoic. "It's okay."

"Your husband worked for a company called Pharmacap."

The widow frowned. "Silly name. I never liked it."

"He started it with Professor Enslein?"

"Yes. Enslein. Gerald said he was very smart. I never met him. And Mr. Haley. 'Moneybags,' Gerald would say."

"I guess you know Pharmacap no longer exists."

Mrs. Durning laughed sardonically. "Gerald poured his flesh and blood into that business. He bragged it would save millions of lives and people would never get COVID again. But it never made a dime."

"Professor Enslein. Do you know what happened to him?"

She shook her head and muttered, "I don't think he liked Gerald very much."

"Why?"

"Just a hunch."

"Do you have a picture of him?" asked Imelda.

"No. We were never ones for pictures. Gerald hated getting his picture taken. Bad acne when he was young. Oh, I'm sorry, forgetting my manners. Do you want something to drink? Lemonade? Tea?"

"No thanks."

The elderly woman cooly appraised her visitor. "How old are you, child?"

"Thirty."

"Seem like a college girl to me. And so pretty."

"Thank you."

Mrs. Durning glanced at Imelda's hands. "Don't see any rings."

The widow's curiosity charmed Imelda. "Haven't found the right guy yet."

"Oh, horseradish."

Imelda couldn't help but laugh, as Mrs. Durning shrewdly had reversed their roles. "Well, in high school, I went steady. My boyfriend wanted to get married as soon as we graduated. The idea was tempting, but it felt too soon to me. He couldn't accept me going away to college and resented me for it. We wrote back and forth for a year and then he married one of my girlfriends. They're divorced now. I still hear from him occasionally. But it's over."

Mrs. Durning raised an eyebrow. "Only one beau? Pretty girl like you? That's all?"

"There was a guy at work," said Imelda. "We dated for a while. It died out. It's not a good idea to date one of your colleagues. And I've been so busy, a relationship seems out of the question right now."

"And if the right guy came along?"

"I went out on a few blind dates, but nothing clicked." She smiled. "My friends say I intimidate men."

"Then you wouldn't want 'em, anyway." Mrs. Durning looked away and touched her wedding ring. When she turned back, there was a tear on her cheek. "Old people are supposed to be tough, hardened from all those years." She reached into her pocket for a tissue and blew her nose, then turned and stared out the window.

"Mrs. Durning," said Imelda.

She didn't reply.

"Mrs. Durning."

"Yes."

"Do you have any of your husband's letters?"

Mrs. Durning turned and glared at her. "Why do you want to know all this?" Her voice took on a jagged quality. "Did my husband do anything bad, anything illegal?"

"No. We're just interested in his work. Anything you can offer would be helpful."

Mrs. Durning glanced at a worn, leather-bound book on the floor next to the couch.

Imelda followed her gaze. "What's that?"

"His diary."

"May I?"

"No!"

Imelda extended her hand. "Please."

The widow reached down and snatched the diary while staring coldly at Imelda. "How dare you come into my house like this? Who do you think you are?"

Afraid the interview would blow up in her face, Imelda replied softly, "I wouldn't be here if this wasn't important."

"I don't care," Mrs. Durning snapped. "That doesn't give you the right."

With a caring expression, Imelda kneeled and looked up at her. "We believe the recent flu outbreaks may be linked to your husband's research. You must have heard about them on the news. People died, mostly elderly, and we don't want anyone else to get sick. That's why I'm here today to find out how it happened."

Mrs. Durning rose from the couch and dropped the diary on the recliner. "I'll be in the kitchen."

Imelda waited until she heard the volume go up on the news show before opening the diary. She moved nearer to the window where the light was better and began reading.

Most of what she found were family events, business meetings, indecipherable notes, and only two references to Enslein. One mentioned publishing Pharmacap's research if the FDA did not approve the encapsulation patent. Scribbled in the margin: "Will they risk the golden goose?"

But what caught her attention was a note about Durning's visit to Enslein's "vacation home" in Rhodes, Greece.

The diary also alluded to after-hour meetings with Durning's lab assistant, Jessica. These pages were dog-eared and discolored. Imelda stopped reading, recalling the tear on the old woman's cheek. Her heart went out to her.

It was almost noon when Imelda closed the diary and returned it to its place on the floor. Mrs. Durning appeared in the doorway, having heard the floor squeak when Imelda placed it there.

"May I borrow these?" Imelda held up the technical papers she had discovered in the back of the diary. "I'll return them."

Mrs. Durning nodded. "Sorry I snapped at you earlier, dear. You know a diary is very personal. Lots of private things get said. I hope you found what you were looking for."

"It was very helpful. Thank you."

Imelda picked up her briefcase, rose to her feet, and started for the door.

Mrs. Durning followed and took hold of Imelda's arm. "Be careful, dear. I don't know why, but I think you're in danger."

Imelda stopped and stared at her. "Why would you say that?"

"Sometimes I get these premonitions. Gerald thought I was a little batty. To him, everything had to have an explanation." She frowned. "I had a similar feeling the day he died."

The interview left Imelda with many unanswered questions. Did the police have any leads? Prints? DNA? Where was Durning on the day he was murdered? Who was with him? Why would Mrs. Durning throw out her husband's computer? Perhaps he used it to chat with his lover. That would make her furious.

The diary was helpful, providing a clue to Enslein's whereabouts. Searching for the professor in Greece was a long shot. But Imelda had a gut feeling that's where he might be hiding.

She could already hear Dunphy's reaction: Imelda wants to spend a few days on the beach while we bust our asses testing samples.

twenty-one

KARTAN PHARMACEUTICAL HEADQUARTERS, NUTLEY, NEW JERSEY

Haley seemed ill at ease behind the desk. His eyes were hard and cold. "You're lucky to get me," he said, leaning back his bulky frame. "My visa didn't come through, so I couldn't fly to Brazil this morning. I'm afraid I disappointed a lot of people today."

"Sorry to hear that." Imelda took the chair in front of his desk, although he didn't offer it.

Haley glanced at his watch. "My schedule's a little tight, Dr. Burke. I hope you understand."

"I'm investigating the recent flu outbreaks and looking for research data on similar viral strains. You worked with Gerald Durning and Gerfried Enslein at Pharmacap. They're experts on flu viruses. I'd like to see their research."

He frowned and shook his head. "Why ask me? I don't have it."

Imelda knew pharmaceutical firms were notoriously paranoid, especially regarding research. But Haley's comment bordered on preposterous. "Nothing's here?"

"No. Pharmacap was a private venture. Kartan wasn't involved."

"But *you* were. And Enslein consulted at Kartan for a few months, didn't he?"

"Yes."

"And you have no records of his work?"

"He took everything with him when he left."

She stared at him coldly. "Mr. Haley. This is a health emergency. The government can subpoena your records."

He gave a throaty laugh. "Be my guest."

"Tell me about Durning."

Haley shrugged. "You probably know about the murder."

"Was he the mastermind behind Pharmacap?"

"No. He was the guy who tested, quantified, and eventually proved Enslein's work. But the creativity, the real creativity, came from Enslein himself. The encapsulated vaccine would've saved millions. But the FDA wouldn't approve it. The pressure was too much for them, I guess."

"Pressure from whom?"

"Pharma. That's why I took this job. If you can't beat 'em, join 'em."

"What about Enslein? Where is he?"

Haley's face went blank.

"In Greece?"

"I heard he vacations there, but I don't have an address, if that's what you're asking."

"When did you last see him?"

"Look, Dr. Burke, I don't have the time right now." He rose from his chair. "Why don't you send me a list of questions?"

"What did Enslein do at Kartan?"

"I really can't talk about that."

"Why not?"

"Confidential." He moved to the door and opened it for her. Haley's assistant was standing there. "Now if you'll excuse me."

"We'll be in touch," she said, as he closed the door behind her.

Imelda arrived at Newark Airport an hour before her flight to Atlanta and called Brockman from the gate. The boss sounded faint and raspy.

"Are you okay?" she asked.

"Didn't sleep last night." He cleared his throat and spoke louder. "I met with Malone in Washington yesterday, requesting relief from all the testing they ordered for us. Malone was adamant, depressingly so. He refused to change the order. We're not getting the support we had hoped for until the other agencies exhaust their leads. And they have plenty. It could be weeks before we're relieved."

Imelda's mind raced. "I need to talk to you about a trip to Greece."

"Is this a joke?"

"No. I'm serious."

"We need you here, Imelda."

"I know, Marv. Get some rest."

He disconnected.

twenty-two

7TH AVENUE YMCA, MANHATTAN, NEW YORK CITY

Rock music blared on the racquetball court as Alex and George fought for the deciding point in their weekly game. Since their cop days, the two men maintained a healthy rivalry and mutual respect. Highly competitive and, while good sports, they hated to lose. "No mercy" was their outspoken mantra.

George slapped a wicked backhand into the corner. Alex made a diving save, placing the ball a few inches from the floor. It skidded into center court, impossible to retrieve. George groaned in despair and grabbed a towel off the bench. "That's it. That's it."

As George wiped the perspiration from his forehead, Alex slapped him on the back. "Good game, partner."

On their way to the showers, George recapped his research on Pharmacap. It disclosed nothing they already knew.

"Do you think Enslein and Haley plan to split the two mill?" said Alex.

"Ha!" spouted George.

"A perfect ploy."

"Maybe so," continued George. "But I don't buy it."

"Why not? Haley looks good at paying for an investigation that goes nowhere."

"Because we're gonna find the son of a bitch."

They paused at the indoor climbing wall, where a few people in harnesses attached to safety lines were attempting to scale it. An instructor observed the climbers from below.

"You used to climb when you were in the service," recalled George.

"Fort Benning." The fond memories brought a smile to Alex's face. "Climbing, rappelling, and bouldering on Mt. Yonah. I loved it."

"Climb anymore?"

"Yeah. I like to climb . . . alone."

"Sound dangerous to me," said George.

"I taught it at Fort Benning. It's the purest form of climbing. We use safety equipment during training. But the purists climb without it."

"I think you're crazy doin' that."

Alex laughed.

They entered the locker room and sat across from each other on redwood benches. Steam from the showers floated overhead. A young man behind them was helping his bashful son get dressed.

Alex untied his sneakers and pulled off his socks. "Anything on Tomek?"

"Five Tomeks in Florida. I searched men under forty with priors and turned up two. The closest one to the Talas plant lives in Palm River. He served nine months at the Durham Correctional Center. *And get this.* His tour overlapped Enslein's."

"The plot thickens," said Alex.

George pulled off his sweaty T-shirt and opened his locker. "No luck on who owns Talas. Baxter Holding is a shadow company, and Cyprus won't divulge the owner's names. I contacted a local attorney on the island who might help."

The men showered, had a light lunch, and returned to the office, where Alex's message light was blinking. It was a voicemail from Corrales. The yacht anchored off *Punta Negra* was the *Minotaur* and flew an Antiguan flag.

Connie mailed Corrales a check for $500, while Alex called TranSea, an offshore company, providing administrative services to vessel owners seeking Antiguan registry.

TranSea refused to supply ownership information until Alex provided his old badge number and police ID. It worked. TranSea revealed Majreen Kavi as the *Minotaur's* sole owner. Her address: a Post Office Box in Rhodes, Greece.

Alex ended the call and informed George.

"She's gotta be the M. Kavi who visited Enslein in prison."

"You think she owns Talas, too?" asked George.

"Possible."

"I don't get it. What interest in seafood could Enslein or Kavi have besides eating it?"

"I didn't see one shrimp in there. It looked like a crystal shop to me."

"Now what?"

Alex leaned back and thought for a moment. "Well, we could stake out Talas and follow Tomek around . . . Or, we could gamble."

George gave him a tentative look. "Gamble? On what?"

"Kavi."

"Seems like a long shot. I'd stake out Talas."

Alex looked at his partner. "My gut says, Rhodes."

George grimaced and remained silent until he could no longer restrain himself. "Going to Greece is crazy. Expensive, far away, and not the best use of our time. You said yourself, Talas is dirty. And Tomek's our best bet of finding Enslein. They probably know each other from Durham. Not much time left for a shot at the bonus, Alex. You gotta believe the odds favor Talas."

Alex sat back in his chair and chewed on his thumb. "Why not do both?"

"Both?" George snorted.

"When I learned about this case, I figured Enslein was out of the country. Living here would be risky for an ex-con, especially an embezzler, and too easy for us to follow the money, which I bet is in some offshore account. Hiding in Greece makes sense. Hard to trace and we have little or no leverage there. His ex-wife said he traveled to Rhodes after they were married. Enslein took a picture of a castle while he was there and hung it in their apartment."

George shook his head with a sour expression. "So what? He might like castles. Waste of time."

"Hold on. Let me check." Alex logged onto the Aegean Airlines' website and searched for flights. "Thursday I can get a nonstop to Athens with a connection to Rhodes. This could take four or five days at most and there's no reason you can't stake out Talas while I'm gone."

"And how am I supposed to finish up with Dookeran? She expects you to make the report."

"Okay. I'll close with her and leave on Friday. And I'll clear it with Haley before I make the reservation. If I'm right, we wrap this up, get our dough, and move on."

twenty-three

KARTAN PHARMACEUTICAL HEADQUARTERS, NUTLEY, NEW JERSEY

A light rain was falling when Martin Haley walked into the parking lot. He was hungry and thinking about dinner as he raised his jacket collar and noticed a man in a tan coat and black watch cap hurrying to catch up with him. It was unusual for someone to be waiting for him when he worked late.

"Haley!" shouted the man. "Haley!"

Haley paused and turned. "Yes."

"Come with me." The man had a sunken left cheek that pulled his lips into an unusual smile. The few syllables he uttered sounded Eastern European.

"Sorry. I'm in a hurry." Haley turned and continued walking. The man grabbed him by the arm and jammed a gun into his gut. Haley froze. "I don't have any money."

A black sedan pulled up next to them. The rear door swung open and dark inside the car. The man pushed Haley into the backseat, followed him in, and shut the door.

Anton Valovitch, wearing a black overcoat, was on Haley's left. The coarse-looking man spoke a few words of Russian to the other man, then addressed Haley in English. "Where is Gerfried Enslein?"

The other pressed the gun barrel against Haley's temple.

Haley trembled. "I-I don't know. I'm . . . I'm looking for him, too."

Valovitch spoke again in Russian.

The gun struck Haley's nose and split his right cheek. The CEO screamed and raised his arms in self-defense. Blood dripped onto his coat.

Valovitch snorted. "Sniveling coward. Gutless piece of shit. Where is he?"

Haley gasped for breath and sobbed as blood bubbled from his nose and mouth. "I don't know. I don't know."

"How can you work with a man and claim to know nothing about him? Liar!" The car eased forward.

Moaning, chest heaving, Haley cradled his bleeding head in his hands and rocked back and forth. "Please. Please. I don't know. I don't know."

The gun struck Haley's ribs, producing a cracking sound. The CEO screamed in pain and gasped for breath. "Please, please don't."

The car stopped, and the door flew open. The man in the tan coat stepped out, pulled Haley into the gutter, and left him cowering there. The car door slammed and the black sedan roared off into the night.

twenty-four

JFK INTERNATIONAL AIRPORT, QUEENS, NEW YORK

Travelers crowded Gate 21 in Terminal 2, waiting impatiently to board the plane. A few wandered aimlessly around the aisles and adjacent food courts. Alex could hear Greek and Turkish above the airport chatter. A voice on the public address system announced the sold-out Aegean Air flight to Athens was a half hour late. A flight attendant was offering $500 to anyone who would give up their ticket. Nobody seemed interested.

First-class and business class had already boarded and the rear of the plane was nearly full. Coach had yet to be filled. The flight attendant called out Alex's group number. He slung the backpack over his shoulder, presented his boarding pass, and got on the plane.

When he arrived at his row, a flight attendant was wiping his aisle seat with a paper towel. An attractive blonde in the middle seat looked up at him. "I'm sorry. I spilled coffee on your chair."

"No problem." Alex smiled and waited for the flight attendant to finish the cleanup, then sat down and fastened his seat belt.

"I asked for an aisle seat," said the blonde. "It was this or come back tomorrow."

"Do you snore?" asked Alex with a straight face.

"No."

"Good. Neither do I." He extended his hand. "I'm Alex."

"Imelda." She shook it.

"Scottish name?"

"Spanish saint. It means powerful fighter."

"Are you?"

"Absolutely," she asserted.

"Good, then you can protect me. I hear Iron Mike is on this plane."

She laughed.

Hatches secured, the Airbus taxied to the runway, number seven in line for takeoff. The pilot announced a short traffic delay but insisted the flight would still get into Athens on time.

Fifteen minutes later, they powered up in a northeasterly direction. Alex pushed back his chair and closed his eyes, needing some rest to be sharp for tomorrow. The idea of finding Enslein had completely captured him. Imelda was thinking of Enslein, too.

He was almost asleep when the flight attendant came by with the dinner menu. Alex told him he'd be sleeping through the meal. Imelda ordered the beef dish and a glass of red wine.

After dinner and a movie, Imelda tapped Alex on the arm. His eyes were closed, but he couldn't sleep, going over his strategy for finding Enslein and a plausible backup plan. He pulled back his legs so she could pass. As she stepped over him, the plane hit an air pocket and she fell backward into his lap. He gently helped her into the aisle.

Alex hadn't held a woman in his arms since Sue Lindsay walked out on him after the Danny Taylor incident. Sue was Chief Arnold Lindsay's oldest daughter. Alex met her at the annual precinct picnic during his first year on the Pinewood force and they fell in love. Sue knew the trials and tribulations of law enforcement officers. The handsome young corporal promised a lifestyle like the one she was used to, and someone who reminded her of her dad, whom she worshiped. Alex was a promising rookie and former U.S. Army

Ranger, who couldn't take his eyes off the tall, athletic brunette with sparkling blue eyes.

They dated for only a month before she told her parents she was moving in with him. This didn't sit well with Chief Lindsay, who, when prodded by his wife, swallowed his pride, and eventually gave in to his daughter's desire.

They had a quiet ceremony under a grape arbor in the Chief's backyard, followed by a honeymoon on Maui. Life couldn't have been better until that fateful day in August.

In the weeks that followed, Alex showed up for work every day and did his job. But the anguish and guilt for killing that innocent bystander festered inside him like virulent cancer. The happy, carefree cop had become a different person—moody, listless, often sitting for hours watching TV or staring at the wall.

Sue panicked, as her well-laid plans vaporized before her eyes. They argued and fought, and when Alex most needed a lover and a friend, Sue pulled back, blaming Alex for their failing marriage and feeling sorry for himself.

A week later, she moved out of their small apartment to live with her parents. And a month after that, she hired a lawyer and filed for divorce. Alex was too depressed to contest any of her demands. At that point, he just wanted to be done with it.

The chief hammered the final nail when he accused Alex of "unacceptable police work that tarnished the image of the entire department."

Bucking the department's tradition of supporting its men, Lindsay called for Alex's resignation. Alex tried to stick it out, but most of his colleagues and the media were against him. A few months later, he quit the force and moved to New York City. He dated for a while, but nothing gelled, so he stopped trying and turned all his attention to Inteletech.

twenty-five

BOYARSKY RESTAURANT, MOSCOW, RUSSIA

The restaurant in the legendary Hotel Metropol was about to close, as refrains from "Kombat," a Russian folk song, drifted in from the lobby. It was darkly elegant in there: six illuminated Greek urns atop tall, round pillars provided the only light.

At a table near the door, an attractive couple talked and sipped their wine. The manager puffed a cigar as he spoke to the server across from him.

Sergei Krakov, a well-dressed man, lean of build and gaunt of face, occupied a corner table. Glancing at the door, he popped a pirozhki into his mouth and washed it down with vodka.

A chilly rain fell as a black sedan with dark, tinted windows pulled up at the hotel entrance. Anton Valovitch stepped out, wearing a black raincoat and matching rain hat. The same clothes he wore when he threatened Haley at Kartan headquarters. He entered the hotel and headed for the restaurant.

Pausing at the door, his eyes swept the room and stopped on Krakov, who nodded ever so slightly.

The professional hitman had a cool, worldly way about him and a self-assurance that came from a record nineteen unsolved assassinations. "Krakov," the Russian mafia determined, "was an executioner to die for."

Valovitch crossed the room and sat across from the hit man, his back to the door. He sampled a pirozhki.

The server approached and Krakov waved him off.

Valovitch handed Krakov an envelope. Krakov slipped it into his jacket pocket. Valovitch got up and headed out the door.

The manager approached the table. "How's everything, Mr. Krakov?"

"Bullets, vodka, cigarettes," Krakov said, repeating Kombat's lyrics. "Shoot where you die." He pointed a finger gun at the manager and pulled the trigger.

twenty-six

ATHENS, GREECE

They approached Athens International Airport over the pristine Saronic Gulf, banked over the coast, and landed at 9:15 a.m. Flight attendants directed passengers not staying in the capital to gates for Cairo, Nicosia, Istanbul, and Bucharest, and others for the Greek islands. The Rhodes flight departed in two hours from Gate 17.

Alex exchanged $300 for euros, bought a bag of popcorn, and spent the time exploring the airport. At the gate for the Rhodes flight, it surprised him to see Imelda curled up in a chair reading a paperback. He sat across from her and held out the popcorn.

She took a handful and smiled at him.

"You're popping up everywhere."

The one-hour flight from Athens to the Diagoras Airport was uneventful, except for a baby girl who cried for most of the way. Holding the baby in his arms, her devoted father paced up and down the aisle, trying to calm her. She stopped crying when they landed.

Passengers deplaned, claimed their baggage, and waited in front of the airport for taxis to take them into town. Imelda, in line in front of Alex, was speaking to an elderly woman standing next to her. The elderly woman was doing most of the talking.

Sharing rides on Rhodes was customary because of the shortage of taxis. The attendant would announce a destination and squeeze up to four passengers in each cab. He doffed his hat to the attractive blonde researcher and shouted, "Knight's Hotel!" Imelda boarded the taxi, as Alex raised his hand and walked forward.

The driver placed Alex's backpack next to Imelda's carryon, slammed the trunk, and opened the rear door, offering Alex the last seat in the taxi next to her.

"The odds of the universe existing are so small, they're practically impossible," she said, while staring at her phone.

Alex looked up at the turquoise sky. "Strange things happen."

Mandraki harbor was clearly visible from the hills outside the town. Two deer sculptures flanked the narrow entrance, where the famous colossus presumably stood. The Turkish coast stretched like a pink ribbon across the horizon. A few riders oohed and aahed at the dramatic scenery.

Heading north, they passed immense stone walls that surrounded the Old Town, dating back some six hundred years to the Knights of St. John. The island's magnificence, however, seemed less important to Alex and Imelda, focused on finding Gerfried Jacob Enslein, the notorious professor.

The taxi stopped in front of the Knight's Hotel. Imelda collected her luggage and entered the elegant and spacious lobby, decorated with bands of black marble topped by lighter terrazzo tiles. Pink and white cherry blossoms adorned the domed sky-blue ceiling.

Imelda checked in and then followed an attendant carrying the luggage to her room. She immediately opened her laptop and got Brockman's email. It included a photograph of the speakers from an old Gordon Conference. The only person who didn't have a smile was Gerfried Enslein.

The accompanying International Procedure Report explicitly instructed Dr. Burke not to engage with the potentially armed and dangerous suspect. If she identified Enslein on the island, her directive was clear. Immediately notify: Adam Morris, CIA Administrator in Langley, Virginia; Brian Hummer, Director of Operations at the Criminal Division of the Office of International Affairs in London; and François Bourdain, Deputy Director at Interpol in Paris.

Hummer at OIA would produce the arrest warrant and documents for a formal request for extradition. Included was their contact information.

twenty-seven

POLICE STATION, RHODES, GREECE

The nondescript, two-story building was often mistaken for a residence. The only distinguishing feature was an official bronze seal over the door.

A cool breeze blew down the hall when Alex walked in to the small office crowded with desks, chairs, and metal file cabinets. Posted on the wall were mugshots of several wanted felons, yellowed from age. Alex wasn't sure if someone had caught these perps or if they were still at large. From somewhere in the back, a police radio squawked static and an occasional alert. A clerk looked up from his work, acknowledging the visitor.

"Hello," said Alex, approaching him. "I'm a . . ."

The clerk turned and summoned the short, gray-haired man sitting behind him. He had sun-wrinkled skin, piercing brown eyes, and a friendly face. He smiled and waved Alex over.

Alex offered his hand. "Alex West."

"Captain Dimitri Trachones." He shook Alex's hand. "How can I help you, Mr. West?"

"I'm trying to find someone, and I was hoping you could help."

"American, yes?"

"Private detective from New York."

Dimitri pushed his work aside and offered Alex a chair. "Finding someone is the same no matter where you are." His cell phone rang. He answered, spoke a few words in Greek, and then hung up. "My wife. She worries." He sat back and reappraised the visitor. "How is the detective business in America?"

Alex smiled and got comfortable. "Could be better."

"We take the good with the bad and make the most of it."

Alex looked around. "Looks pretty good in here?"

"Off and on, depending on the weather and the time of year." Dimitri nodded to a rear door. "We can talk better there, have a drink."

He got up and beckoned Alex to a backroom. Alex smiled and willingly accepted the surprising invitation. The room was empty except for a round wooden table and four chairs. Two glasses and a half-full bottle of ouzo on the table implied this wasn't a rare occurrence for the captain.

They sat across from each other and Dimitri brimmed two glasses. "Welcome to Rhodes, Alex. To our health. *Yamas*, in Greek." He clinked Alex's glass.

"*Yamas*," said Alex. "Are you always this welcoming with foreigners?"

"No. But an American sleuthhound is a rare treat for us."

Alex grinned.

Dimitri downed his drink in one gulp. "Let me tell you about my island. Here, the most common crooks are tourists. It would surprise you how many think they can get away without paying for dinner or a hotel." He refilled their glasses. "I am sorry to say sometimes these people are Americans." He sighed. "We have Greek criminals as well. And they are the dangerous ones because they know the island and the laws." He pointed at the floor. "Those who have a taste for evil follow it to the end and never stop because the devil is inside of them." He raised his hands in acquiescence. "Ah, forgive me. I like to talk. So, my friend, you were looking for someone?"

Alex nodded. "A man named Gerfried Enslein." He produced the professor's headshot.

The captain studied it and rubbed his stubbled chin. "No, but I will look him up." He jotted down the name as Alex spelled it.

"There's also a woman. Majreen Kavi. I think she knows him."

Dimitri arched an eyebrow. "That is easy. She owns the Havasi, a private nightclub close to here."

"And the *Minotaur*?" added Alex.

Dimitri swirled the liquor in his glass. "Madam Kavi showed it to me herself. Beautiful. Designed like a penthouse."

"Introduce me."

"Tonight at the club," he said. "You are welcome as my guest."

"Nice," said Alex. "I'm staying at the Knight's Hotel."

"I will meet you in the lobby at eight."

Alex got up and stopped. "I need a favor, Dimitri. I'm licensed to carry, but . . ."

Dimitri's face tensed. "It is illegal for a tourist to carry a weapon. This island is a peaceful place."

Alex opened his wallet and presented an expired ID and a concealed carry permit. "I'm an ex-cop. Left the force three years ago."

Dimitri carefully studied the ID and the permit. "You are the first to ask for this."

Alex said, "Odds are against me using it. For an emergency, if it happens."

"Hmm." The captain poured himself another ouzo. "I think maybe it will be okay, as long as you are with me." He left the room and returned with a well-worn SIG P226 in a vertical shoulder holster and a box of rimless shells. He jotted something on a piece of paper and gave it to Alex. "Sign this and return the gun before you leave."

Papanikolaou Street was overflowing with traffic and tourists, and the yeasty aroma of baked bread floated in the air. The afternoon sun blazed fiercely, and the morning breeze had given way to a hot and muggy day.

Alex walked toward the harbor, past the open-air market and several small cafes, the SIG and holster wrapped tightly in newspaper under his arm. He followed the path to the Old Town, observing its stone walls, cobbled streets, and 14th-century buildings. In any other circumstance, the medieval architecture would be of interest, but today he didn't think about it. At D'Amboise Gate, he took a taxi back to the hotel.

Guests filled the lobby, many of whom were waiting for friends, colleagues, or planning dinner. Alex checked in at the desk for messages, but there were none.

He dialed the office and got George, whose businesslike tone implied he had yet to forgive Alex for his impulsive Greek holiday. But George became more accepting of Alex's decision after learning he had located Kavi. George said he'd head for Palm Grove tomorrow to report on Tomek, and they ended the call.

After a cold shower, Alex stared somberly at the SIG lying on the bed. Since that fatal morning outside the convenience store, he hadn't fired a gun. Faced with a life-or-death situation, he wondered if he'd have the guts to pull the trigger.

For his outing to the club, he chose dark blue slacks, a white shirt, and a blazer to conceal the holster. Then he field-stripped the SIG, checked the bore, and pushed fifteen rounds into the magazine. Cocked and locked, he placed it in the holster, shrugged it on, and clipped it to his belt. He didn't think he'd need it, but wanted to prove to himself that he could carry.

Dimitri was all smiles when he met Alex in the lobby, dapper in a tailored gray suit and a sports shirt. "I checked the name," he said. "Enslein is not a resident here."

"I didn't think it would be easy," said Alex, as they walked outside and waited for a cab.

They rode several blocks to a large, neoclassical building with a columned portico, tall, ornate arches, and a white marble facade. Twelve-foot-high mirrors in gilded frames bracketed the foyer. Two muscle men, stripped to the waist and wearing Turkish pantaloons, stood barefoot on each side of the door. Curved scimitars hung from their belts as they measured Alex and Dimitri with faces carved in stone.

A severely attractive, dark-haired woman in a Beladi dress welcomed members and guests as they entered and her face lit up when she saw Dimitri. Greeting him warmly in Greek, she switched to English when he introduced her to Alex. "We have a few American members," she chirped in a British accent. "They enjoy our club, and I hope you will, too."

"I'm sure I will," replied Alex, checking out the clientele—mostly well dressed, older men escorting younger women. "Is Madam Kavi here tonight?"

"Yes. Is she expecting you?"

"No, but I'd like to meet her. My name's West. Alex West."

"She's dancing tonight, Mr. West. After her act, I'll introduce you."

A scantily clad woman led Alex and Dimitri through double bronze doors into the grand salon, where patrons occupied small tables surrounding a stage and dance floor. She offered Dimitri a reserved table in front. Velvet curtains, plush seating, and elegant lighting created a warm and inviting ambiance as chatter and laughter filled the air.

A three-man ensemble playing traditional Greek instruments,

entertained the crowd, and Dimitri identified the qanun, resembling a zither; mizmar, a wind instrument; and a two-stringed lute or rebab.

They ordered bourbon as the sweet, pungent smell of Turkish tobacco and marijuana wafted through the air. Alex took a breath and smiled.

"Hashish," said Dimitri, nodding.

"Legal here?"

"No. That is why Madam Kavi treats me so well. I do not mind so long as it stays inside." He paused as their drinks arrived. "She has a reputation. 'Ee Seereeness.' I think 'siren' in English."

Alex nodded. "Lures men to their destruction?"

Dimitri smiled coyly. "Only what I have heard."

The lights dimmed, and three men, playing hourglass-shaped drums, pounded out a roll. An exotic, dark-haired woman dressed in red, gold, and green veils artfully tucked into a gold-sequined bra and belt appeared on stage as the lights got brighter.

She gracefully circled the floor and acknowledged the applauding audience with a smile. Then she stopped and struck a dramatic pose, twisting her torso and extending her arms over her head.

Dimitri had a cheery expression on his face. "Now you know."

The dancer moved sensually to the beat of a soft, dreamy rumba, performing subtle turns on the balls of bare feet. The musicians escalated the tempo as she swayed her hips and arms while moving fluidly around the floor. She removed the side of one veil, using her eyes and the movement of her free hand to direct attention away from it. Dancing with half the veil free, she freed the other side, and it fluttered to the floor.

One by one, Kavi discarded the veils, as the music increased in tempo and volume. She performed belly rolls and figure eights, combined with sweeping arm gestures and stomach shimmies. She'd freeze at unpredictable moments, holding a pose for dramatic effect.

As the beat became more pulsating and intense, the dancer responded, layering her movements with the captivating powers of artful expression and seduction.

Losing herself in a suggestive incantation, Kavi continued to shed veils that drifted to the floor like hydrangeas budding at her feet. Beads of perspiration sparkled like diamonds in the lights.

As the music faded, she gracefully removed the last veil and, spinning around the floor, draped it around Alex's neck.

The music stopped, and the lights went out. The crowd erupted in cheers and loud applause.

Dimitri laughed. "Be careful of her song."

"I'll wear earplugs."

When the lights came on, Kavi was gone. The hostess in the Beladi dress approached their table. "How do you like the Havasi, Mr. West?"

Alex sniffed the veil's musky scent. "Intoxicating."

"I'll introduce you now."

She led Alex through the grand salon to a rear hallway and up a spiral staircase leading to Madam Kavi's office and dressing room.

"She's changing," said the hostess, opening the door. "Please go in and make yourself comfortable." She bowed politely and departed.

Persian carpets and colorful pillows of varying sizes layered the floor. Star-shaped mosaics on the tile ceiling glowed colorfully in the flickering light of the suspended oil lamps. A cedar scent pervaded the air, and perched on a gold stand, a green parrot with red chevrons on its wings whistled and one-eyed the visitor.

As if summoned by the parrot's high-pitched trill, Kavi suddenly appeared in a scarlet robe, carrying a bowl of assorted fruit. Lamplight glistened off her long dark hair and luminous eyes. Gold rings adorned her fingers and toes. Up close, her exotic beauty was more enticing than before.

She settled on a pillow and placed the fruit bowl next to her. "What can I do for you, Mr. West?"

"You're a wonderful dancer."

She flashed a radiant smile. "Thank you. You're an American, I gather."

"Yes. Arrived today."

She leaned back. "I have a passion for Middle Eastern dance. My performers and I create works that reflect our cultures. Preserving them is our artistic mission." She arched her eyebrows. "But I don't think you came here to speak about dance."

"Well, I wondered about the veil."

She smoothed an imaginary wrinkle from her robe and looked into his eyes. "It was my way of welcoming you." She pursed her lips. "Did I embarrass you?"

"No. Your graciousness delighted me, Madam Kavi."

"Majreen."

"Majreen . . . I represent an American client who admires your yacht. He'd like to buy it."

She frowned and bent forward. "Where did he see it?" Her voice assumed a slightly darker tone.

The sudden shift in her demeanor caused Alex to regret getting down to business so soon. But now there was no turning back. "I didn't ask."

"How did he know it belonged to me?"

"No idea."

"I hope you didn't come all the way to Greece for this, Mr. West. It's not for sale." Stated with a penetrating stare.

"He's a very wealthy man, Majreen. Price is no object."

"I'm sorry, Mr. West. Inform your client that the *Minotaur* is not available at *any* price." She looked away. "Some things are more precious than money."

"I agree."

She eyed him warily. "What do you do, Mr. West?"

"Find people like you."

"Strange way to make a living."

"So's dancing with veils."

She tucked her feet under her and draped a hand over a thigh. "Are you with the police?"

"Private investigator."

She picked up the fruit bowl and held it out to him. When he reached for a grape, she took hold of his right hand and didn't release it. "I hope you don't mind. I practice palmistry." She studied his open palm. "Ah. Strong-willed and earn your living with your head."

"I'd like to think so, but my feet do most of the work."

She released his hand and gestured to the other. He held his left palm out to her. She traced the heart line with her finger. "Hmm."

"What is it?"

"Are you afraid of me, Mr. West?"

"Why do you ask?"

"You carry a gun."

He smiled. "You got that from my palm?"

A wry sneer creased her lips, as if the answer should be obvious. Moments passed before he broke the silence.

"My client requires it."

"Surely, you don't feel threatened here," she said.

"Hospitality couldn't be better."

"First time on Rhodes?"

"Yes. Have you always lived here?"

"Born in Istanbul," she proudly avowed. "This is my second home."

"Dancing is your profession?"

"Yes. And I own and manage the Havasi." She rose to her feet as her robe slightly parted. The parrot whistled. "The show must go on, as they say."

"Does he talk?" asked Alex, rising to his feet.

"Only when it suits her."

The parrot flapped its wings, dislodging a few feathers into the air. One landed in Alex's hair.

Kavi extended her hand with a grim expression. "Goodbye, Mr. West."

He shook it. "If you change your mind about the yacht, I'm staying at the Knight's Hotel."

"I don't think so." She vanished behind a curtain.

The door to the dressing room swung open, and the hostess appeared and accompanied Alex to the bar, where he joined Dimitri.

"You survived, I see," said Dimitri, with a wily look.

"More or less." Alex took the stool beside him and signaled the bartender for two beers.

"A very private woman," said Dimitri.

"Where does she live?"

"The Housing Bureau has records. Not public."

Alex turned to him. "You could check for me."

"We are famous for our hospitality." Dimitri's phone rang. He looked at it and frowned. "My wife." He didn't answer. "She knew where I was going and got jealous. Greek women inherited jealousy and envy from the ancients. You should know that before you marry one. I will call the Bureau tomorrow and find out where Madam Kavi lives . . . Good night, my friend." He slid off the stool and gave Alex the Hellenic Army salute before walking out.

Alex sipped his beer and thought about Kavi. Her knowledge of the gun caught him by surprise. A metal detector in the entryway?

Bulge under his jacket? And what was her connection to Enslein—Lover? Friend? Psychic? Trophy? He had to be nearby.

Glancing at his palm, he wondered what else she saw there. Challenges? Limitations? Danger? He dismissed the whole idea. "It's just a palm."

twenty-eight

KNIGHT'S HOTEL, RHODES, GREECE

Imelda checked her messages and spent the afternoon on the computer reviewing test results with Atkinson. After a short walk and workout in the hotel fitness center, she called room service for a bowl of bream soup and arugula salad.

She was wide awake when she finished eating, and it was much too early for bed. Upon arriving at the hotel, she noticed a sign for the casino that caught her attention. "An hour of fun—no more," she told herself.

She opened the closet and chose a white blouse, a plain but elegant red skirt, high heels, and a red scarf. Not accustomed to wearing makeup, she proudly wore eyeliner, lipstick and perfume. It'll do, she thought, studying her reflection in the bathroom mirror. No one would have recognized her as the same woman who checked in the other day.

Her room opened to a small wrought-iron balcony. Stepping outside, she gazed at the breathtaking view of the ancient harbor. A soft breeze blew through her hair and the aroma of bougainvillea mingled with the salty scent of the sea.

She checked her hair one last time, walked out, and took the elevator to the lobby. On her way to the door, she noticed the concierge speaking to a well-dressed man with a thick Russian accent. The concierge accepted a tip and bowed.

"Thank you, Mr. Krakov."

Oil paintings, Persian carpets, and crystal chandeliers were on display in the busy casino. Imelda signed in, paid the exorbitant entertainment tax, and purchased a hundred euros in chips. The salon buzzed with Europeans, Americans, and Arabs, indulging in roulette, blackjack, and baccarat.

She stopped at a roulette table, where a croupier picked up the ivory sphere, spun the wheel, and flicked it around the outer rim against the spin. Two men on either side of the table assisted bettors. An inspector, with the uncanny ability to identify and remember all the players and their bets, presided over the game.

Imelda's interest grew when she saw Alex in the favored center position, flanked by two well-dressed older women. She debated greeting him, but waited for a vacancy instead, and took the chair across from him. At first, he didn't recognize her without the jeans and sweatshirt until she smiled. Her lovely appearance completely captivated him.

"Small world," he said, placing a small stack of chips on black.

"Too small," she replied, setting a similar stack on red, and gave him a wry grin.

She wasn't a gambler but would follow the Martingale system, doubling her wager after a loss. If she lost four bets in a row, her chance of losing the fifth time was only about three percent. Amazing the things she recalled.

The croupier picked up the ivory ball, gave the wheel a substantial twist, and flicked the ball against the spin. Dropping off, it landed on thirty-four red. The croupier scooped up Alex's losing chips and paid Imelda.

Over the next hour, she played her system, and Alex played with his hunches. Imelda's stack increased as Alex's dwindled. Down to his last five chips, he placed them all on twenty-two.

Abandoning her system, Imelda stacked all her chips next to his, making an impressive pile.

The ball spun. The croupier shouted, "No more bets!"

They all stared with glittering eyes and waited. The ball drifted down the wheel, bounced twice on the ridges above the numbers, hopped in and out of twenty-two, and landed on the eight.

Alex pushed back his chair and caught her eye.

Tall, frosted mirrors, polished chrome molding, and gray marble counters showcased the casino bar. Its blue circadian lighting kept customers alert instead of tiring. Solace for the losers, perhaps, to keep on playing.

Servers scurrying in and out carried free drinks to the big spenders, wagering the drunker they got, the bigger the tip.

At the bar, Alex got bourbon and Imelda ordered a local red wine. He raised his glass. "To better luck next time."

"I thought I did okay," she replied with an air of satisfaction.

He sipped his drink, wondering if he had something to do with that. "I liked your system. Why'd you stop?"

"Bored." She reached over and removed the feather from his hair. "Pillow fight?"

He laughed. "Now you know I didn't shower today."

"What bird is this?" she said, examining the feather.

"Parrot. I think she recognized me."

She frowned. "Really? From where?"

"When I was in the service, I brought one home from Tokyo for a friend."

She placed the feather on the bar. "Same parrot?"

"I think so. Some live to be a hundred, you know. Many outlive their owners and move around a lot."

"Wow!" she said with a dubious expression. "What a coincidence."

"Yeah. She got all excited when she saw me and flapped her wings. Feathers flew. I guess one landed in my hair."

"*Fascinating.* She must've really liked you."

"Yeah, I think she did."

She leaned back, wrinkling her brow. "I don't believe a word of it, but I like the story."

"You know, I hardly recognized you tonight without the—" He spun his finger.

"I never dress for flights unless I have to."

"Their loss."

"Thank you."

He nodded at her. "What do you do, anyway?"

"Work for a government agency, research mostly."

"On Rhodes?"

"Island investigations are really hot right now."

"Who knew?"

"Yourself?"

"Private investigator."

"Hmm." She gazed at the ceiling. "When I think of private eyes, I think of old movies and pulp novels. You know, men in trench coats working for a sultry blonde." She flirted and batted her green eyes.

He frowned and shook his head. "Pure Hollywood. It's just like any other business, managing expenses, and driving sales. You know those planes that fly banners over the beach?" He swept his hand through the air. "Inteletech! Find your husband, cell phone, dog, or cat. 1-800-SLEUTH."

"Does it work?"

"Don't know. I can't afford it."

She smiled.

They discussed the island, food, weather, and music, but not their missions. During a break in the conversation, she excused herself and headed to the restroom. As she walked away, he couldn't help looking after her, as did several other patrons. She had a shapely rear and well-toned, slender legs, the kind you see on swimmers and dancers. He envisioned her as a knockout on the beach. She turned and caught him looking, while he decided she expected it.

The door to the women's restroom was across from the baccarat table, where Imelda stopped next to a man observing the action. One disgruntled player scooped his chips, calling it quits.

"Poor guy," said the observer, turning to Imelda. "Not his night."

"Mine neither," said Imelda, frowning. "I just lost a hundred euros."

His face lit up. "American?"

"Yes."

"Cleveland." He held out his hand. "I'm John."

"Imelda. Nice to meet you, John."

"Enjoying the sights?"

"Not yet," she said.

"What do you do?"

"Work for the government."

"I'm with the Power Company." He made a face as if the job were beneath him.

She nodded. "How'd you wind up in Greece?"

"I came to visit relatives and never looked back."

"Well, good luck, John." She turned and entered the restroom.

John was waiting there when she walked out. "Listen, I know a party at the Knight's Hotel. Should be fun. Wanna join me?"

She gestured toward the bar. "Sorry, I'm with a friend."

"Bring 'em along. I promise you'll have a good time."

"I'll see if he's interested." She returned to the bar but couldn't find Alex. The bartender told her the gentleman had taken a call and left. There was no note.

Some fifty people in casual and formal attires mingled in the VIP suite at the Knight's Hotel. A gaily costumed trio entertained the crowd with lively Turkish music.

John nodded to a gray-haired man with tired eyes and a short, curly goatee, holding court in the center of the room. "That's Orhan Erkin, the Turkish ambassador. He throws parties like this every summer." John winked. "Pay my respects."

When John departed, Imelda took a walk around the suite, where a festive mood prevailed. A few couples danced, while others on the balcony absorbed the harbor view.

Guests cast admirable glances at the attractive blonde. She smiled when John caught up with her. "Sorry about that. He's an important guy. Gotta schmooze a little."

"You know all the people living here?"

"I should. I bill 'em for electric every month."

"Gerfried Enslein?"

John scrunched his face. "Never heard of him."

The band struck up a catchy tune. A short, stout woman pulled John onto the dance floor. "Be right back," he shouted over his shoulder.

Imelda took the moment to join the small group around the ambassador, including the well-dressed Russian she had seen earlier in the hotel lobby. The ambassador stepped aside to make room for her.

"Splendid party," she said, grinning.

"I'm glad you are enjoying it. I'm Ambassador Erkin." He turned to the middle-aged woman standing beside him. "Daria, my wife. I'm sorry. You are?"

"Imelda Burke."

Daria scrutinized Imelda's face and figure, either envious of her beauty or just checking out her style. "What brings you to Rhodes, Ms. Burke?"

"I'm on vacation."

"We've been coming here for years," she said. "We enjoy the beaches and the Old Town. You're American."

"Yes. While I'm here, I'm trying to locate an old acquaintance."

"Oh?" remarked Daria, perking up.

"Gerfried Enslein, a professor," said loud enough that others overheard.

For an instant, the group grew silent, and Daria's lofty expression shifted to an icy stare. The ambassador said something to the Russian and the tall, dark-haired man standing across from him. The Russian replied in Turkish, and everyone except Imelda and Daria laughed.

Imelda acted as if nothing had happened and focused on the others. But the knot in her stomach and the sudden hush in conversation revealed her gaffe at mentioning the professor's name.

During a lull in the conversation, she thanked the ambassador and Daria for their hospitality and excused herself. At the bar, she found John and thanked him for inviting her.

As she headed for the door, the Russian stepped in front of her, a thin smile on his lips. "I am sorry, miss. I did not get your name."

"Imelda Burke."

"Sergei Krakov." He waved at the festivities. "The party is just beginning."

She frowned and politely stepped around him. "It's been a long day and I'm a little jet-lagged."

"I saw you in the hotel lobby. Perhaps we can have a cocktail tomorrow or dinner. I am here alone."

"I'm sorry. I'm very busy tomorrow. But thank you anyway."

He bowed his head. "I hope to see you again."

"Yes," she said, walking out the door.

twenty-nine

KNIGHT'S HOTEL, RHODES, GREECE

Half asleep, Imelda rolled over and noticed her message light was blinking. She picked up the receiver and listened to Alex's apology for missing her last night. He said he had an important call while she was in the restroom and the reception was so poor he went outside to take it. He asked the bartender to tell the blonde that he'd return in a few minutes. The bartender forgot to mention it.

Imelda made a mental note to call Alex and explain her side of the story. She didn't want to end their friendship on a sour note.

After breakfast, she stopped in the lobby to get a street map and noticed a big, hulking man reading a newspaper. What struck Imelda was the size of the man's hands, almost twice the normal size—thick, muscular fingers and broad, fleshy palms that seemed too large for the paper they were holding. Gant glanced up at her as she walked past, like a cat appraising a mouse before the pounce.

At the ambassador's party, Marcos, Kavi's brother, overheard Imelda talking about Enslein. He informed Enslein, who ordered Gant to follow her.

The Housing Bureau was one large room on the ground floor of the municipal building three blocks from the hotel. The hand-written sign on the door declared it would open at eleven.

With time to kill, Imelda embarked on a brief sightseeing tour and headed for the harbor, a beehive of activity. Delivery trucks, cars, and mopeds streamed on the shore as the morning ferry unloaded its usual allotment of day-trippers. Visitors swarmed the small seaside cafes and wandered along the harbor. A few ventured out to the long breakwater with its three distinctive windmills.

Following the crowds, Imelda continued to the arched gate of the Old Town. As she neared the fountain in Museum Square, she came upon a small group of tourists.

She overheard a man in a Yankees T-shirt speaking to a young woman as he pointed at the high stone barrier behind him. "You can see the whole Old Town from up there." He turned to Imelda. "They sell tickets in the Palace of the Knights."

Imelda thanked him with a smile and strolled around an open-air market, where one could buy almost anything. She stopped by a stall and picked up a crescent-shaped shell fluted like a Greek column.

"Argonauta," said the proprietress, continuing to describe the parchment-like shell in Greek.

"I'm sorry," said Imelda. "I don't understand."

A woman nearby translated. "She says it's very rare."

The proprietress pointed to the shell's intricate pattern and handed it to Imelda.

As Imelda examined the shell, she spotted the hulking man from the hotel lobby looking in her direction. When Gant saw her staring, he turned away. She waited to see if he'd look back in her direction. When he didn't, she returned the shell to the table. "Thank you. It's exquisite."

The proprietress presented Imelda with a pink moon shell, coiled like a corkscrew.

"No, thank you," said Imelda. "I like the Argonauta." Shouldering her bag, she headed toward the Housing Bureau.

Upon returning, Imelda noticed that the closed sign was still on the door. She sat on the steps and waited. Ten minutes later, a casually dressed young man appeared and quickly climbed the stairs. He acknowledged the visitor with a nod and unlocked the door.

"Good morning," she said, following him in.

He drew the shades and opened the windows. "English?"

"American."

"You are lucky Leonidas is not here. He does not speak a word. *I* studied at the university." He moved two books out of the sun. "Heat is not good for books." He looked at her and waited.

"I'd like some information about a property owner."

"Do you have a letter?"

"A letter? No."

"You need a letter from the secretary. The records are private."

"The secretary?"

"At County Hall."

Imelda remembered walking past it. "Will they give me a letter?"

"Are you a Greek citizen?"

Imelda's face dropped. "Look, Mister . . ."

"Anatole. Call me Anatole."

"I came all the way from America, Anatole. I'm looking for an old acquaintance who owns property here." She lowered her eyes. "I didn't know the procedure, and I don't have any Greek friends. Couldn't you, well, couldn't you make an exception in this case?"

Anatole frowned. "I could get into trouble."

"No one will know."

He shook his head. "I cannot let you look at the book."

"Suppose I give you a name. You can check it for me, couldn't you?" She looked into his eyes with a captivating smile he had rarely seen before.

Anatole blushed shyly. "Are you staying here?"

"Yes."

He shuffled some papers and gave her a tentative look. "My uncle, he owns a restaurant nearby. If I help you, maybe we can have dinner there, okay?"

"Yes. That would be nice."

He beamed. "Tonight. Seven o'clock?"

"How's eight?"

"Eight. Okay." He smiled.

"I'll meet you in the lobby of the Knight's Hotel," she said, wondering if she had made another foolish mistake.

Anatole glanced at a directory on the corner of his desk. "I suppose I could check *one* name."

"Gerfried Enslein." She spelled it for him.

He opened the book, as she leaned over the desk, noticing the entries were in Greek. When Anatole caught her looking, he quickly closed the book. "You must sit over there, please." He pointed to a chair by the window.

She took a seat as he flipped through the pages, then looked up and frowned. "I am sorry, he is not here."

"Is it possible he's here but not listed?"

"If he owns the property, he must be for taxes. What does he do?"

"He's a famous biologist, born in Switzerland. I'm pretty sure he lives here," she insisted.

"Maybe he is a renter or a guest," said Anatole, studying the book, "or the property is in a different name."

"It's important that I find him."

"My boss might know," he said. "I will ask him and tell you at dinner."

She got up and shook his hand. "Thanks, Anatole."

"*Parakalo.* I will meet you tonight at eight."

Stepping out the door, she caught sight of the hulking man sitting on a bench reading the newspaper. She hurried down the stairs toward the market, convinced the man was following her. At the end of the block, she ducked into a coffee shop and waited for ten minutes. Venturing outside, she anxiously looked around. He was nowhere to be seen.

thirty

MONOLITHOS CASTLE, RHODES, GREECE

Enslein sat on a chair as Kavi helped him ease his bony legs into the orange Hazmat suit and sewn-in socks. Enslein had tried to dress himself and became frustrated when he couldn't, reluctantly having to rely on Kavi.

Heavier and more difficult to get into than other suits, orange Hazmat garments protected against nuclear threats and extreme biohazards.

Flexing his arms and legs, he slowly stood up. "I blame Chu for this."

Kavi raised the back of the suit as she pushed his right arm into the sleeve and glove. Then she pulled the hood over his head and checked the seal around his face as he inserted his left arm into the other sleeve.

"No gaps or holes." He stared into her unsympathetic eyes. "One leak and I am finished. All of us would die."

She smoothed the seal around his face and adjusted the self-contained breathing apparatus. "Why you?" she said. "Let Chu take care of it."

"He had an asthma attack. The suit will choke him."

"It's just a mouse."

"An infected mouse that could kill us all if we do not find it. Would you take the chance?"

He stepped into safety boots as Kavi supplied the face-piece and zipped him up. She sealed the Velcro flaps.

Enslein stretched his hands and feet, checking for fit and comfort, and waddled toward the stairs. Then he stopped and turned to her. "This should not take too long."

"What are you doing down there?" she asked. "In your secret lab? You never talk about it."

"No one has ever done what I am doing. No one is smart enough to pull it off."

"To pull it off? Is this some kind of game?"

"Yes. And I will win it. They will pay a fortune for their arrogance and pride."

She watched as he approached the stone stairway leading to the laboratory. The stairs were rough and jagged; the only light came from a window at the top. He took his time descending and paused on a step before continuing down.

At the laboratory door, he typed 541AD on the keypad. A tribute to the year the Plague of Justinian reached Constantinople, the former capital of the Roman Empire, and killed over 10,000 people per day. Corpses stacked like kindling rotted and festered in the public squares.

The door clicked open, and the lights went on. He entered the lab amidst an impressive array of sequencers, spectrometers, imaging systems, and histology tools. The door wheezed shut and silence filled the room.

Like a zombie, he crept around the lab in search of the afflicted mouse. It was nowhere to be seen. He crouched down and peered under the cages, and finally spotted it lying lifeless on the floor.

He picked it up by the tail and studied it. The eyes and mouth were wide open, as if it passed in excruciating pain.

He carried it to the propane incinerator and dropped it in. Then he closed the lid and flipped the switch. In two hours, it would be a harmless ash.

thirty-one

THE HAVASI NIGHTCLUB, RHODES, GREECE

The open-air cafe across the street proved a perfect place for spying. Alex sat there for an hour, wondering if Kavi would appear and angry with himself for not following her when he was there. He considered going back to the hotel, but with his luck, she'd show as soon as he had left.

At a brisk pace, a woman in a red dress headed toward the side door of the nightclub. Alex dropped three euros on the table and quickly crossed the street and followed her.

She unlocked the door and entered. He ran and caught the door before it shut. Motionless, he listened to the fading click of leather heels on the white tile floor. When the clicking stopped, a door slammed shut, and he walked inside.

Retracing his steps through the grand salon, he climbed the stairs to Kavi's dressing room. At her door, he paused and listened. It was quiet inside.

The lights were on when he walked in and the parrot was awake. "Nefis ekmek. Good bread," she said. "Nefis ekmek. Good bread."

Alex put his finger to his lips. "Shh. Shh." The parrot stopped chattering and one-eyed him.

Spread across the vanity were Kavi's makeup, hair clips, combs, and tubes of lotion. Dance costumes, gowns, and shoes lay scattered on the floor. He looked behind the curtain and saw a door that opened to a small room with a cot, desk, laptop computer, and a file cabinet. The laptop was password protected. It took Alex only a minute to access the Recovery Manager, change the password, and log on.

The homepage revealed icons with English captions: Memberships, Financials, Music, Rehearsals, Miscellaneous, and Personal.

He clicked on Memberships and searched for Enslein. Not there. He tried Personal, but it was blockchain encrypted so he couldn't get in. He clicked on Financials and scrolled through tax and insurance statements and ownership contracts. Among the contracts was one from Enslein, transferring the title of the *Minotaur* to Majreen Kavi.

A creaking sound came from the dressing room. He closed the laptop, opened the door, and cautiously stepped out. An arm seized him from behind, choking off his breath. He dropped to one knee, grabbed the arm, and flipped his assailant to the floor.

An Asian woman sprang to her feet and twisted into a martial arts posture. Confident and in control, she calmly circled him. The parrot's whistle and her flinch were all it took. He seized her by the arm and slammed her to the floor. Out cold, he left her there and quietly retraced his steps.

thirty-two

KNIGHT'S HOTEL, RHODES, GREECE

Wearing a black skirt, red blouse, and black flats, Imelda relaxed at the bar, nursing a gin and tonic. She avoided looking at a young man who couldn't take his eyes off her. To her left, a couple kissed and toasted their arrival. Four women standing by the door discussed their dining options but couldn't seem to agree on where to go. At the desk, a woman holding a nervous Norfolk Terrier waited impatiently for her room key.

Anatole walked in, looking older and more confident than before. He wore a dark gray jacket, tan pants, and a white shirt, opened at the collar. When he saw Imelda, he waved and joined her at the bar.

"Hello." He stepped back with a bashful smile. "I am sorry, but I never learned your name."

"Imelda."

"Imelda, you look . . . very nice tonight."

"Thank you." She signaled for the bar tab and initialed it. "Shall we go?"

"We can walk," he said, as he proudly escorted her through the lobby into the warm and humid night. "This part of town has no cars or scooters, and the restaurant is near to here."

They proceeded side by side down the street to an intersection where they crossed a stone bridge over an empty moat. Ahead, a pointed archway and tall trees overhung the cobbled path leading to the Old Town. Imelda felt like she was entering a dark, forbidden fortress.

Anatole stopped at the clock tower on Sokratous and pointed to a glow in the distance. "Carnival tonight in the Turkish quarter. Snakes, jugglers, and magicians. If you like, we can go after dinner."

She smiled but didn't speak, as they walked under a succession of stone arches and crossed a narrow street.

"I know a shortcut." He led her to a winding alley that ended at a brightly lighted square where strings of colored lights welcomed diners to a charming open-air restaurant. The appetizing scent of grilled fish filled the air. Off to the side, a quartet played Greek music. A few people danced.

When Paulus, the headwaiter, saw his friend's date, his eyes widened. "No! I don't believe it! You have a date!" he said in Greek.

Anatole made a face, and in English introduced Imelda.

Grinning, Paulus led them to a pre-set table and recommended a carafe of white wine, eggplant salad, and a local fish served whole for them to share.

"Charming," said Imelda, taking in the scene.

Anatole smiled self-importantly. "They spoil me here."

The diners applauded as the musicians concluded their set, and the guitar player joked with the crowd. Paulus returned with a breadbasket and salad, and poured the wine, which they tasted before starting on their salads.

"I spoke with Leonidas," Anatole said, popping a slice of cucumber in his mouth. "He never heard of Enslein. When I told him he was Swiss, he searched again and found Gerfried Enslein with a Swiss passport, living on the other side of the island."

Imelda's eyes lit up. "That's great! Thank you, Anatole."

"It is nothing."

"No," she replied. "This is very important to me." She removed the Rhodes map from her purse and opened it on the table. "Show me."

Anatole pointed to Monolithos, a small village on the western side of the island. "Enslein lives in a castle there. It has no address because it is the only one in Rhodes. He must be very rich."

"Who owns the castle?"

"I did not ask."

"Please do." She drew a circle around Monolithos, then folded the map and returned it to her purse.

At that moment, Paulus delivered the fish, sizzling on a black metal plate. Skillfully, he separated flesh from bones and served each of them a filet. Then he doled out roasted potatoes and topped off their wineglasses.

Imelda took a bite. "Mmm. Very nice."

"I am sorry to be so curious," said Anatole. "But are you married?"

"No. But I'm seeing somebody."

He gazed at her in his bashful, unassuming manner. "I do not work every day, so I could show you around. Rhodes is beautiful. I bet you have not seen Lindos. That is my favorite. Or Rhodini. Ah, I know what you would like. Petaloudes, Valley of the Butterflies. We could drive there on our way to Monolithos."

Imelda smoothed a napkin on her lap. "It sounds beautiful, but I'm only here for a short time. And thanks to you, I can find my friend."

His smile faded. "I understand."

After dessert, Paulus returned and scribbled the bill on a piece of brown paper. Anatole reached for it, but Imelda snatched it first.

"Please. You've been so nice."

"Thank you." He stood up. "Can I take you to the carnival now?"

"I think I'll stay and listen to the music. Are you okay with that?"

A flicker of sadness swept his eyes. "You should come and meet my friends. We have fun."

"You join them. Please. I'm okay."

Anatole nodded regretfully, wrote his phone number on a napkin, and gave it to her. "Call me if you change your mind."

She put the napkin in her purse. "I will."

He shook her hand.

"Thank you," she said. "For all your help."

Imelda waited for him to depart and then poured herself another glass of wine.

Only a handful of diners remained when she paid the bill, plus a generous tip, and waved goodbye to Paulus. Pausing in the empty square, she tried to recall which alley they came in on. In the dark, they all looked the same to her. She tried her phone to get directions. But it had no service there. The pathway on the right seemed recognizable, and she took a chance.

It ended on an unfamiliar street. But she was relieved to see the tall, white minaret of the Mosque of Ibrahim in the distance. Using it as a polar star, she navigated in that direction.

The medieval architecture, so striking during the day, took on an eerie aspect at night. Pennants hovering from towers resembled ghostly apparitions, and ancient buttresses and arches cast frightening shadows on the streets and walls below.

Her heart skipped a beat when a clang broke the silence. Straining her eyes, she stared into the shadows and breathed a sigh of relief when she saw a boy carrying a trash can.

She crossed Sokratous Square and glimpsed the glittering lights of D'Amboise Gate, reassurance she was going in the right direction. She quickened her pace, eager to return to her hotel.

When she passed an alley, Gant lunged out from the shadows, terrifying her. She jumped back as he seized her arm. She twisted, breaking free, and ran back the other way.

Sprinting for a block, she came upon a man in uniform, sleeping in a chair, a peaked cap covering his eyes.

"Help!" she shouted. He didn't move. She shook him by the shoulder. His head slumped to the side, revealing a deep gash on his throat and a jacket soaked in blood.

Horrified, she ran toward the clock tower as the tread of heavy footsteps thumped behind her. The street ended on a flight of stairs. She charged up three steps at a time, dislodging an empty soda can that clattered down behind her.

She stopped on the terreplein atop the wall and caught her breath. The dark and empty space between the parapets encircling the Old Town was vast and made of earth. Heavy footsteps from the staircase shattered the tranquility.

Propelled by fear, she ran along the terreplein and almost lost her footing when it ended at an unprotected ledge. Bracing against a parapet, she looked down at the grassed-over moat some forty feet below.

A pitch-dark stairwell led her to the street, where she pushed through the heavy wooden door into the Turkish Quarter.

The maze of narrow, winding streets and alleys confused her. Afraid to stop, she ran down a nameless alley, past boarded-up shops, ending at an intersection. She continued on, searching for someone who could help.

The dark quarter's labyrinthine corridors drew her deeper in, evoking a sense of dread and isolation. She entered another alley, startling a black cat that wailed like a hungry baby and disappeared under a wall. The alley ended at a wide-planked door, where a dim light flickered from above.

Lifting the latch, she stepped into a courtyard open to the inky sky. White sheets hanging from ropes partitioned the space into small rectangles, each containing a bed where people slept.

A bony hand gripped her shoulder, and she turned and stared at a grotesque face and toothless mouth that moved, but didn't speak.

"Help me," Imelda cried, pulling away. "Help me." The old man gaped at her and pointed to the door.

She turned and ran through the courtyard, dislodging sheets and waking people as she went, escaping through a narrow archway leading to an ancient square with marble colonnades.

Streamers, confetti, and food containers blanketed the way. Imelda hurried across, colliding with a woman who dropped a basket of metal trinkets that rang like wind chimes on the stone.

Imelda pleaded for help. The woman stooped, collected her wares, and cursed at her.

Across the square, two men sat beside an unkempt bear with sunken eyes, chained to an iron ring fastened to a wall. The men stopped talking when they saw her; the bear got up and snarled at her.

"Please," she said, reaching out to them. "Help me."

The older man spoke Arabic to the bearded, younger man.

Imelda ventured closer. "Someone is chasing me. I need your help."

"What?" asked the bearded one.

"Police! Call the police!"

He translated for the other, who grumbled an incomprehensible reply.

"Someone is chasing me!" She gestured nervously behind her.

The bearded man rose to his feet. "Money!"

She opened her purse and handed him several large bills, which he stuffed into his jacket pocket.

She looked around in desperation. "Please. There's no time." She feared they didn't understand. "We have to go," she pleaded. "Now! He's coming!"

The bearded man yanked the purse from her hand. She grabbed for it, but he pushed her away and shook its contents onto the cobblestones. He seized her wallet and her phone.

From out of nowhere, a trunk-like arm propelled him into the air. He landed on his back, squirming and moaning in pain.

Petrified, the older man locked eyes with the imposing giant standing in his path.

As Gant lunged for Imelda, she sprang back and failed to see the chain. Tripping, she fell backwards and struck her head on the stones, knocking her unconscious.

The bear snarled, raised its claws, and charged. Gant jerked it away as if it were a toy. The bear whimpered and retreated to the wall. A hush fell over the square.

Imelda awoke from the jolting and rocking motion while sitting in the back seat of a limo. Seated next to her, Gant held her by the arm. She had a pounding headache and felt lightheaded. Attempting to break free, she felt his grasp tighten like a vise, and feared he'd break her arm.

They drove for what seemed like miles, over rough roads that bounced her side to side. The passing blur of trees and small farms and houses was all she saw.

The sky turned crimson, as gray clouds swept east toward Turkey. She saw a sign for Paradisi and recalled it was a village somewhere on the coast as they took a left turn at a roadblock heading inland.

The limo slowed and pulled onto a shoulder because two cars blocked the road ahead. A man and woman, standing in the middle of the road, quarreled with an older man. Ignoring the driver's shouts, they refused to move their cars.

Distracted by the altercation, Gant leaned forward, relaxing his grip on Imelda's arm. She slid her left hand through the space between the front seat and the driver's door and released the door locks. Throwing open the rear door, she made a break for it. When Gant reached for her, she was already out.

Her legs felt like rubber as she rushed down an embankment into a lush, wooded area, running as fast as she could. She ran for several minutes until her legs gave out. Collapsing behind a boulder, she gasped for breath and looked back for her pursuer. Not seeing him, she got up and trotted, following a brook through tall trees and tangled bushes.

When an orange-and-black-winged butterfly landed on her arm, she swatted it, and it fluttered to the ground. More butterflies appeared. She recalled Anatole's mention of a valley of butterflies. Is she there?

A crack that sounded like a broken branch alerted her, and she caught sight of her abductor some fifty yards away, heading in her direction.

Imelda ran alongside the brook to an algae-covered pond, home to thousands of butterflies blanketing the ground and brush into a pulsing mantle. When she appeared, they filled the air, forming a swirling cloud around her, like a tornado.

She stopped running, unable to see more than a foot in front of her. The teeming insects assaulted her eyes, nose, and mouth as she waved her hands to fend them off. Stumbling over a rock, she fell into the pond as a maelstrom swarmed above her.

Gant strode into the water, disrupting the whirling mass. He lunged at her but missed. Stumbling out of the pond, she scrambled up the bank into the outstretched arms of the limo driver.

She fought and flailed, but couldn't break his grip. Gant carried her kicking and shouting back to the limo, where she was bound, gagged, and blindfolded.

Heart pounding in her rib cage, Imelda lay on the back seat, sore, tired, and thirsty. The sour odor of sweat, foul breath, and sodden clothes polluted the surrounding air, and they continued on.

As the road became rougher, the car bounced, slowed, and eventually stopped. The lack of motion frightened her, triggering thoughts of torture, rape, and murder.

The driver shouted something in Greek, followed by a metallic squeaking like a rusty hinge. As it inched forward over what sounded like wooden planks, the limo stopped.

The door opened and she could smell the sea. Gant removed her bindings and led her blindfolded, about twenty paces.

Someone removed her blindfold. Blinking from the glare, she saw an ancient fortress overlooking the sea, dark and strangely menacing.

Gerfried Enslein stepped in front of her. His relaxed manner and faraway look gave her the impression his mind was on other things. Yet, when he stared at her, his gaze was chilling and unnerving.

He looked her over like a scientist examining a rare specimen and touched her cheek. His hand felt cold as ice. She pulled away.

"You know who I am," he said in a guttural voice. "But I do not know you."

She shot a glance at the massive block of a man at his side. "I demand to be released."

Enslein slapped her face.

She glared at him.

"Who are you?"

She didn't answer.

"Your name!" demanded Enslein.

"Imelda Burke."

"Why are you looking for me, Imelda Burke?"

"I studied your work and wanted to meet you."

With a sullen cast of face, he turned and walked away. Gant seized her by the arm and pushed her through a long stone passageway, down a flight of stairs, and through a door leading to the armory, a large stone chamber filled with instruments of torture and wooden crates stuffed with books, statues, and paintings, items Enslein had purchased when he bought the place. Longbows, crossbows, and swords adorned the walls. A suit of armor posed before a rack, as if it were defending it.

Gant shackled her ankle to the wall and tossed her a blanket. Before he left, his lustful eyes appraised her.

She glared back at him. "I'm an American citizen! They know where I am!"

He walked out and locked the door. Hazy darkness filled the room. She gasped and felt as if the walls were closing in on her.

thirty-three

MONOLITHOS CASTLE, RHODES, GREECE

Enslein preferred the castle's solar suite, not for its tapestries, furniture, and wall lamps enhanced with precious gems, but for its golden sunsets in the sea. He gazed at Kavi sitting beside him as she lit a cigarette. "Who was that woman?" she asked.

"Imelda Burke, if that is her name."

"A foreign agent?"

He laughed. "Expect the marines, my dear."

Kavi took a drag, reclaiming through her nostrils the lines of smoke leaking from her lips. "Someone talked?"

"I worry about Valovitch."

The sudden mention of the Russian's name made Kavi rise and pace the room with slow, deliberate strides. "What does *he* know?"

"You and me, and possibly this castle."

"Sometimes I think we made a mistake not going back with him," she said. "For two years we made a fortune selling drugs. It was safe. An easy set-up."

"Easy for Valovitch," mocked Enslein. "We did all the work."

"Well, you got even, didn't you?" she smirked.

thirty-four

THE HAVASI NIGHTCLUB, RHODES, GREECE

The hostess at the front desk smiled warmly when she saw him. "Mr. West! What a pleasant surprise!" She was alone in there, except for a man vacuuming the rugs.

"Hello again," said Alex. "I'm sorry. I never got your name."

"Rhea. How can I help you today?"

Alex sat beside her. "I had a good time, and I'd like to become a member."

"Sure." She reached into her desk, withdrew an enrollment form, and handed it to him. "It's basic stuff—name, address, occupation. Madam Kavi approves all the new members. When you're accepted, there's a membership fee." She handed him a pen.

Alex took his time filling out the form as she watched him thoughtfully. "Is Madam Kavi here?" he asked in a casual tone.

"No. She usually arrives about three. Likes her beauty sleep."

He signed his name and handed her the completed form.

Rhea read it and wrinkled her brow. "Private investigator? Why do you want to join our club, Mr. West?"

"Like I said, I had a good time the other night. And I like the staff." He smiled at her.

"Thank you." She placed his application in a drawer and looked up at him with sadness in her eyes. "This is my last week."

"Oh?"

"Mr. West, I want to be honest with you. This club is . . . Well, I heard some members may be involved in . . . in illegal things."

"Does Madam Kavi know?"

She shrugged. "The drugs, the people . . ."

"Who?"

"Foreigners mostly. They frighten me."

"They seemed okay when I was here."

"It's during the after-hours when . . ." She looked away and stopped speaking.

Alex said, "I'm sure Madam Kavi will be sorry to lose you, Rhea. Did you tell her yet?"

"No. I plan to tell her today."

"Where does she live?"

"On the other side of the island."

"I heard it's beautiful there. Do you have an address?"

"No. I've never been there. A very private person."

He showed her Enslein's photo. "Ever seen him before?"

She studied it for a moment, and then her eyes lit up. "Yes. Once. He came to the club with her. A strange, quiet man. Pale and very intense. 'An old friend,' she said."

"His name is Gerfried Enslein."

"I don't know the name, but I'd never forget the face." She returned the photo as Alex's cell phone rang.

"Excuse me," Alex said, stepping into the hall. "What's up?"

"Bad news," said Dimitri. "They killed a night watchman in the Old Town yesterday. Cut his jugular. Nobody knows how it happened. And someone took the property transfer book during the break-in at the Housing Bureau."

"Just when we needed it," said Alex. "There must be an online version, right?"

"Yes, but I do not have the password."

"You're sure?"

"I promised to help you, Alex. Do not worry. One more thing. A fisherman discovered a corpse on the beach near Monolithos. I am going now. Can you join me?"

"I'll be waiting in front of the Havasi."

thirty-five

MONOLITHOS CASTLE, RHODES, GREECE

melda opened her eyes, and for one terrifying moment didn't know where she was. No matter how she moved, her clothes stuck to her clammy skin and a dull pain throbbed in the back of her head.

Wiping sweat from her brow, she leaned against the wall, and blamed herself for her predicament—cover blown, life in danger, and mission compromised. She had talked too much and didn't think.

The sound of heavy footsteps approached the armory door, followed by the jangling of keys and the dull clank of a moving bolt. The door creaked opened. Enslein entered, walked to the table, and picked up a helmet-like object. He turned to her and displayed the blade mounted on the helmet's faceplate. "It is called a brank. If the victim moves their tongue, it will puncture it or slice it off."

He swept his arm in an all-consuming gesture. "This used to be a museum open to the public. I bought all the artifacts and added to the collection. Naturally, I wanted to learn more. It *is* quite fascinating." He approached her, holding the brank. "Why did you lie to me, Imelda Burke?"

"I didn't lie."

"Why would a nobody come so far to ask about my work?"

She glared at him. "No one knew where you were."

"You found me!" He shifted the brank in his hands. "Why go through all this trouble to locate an old man retired on an island who only wants a little peace in his life?"

"I heard about you and wanted to meet you."

He placed the brank on the table and fingered the other objects lying there. "Many of these are valuable antiques, some used. Thumbscrews. Pincers. Daggers." He paused before the rack, admiring it. "The arms are the first to go. The humerus pops out of the shoulders. Tendons snap. Extensor and flexor muscles tear. Arteries fail." He stopped and smiled at her. "Primitive, but quite effective."

"Only a sick, demonic person would collect such things." Revulsion etched her face.

He gestured to an upright cabinet on a metal base. "My friend, the maiden." Slowly, he cranked open the spring-driven lid; it creaked from the increased tension, exposing razor-sharp spikes glistening in the hazy light. "The only one of its kind invented by Karras, the man who built this castle. I do not suppose you would like to sleep in here tonight."

He took a few steps toward the door and stopped. "Ms. Burke, vulgar business is something I absolutely detest." He departed and secured the door behind him.

Seizing the chain with both hands, she pulled but couldn't budge it. The manacle dug sharply into her ankle.

thirty-six

THE HAVASI NIGHTCLUB, RHODES, GREECE

D imitri's Opel had seen better days: a dented front fender, cracked windshield, and no AC. Alex slid into the passenger's seat and wondered how his friend could stand the heat in there. He rolled down the window and stuck his finger through the bullet hole over his head. "Lucky it doesn't rain too often."

"In January," smiled Dimitri. "Not a drop right now. We take the main road toward Afandou and Archangelos, then on to Lindos, and through the mountains toward Agios Isidoros. You will see the beauty of our island."

At higher elevations, it grew cooler, and a slight breeze picked up from the west. With trucks and tractors crowding the narrow roads, Dimitri slowed down and took a moment to point out a hawk riding the thermals, its wide tail distinctive in the clear blue sky.

"A break-in, a robbery, and now two fatalities," Dimitri mused. "Bad news for Ródos. We sell some grapes, figs, olives, and jewelry. But without the tourists . . ." He waved an anxious hand.

"It seems more than a coincidence that someone stole the property transfer book the day before we needed it," said Alex.

"We will get it back. We are checking the airport and the docks and piers."

Alex nodded. "What about this corpse?"

"A fisherman in Monolithos found the body near the cliffs. He thinks the man was climbing and somehow fell on the rocks below."

"ID?" asked Alex.

"The fisherman was afraid. He did not touch him."

In silence, they drove on for several minutes and crossed Sianna Mountain, offering a spectacular view of the sea. The water was calm, like in a travelog, almost too splendid to be real.

A half-hour later, they took a narrow dirt road to the small fishing village, leaving in their wake a swirl of yellow dust.

White cottages lined the road behind split-rail fences, where fishnets and buoys hung intermittently. In front of the cottages, several men and women sat on benches repairing nets, lines, and lures. They eyed the car suspiciously, then returned to their work, chatting among themselves.

Dimitri stopped and asked a boy if he knew Spiros Stamatakis. The boy pointed to a cottage at the end of the road. Dimitri thanked him, drove up the hill, and parked in front.

Sitting on the front stoop, Stamatakis rose to his feet as if he were expecting them. His baggy shirt and pants billowed in the offshore breeze. He was tall, thin, and dark-haired, with a lined and pious face, weathered brown from the sun, reminding Alex of a prophet or a seer. Alex and Dimitri got out of the car and approached him. Dimitri called out his name, and Stamatakis answered in Greek.

The captain introduced himself and Alex and explained the purpose of their visit. When Stamatakis learned Alex was American, he addressed him in English.

Alex shook his hand. "You speak English very well, Mr. Stamatakis."

"I learned when I was in the Merchant Marine. Traveled all over the world. Please call me Spiros."

Dimitri removed a notebook from his pocket. "You said you found the body yesterday. What time?"

Spiros looked away. "Maybe ten o'clock at night."

"What were you doing out so late?" asked Alex, wondering how he could find a corpse in the dark.

"The beach is peaceful at night. And the moon was full, casting my shadow on the sand."

Dimitri spoke Greek with Spiros, then turned to Alex. "He will take us to the body."

The fisherman nodded and walked off at an easy pace, not bothering to see if his visitors were following. He led them along a winding, grassy path toward the sea.

On the beach, they turned north for about a mile, passing amber-colored cliffs. The tide was low and sea birds flittered on the hardened sand, searching for food.

Spiros pointed to the rocky area at the bottom of a cliff. Wedged between the rocks was the body of a middle-aged man, his head split-open, twisted to the side, and spider crabs were feeding on the brain.

"Scavengers." Dimitri drove them off with a piece of driftwood and examined the body, stiff from rigor mortis. The dead man wore a gray suit, a blue shirt open at the collar, and expensive leather shoes that gleamed.

Dimitri peeled back the victim's jacket collar to reveal Armani on the label. "A wealthy tourist." He checked for clues of who he was and how and why he got there, yielding no results. "It may have been a robbery." He took several pictures of the body and surrounding area and then secured the crime scene with yellow tape.

Alex examined the victim's neck. It had no bruises, contusions, or ligature marks. He ran his fingers over the neck bones and felt the second vertebra. Something or someone had shattered it into pieces.

"I think someone killed him earlier and then dumped him here," said Alex. "Neck fractures from falls are often three or four vertebrae closer to the spine. This was an intentional fracture. And hardly any loss of blood."

"How do you know that?" said Dimitri, studying the corpse.

"Combat school. I'll show you." Alex stood next to Dimitri and placed his right hand on Dimitri's chin and his left hand on the back of Dimitri's head. "Now, if I push your chin up and away with my right hand as I pull your head down with my left, I break your neck. Just like that. You can practice on your wife."

Dimitri smiled. "Thank you, Alex."

Spiros called out to them from the beach, waved a farewell arm, and headed back to the village.

Dimitri watched him walk away. "A penitent man." He called the office for an ambulance and coroner. "The medical examiner will tell us more . . . Walk around with me."

They combed the crime scene for over an hour and found nothing of interest. Rather than return to the village, they climbed a narrow path to the top of the cliff.

Catching their breath, they looked down at the sea, morphing from emerald green at the shoreline to darker hues of blue and indigo on the horizon. The island's beauty clashed with the gory scene below. Alex cast a stone into the void and watched as it plummeted to the rocks below. "One twist was all he needed."

Dimitri smiled. "You seem convinced it was murder."

"He wasn't dressed for hiking."

thirty-seven

MONOLITHOS CASTLE, RHODES, GREECE

A young man in a yellow Hazmat suit injected small quantities of adenine into one of four petri dishes. Beside him, liquids swirled in flasks under sealed glass hoods. He looked up from his work and acknowledged Enslein in his orange Hazmat suit.

"Professor."

"Chu. Good news, I trust."

"Yes. We mutated the virus and increase potency three-fold."

Enslein lifted a culture tube and gently swirled its contents. His eyes glowed with admiration. "A glimpse of the future, Chu. Not a tank or missile, but a pathogen so small, yet powerful enough to bring the world to its knees. A weapon of mass destruction, far greater than any nuclear weapon."

Enslein glanced at Chu's records. "Now then. How is it coming?"

"The copolymer worked perfectly. It will surprise you how effective it is."

Enslein scowled. "I invented it, you fool."

Chu led the professor to several cages harboring mice, monkeys, and rabbits. The mice ran back and forth as if sensing an impending danger. Two white rabbits, their heads oddly distorted by bulbous tumors, lay on their sides, with pink, lifeless eyes. The monkeys sat and watched them with darting eyes.

Chu inserted his right hand through a glove box into a ventilated enclosure and seized a mouse by the tail. It twisted in mid-air and churned its legs, trying to get free. Chu dropped the rodent onto a small piece of paper and it ran off to the corner of the hood. There, it trembled violently as it struggled to take a few more steps, and a moment later, it was dead.

"Three seconds," Enslein said.

Chu withdrew his hand. "This strain is effective. Encapsulation protects ninety percent of the viral population. Death rates are over sixty percent even after exposure to higher levels of heat, stress, and oxygen."

Enslein smiled as he followed Chu across the room to a hood containing three pint-sized, stainless-steel cylinders.

Chu's assistant thrust her hands through two round glove holes and injected a cloudy liquid into a cylinder, trembling slightly while fastening the cap.

"Careful," said Chu. "One false move and we lose several weeks of work."

"Yes, sir." The assistant opened the second cylinder and repeated the process.

"Ship them tomorrow," Enslein said.

thirty-eight

BIOLOGICAL WEAPONS GROUP
HEADQUARTERS, ATLANTA, GEORGIA

BWG had been in overdrive since the DC meeting. Dunphy's and Atkinson's teams had tested hundreds of bio-samples from various government agents around the world and they found no virus resembling the Norwalk Agent.

Every evening, Malone phoned Brockman for an update, and for the first time, the Secretary of the Department of Homeland Security admitted that the search and screening of suspected terrorists had proved more difficult than expected.

Many suspects lived in hostile countries, slowing down the investigative process. And expert legal teams, armies, or militias protected others. Malone's assumption that Vector could be found by the end of June seemed like lunacy now.

Still, Brockman drove his team to the limit. Their future depended on it. Atkinson slept on a cot in the lab, and Dunphy worked sixteen-hour shifts without a break. Even Brockman, who had to watch his health, toiled like a man twenty years his junior.

As usual, the BWG team made it a point to share one sit-down meal each day, usually brunch. It gave them time to blow off steam and talk about something besides Vector and the Norwalk Agent.

Atkinson sampled the mushroom omelet and muttered, "A few days on the beach would be nice."

"Surf and sand," mused Dunphy. "Speaking of the beach, what's the word on Imelda? We could use her here."

"She left a message on Saturday that she'd call Monday with an update," said Brockman. "She never did. I tried her cell and texted her twice. She didn't reply. When I called the hotel, I was told she hadn't been back to her room since Saturday."

Dunphy pushed his half-empty plate into the center of the table. "What did she say the last time you talked?"

"She was waiting for someone to help locate Enslein."

"What if something happened to her?"

"Sanford has officers in Greece," said Brockman. "I asked him to check on her."

"Don't hold your breath," said Atkinson.

thirty-nine

RHODES, GREECE

A lex jogged past the Hall of Justice and took a right. A small black and white dog ran alongside him for a block and stopped when he circled back to the hotel. It was only a brief run, but enough to work up a sweat and clear his head.

Returning to the hotel, Alex played a voicemail from Dimitri and was relieved to learn Majreen Kavi owned the castle near Monolithos.

Dimitri had identified the corpse on the beach as Sergei Krakov, a member of the Russian mafia wanted for drug smuggling. Krakov's wallet, money, passports, and the stolen Book of Property Transfers were in his rental car, parked in a garage near Monolithos.

Alex recalled Marsha Farmer's statement about Enslein's frequent trips to Russia. Maybe Enslein supplied Krakov with drugs, they had a falling out, and Enslein killed him.

Alex feared Enslein may have fled the island by now, but he had to be sure. His gut said the professor was still living with Kavi at the castle.

Alex drove a rental to Lindos, stopped to eat, and then headed west across the mountains. When the castle came into view, he stopped to admire its architecture, more impressive in real life than the photo in Marsha Farmer's apartment.

As he crossed the drawbridge and braked at the gatehouse, two men stared down at him from the tower above.

Alex shouted up at them. "I'm looking for Madam Kavi!"

A guard with a machete strapped to his belt emerged from the gatehouse and approached the car. "Not here," he said, shaking his head.

"Gerfried Enslein."

"Private property." The guard fingered the machete and stared coldly at Alex.

"I'm Alex West. I have a buyer for Madam Kavi's yacht. Tell her that."

The man pointed toward the road and waited until Alex backed over the drawbridge, made a U-turn, and proceeded toward the main road. When the castle was out of sight, Alex stopped and phoned Dimitri, explaining what had happened. "Could the records be wrong?"

"Not likely," said Dimitri. "They update them every year."

"Call the castle and ask for her," urged Alex.

"No landline there."

"She must have a cell phone," said Alex. "Isn't there a way to get the number?"

"It may take a day or so."

"If I can verify Enslein lives there, I'm out of here."

"I am sorry, Alex."

Alex hung up and sat muddled in thought. Even if Dimitri got Kavi's phone number, there was no guarantee Enslein was there. And if he was, who'd admit to it?

Rather than return to the capital, Alex took a right at the fork toward the fishing village and parked in front of Spiros' cottage.

The door was closed, shades drawn. Alex knocked on the door and waited. Silence, then shuffling footsteps. The door opened, and the fisherman stood before him, unshaven, with bloodshot eyes and a mournful expression. Alex followed him into the kitchen, cluttered with dirty dishes and empty beer bottles. A sour odor filled the air.

Spiros slumped in a chair and hung his head, hands folded on his lap. "Since I found that body, I haven't been able to sleep. My father died when I was seven. I found his body on the rocks, just like that man. My father was alive when I found him. I cried for help, but the sea drowned out my voice. I was afraid to leave him and unable to help him. I sat on the rocks, frightened, weeping as my father slowly died before my eyes." He wiped tears from his eyes. "Finding that dead man was a curse! Why did *I* find him? Why was *I* on the beach?"

"I used to be a cop," said Alex, "and saw some awful things. But they don't portend the future."

"I feel like God is punishing me," gasped Spiros. "My sins."

"Everybody lives with sad memories," said Alex, "things we caused or did, hidden in our minds, emerging when we least expect them, like phantoms in the night. They can destroy us if we let them. But God is forgiving, Spiros. Remember that."

Spiros nodded and wiped a tear from his eye.

Alex looked into Spiros's eyes. "A few years ago, I killed a boy by mistake. I couldn't sleep for weeks—kept hearing the shot, and playing that scene over in my head. I went to the funeral and stood off to the side. The boy's mother could have been my mother, and I saw the pain and heartache on her face. It broke my heart. There isn't a day goes by that I don't think about her and her son."

Alex removed from his pocket a keychain holding a .32 caliber slug and held it up for Spiros to see. "The bullet that killed the boy."

forty

MONOLITHOS, RHODES, GREECE

The hot summer sun bore down mercilessly as Alex hiked along the sandy beach. He stopped at the vertical cliff beneath the castle wall, sat on the sand, and studied the rock face.

Juts and crevices in the stones resembled the lines and wrinkles in a human face carved out by centuries of wind and rain. Ledges and fissures in the rock defined the thoughtful brow; black holes, like eyes, conveyed a sense of depth and understanding; and a turned up crack, a gentle smile of confidence and reassurance.

The rock face spoke to him. "Are you insane?"

It's the wind, Alex thought, or the twittering birds, or the sound of waves lapping on the sand.

He assessed the cliff. Scaling the first hundred feet seemed easy, with lots of cracks and shelves. Higher up, he could use vertical channels or chimneys to reach the top. The climb wasn't technically more difficult than others he'd made at Ranger School. The challenge: going up there alone at night.

He wondered why he'd risk his life on a missing person's job? Certainly not for money. Maybe just to prove that he could do it.

It was almost 6:00 p.m. when he drove back to the capital. Lights were burning in the police station when Alex knocked once and opened the door. Dimitri was alone at the front desk, rummaging through items in a cardboard box. He greeted Alex with a grin. "Just the man to keep me company."

Alex pulled up a chair. "How's it going?"

Dimitri held up two driver's licenses and three passports. "Krakov's. We found them in the car, with two thousand euros in cash, one change of clothes, a Makarov semi-automatic, and nothing to explain what he was doing there."

Alex peered into the box. "Mind if I have a look?"

"Be my guest."

Alex sifted through the items. Upon opening a passport, he came across a small envelope containing Russian writing. The envelope contained two wallet-sized photographs. He showed them to Dimitri.

The captain's jaw dropped when he saw Kavi's headshot. "What is she doing in there?"

Alex pointed to the other picture. "You know this creep?"

"No."

"Professor Gerfried Enslein."

forty-one

VLADMIR OBLAST, RUSSIA

Valovitch stared wooden-faced at his cell phone. "Krakov should've called by now."

Leonid checked his watch. "Only an hour late."

"This was supposed to be easy."

"Maybe Enslein . . ."

Valovitch sneered. "He's a fool thinking nothing would happen." He walked to the window, looked out at the dense fog, and noticed the temperature was dropping. The weather fit his frame of mind, and he gnawed a piece of nail from his thumb and spit it onto the floor. "Nobody steals from me."

forty-two

BIOLOGICAL WEAPONS GROUP HEADQUARTERS, ATLANTA, GEORGIA

M arv Brockman avoided Lou Sanford every chance he got. Above all, it pained to ask him for favors, but Imelda was in trouble and he had to make the call.

Sanford was on a conference call and returned Brockman's call ten minutes later. "Make it quick, Marv. I'm in a meeting."

"It's Dr. Burke."

"You told me," Sanford said annoyingly.

"She hasn't called. And we haven't been able to reach her. She could be in trouble. You mentioned an officer in Greece."

"He's on assignment."

"It'll take one of our people eighteen hours to get there. Your man can be there in two hours."

"Our case officers are currently engaged and on the clock. But I'll see what I can do." The phone went dead.

forty-three

MONOLITHOS CASTLE, RHODES, GREECE

In the dim and unsettling half-light, Imelda stirred awake, feeling stiff and achy as she breathed the stale scent of mold and dust in the armory air. She rubbed her ankle and heard a noise from somewhere in the room.

"Who's there?" Imelda's voice aired thin and tired.

Something moved in the shadows, followed by snickering laugh.

Enslein got out of bed and called Tomek, who answered on the second ring.

"How is the weather, my friend?"

"Hot and humid."

"Do you know what day it is?"

"July 7th."

Begin phase two!" Enslein slammed down the receiver.

forty-four

FORT KNOX, KENTUCKY

Commanding General Jami Cobb suddenly changed the daily routine at the bullion depository. Several visitors, introduced as special FBI agents, were overseeing the transfer to a staging area of 1,000 gold bars, each worth almost one million dollars. They stacked the bars on wooden pallets, sealed in black plastic.

White House shipping instructions surprised Cobb. The President demanded bars from foreign banks paid to the U.S. government in swap arrangements. These bars, Cobb knew, were untested for purity.

Cobb recalled rumors that some swapped bars contained gold-coated tungsten that weighed the same as gold but were worth ten percent of the value. He never mentioned it to anyone and didn't question orders from the White House.

forty-five

MONOLITHOS CASTLE, RHODES, GREECE

A lex sat in the shadows at the base of the cliff and took a gulp of water. He checked inside his backpack to make sure he had everything: penlight, rope, grapnel, gun, phone, and water.

The castle lay in slumber under a giant moon flecked by cirrus clouds. A perfect night for a climb—plenty of light and a cool breeze off the water. He stared at the cliff, fixing it in his mind.

At Fort Benning, Alex had solo climbed at night, knew the risks, and was confident in his ability to manage them and minimize their impact on his climb. He found pleasure in taking risks; they opened doors for him and built self-confidence. Without them, he decided, he'd never know what could've been.

Tightening the straps on the backpack, he took a breath and began the climb. After crossing the loose rocks, he tackled the cliff, relying more on legs for support and conserving upper-body strength. Cracks were perfect for jamming his fingers, hands, and fists. At forty feet, he discovered a crack wide enough to accommodate his hip.

Resting, Alex looked out over the Aegean, bathed in the moonlight glistening off the water. The view invigorated him as he eyed the ledge above that arched to the right, leaning and overhanging. The line of footholds that crossed to its base sloped up severely with only one small handhold. The traverse was difficult but not impossible.

Alex moved to the right, planted his right foot in a solid foothold, and extended his right hand for a crack almost beyond his reach, stretching into a spread-eagle position, nose to the stone. Letting go with his left hand, he shifted his feet, positioning himself just below the ledge.

Resting for a moment, he thought about his next move, confident in his physical ability to pull it off. He lunged for the ledge, seized it with his left hand, and hung there, muscles bulging, veins popping.

Gravel spilled on Alex's face as he reached up with his right hand, pulled himself onto the ledge, with air flooding his lungs in great rushes. Small, white birds nesting above peered down at him as he planned his next move: traverse the ledge to reach the chimney.

He took three steps and stopped when he noticed a fissure near to where he was standing. If that section fell, he'd fall with it. Stepping forward, he heard a crack; his added weight had caused the fissure to widen.

As part of the ledge fell away, he took a running jump, sailed over the rift, and landed on the other side. For a horrifying moment, he teetered there before regaining balance. A gust of wind would've doomed him, as sweat poured from his body.

He climbed into the chimney, feet on one side, back against the other, and started up, moving one leg, then shifting to the other leg to complete the sequence. He repeated this until the chimney widened and he had to extend his legs and arms to support his upper body. Reaching the top, he stood there as the castle loomed above him.

Some twenty feet above were two openings in the castle wall. The trick would be to swing the grapnel into one of them and snare it on something secure enough to support his weight. Tape would muffle any sound from steel striking stone.

Placing his right foot near the edge of the cliff, he held the coiled line in his left hand and the grapnel in his right.

Releasing the tri-hook on the upswing, it hit the wall about a foot too high, and he was lucky to catch it in its fall.

He moved farther out on the ledge, coiled the rope, and tried again. The grapnel cleared the opening and pulled the rope inside. Alex took up the slack until he felt resistance and jerked it hard. Secure.

Hand over hand, he pulled himself up, using his feet against the wall for support, and stopping at the opening, large enough to squeeze through.

Lifting his upper body, he turned and sat on the sill, legs dangling outside. Wind blowing across the vent sounded like the bass note on a pipe organ.

He leaned back and aimed the penlight into the darkness, where he saw a narrow, earthen passageway eight feet below separating the outer and inner castle walls. Unstrapping the backpack, he dropped it in the passageway, where it landed with a thump.

He lifted his body, kneeled, and pushed his legs through the vent. Then, hanging by his hands from the sill, he let go and landed on his feet.

Alex stood still and inhaled the rich, clean smell of cold, hard stone. The wind blowing across the opening was the only sound he heard. Holstering the gun, he put the penlight and phone in his pocket and left the backpack under the vent as a marker for his return.

forty-six

MONOLITHOS CASTLE, RHODES, GREECE

Lixin, the castle's chef, had pre-cooked five kilos of potatoes ready for frying. He hummed Elva Hsiao's "My Exciting Solitary Life," as he filled a large steel pot with cooking oil.

Lixin added kindling to the stove. When it flared up, he dropped in three logs and set the pot over the flame. In a half hour, the oil would be hot enough for frying. The fire cast a reddish glow on the chef's unshaven face as he slumped on a chair in front of the stove and closed his eyes.

Alex headed for the red, flickering glow coming from a circular opening on the castle wall. He peered inside, seeing the back of the large, wood-burning stove, and crawled into the kitchen.

A log crackled. Lixin blinked twice, jumped to his feet, and shouted at the intruder. Alex raised his hands in a supplicating gesture. "New employee. New employee."

Lixin seized a nine-inch cleaver from the chopping block and threatened Alex with it. Alex backed into a corner, withdrew the SIG from the holster, and pointed it at Lixin's head.

The chef charged. Sidestepping, Alex slammed the grip against

Lixin's head, knocking him unconscious. Then he dragged him into the pantry and locked the door.

It was quiet, very still. Alex slowly opened the kitchen door and looked out into a long, deserted hallway. A light was on at the far end and he slowly made his way toward it, passing a spiral staircase on this left.

Gant stayed behind as Enslein crossed the armory and peered down at Imelda sitting on the floor.

"Last chance," he said. "Why were you looking for me?"

She didn't answer.

"You overestimate my patience."

Imelda rattled the chain. "My friends will find me."

"How did you know I was here?"

She stared at him and didn't reply, as he shook his head and walked out.

Despite the distance and poor lighting, Alex could still identify Gerfried Enslein as he departed the armory. He swiftly retreated into the doorway and waited. One minute later, he peered out and discovered that the professor had disappeared.

Unattended, the cooking oil expelled a bluish smoke that floated up and spread across the ceiling. Lixin smelled it from the pantry. "Fire! Fire!" he shouted, and banged his fists against the door.

Two minutes later, the boiling oil splattered onto the stove and woodpile, spawning an orange fireball. A symmetric plume of flame quickly enveloped the wooden cabinets above the stove and ignited kindling stacked nearby. Creosote in the old, cracked chimney flared as flames spread onto the adjoining beams and wallboard.

RICHARD ZANETTI

Gant unlocked the manacle securing Imelda's ankle. Alarmed by his malicious smirk, she quickly slid away from him. He grabbed her by the arm and lifted her onto the rack. She punched and kicked him as he forced her down and tied her wrists to the top bar of that horrific device.

"Let me go," she said. "Tell Enslein I escaped. The police will know you helped me."

He tied her ankles to the bottom bar and placed his hand on her breast. She spit into his face.

Alex headed toward the light coming from the doorway and heard a bone-chilling scream. He sprinted towards the door and witnessed a man assaulting Imelda Burke, who was bound to a table.

"Bastard!" she shouted. "Rot in hell!"

Gun drawn, Alex ran across the armory. "Stop! Get away from her!" He aimed the SIG at Gant's titanic head. "Against the wall!"

Gant slowly backed away. Alex stepped forward, leveling the gun. "Against the wall!"

Gant retreated as Alex untied Imelda's wrists and ankles. She rolled off the rack, blocking Alex's line of fire.

Gant charged, pushed Imelda onto the floor and knocked the SIG out of Alex's hand. Seizing Alex by the arm, Gant flung him over the rack. Alex rolled to break his fall. Before he could recover, Gant was on top of him, raising a massive boot to crush his skull.

Alex used his hip to deliver a powerful blow to the giant's leg. Gant pitched backward, colliding with the iron maiden. It rocked and fell to the floor with a deafening roar.

Regaining his footing, Gant snatched a cat-ó-nine tail from the wall and swung it over his head with a high whistling sound. Stepping forward, he lashed Alex across the chest, then lashed him again, driving him back into a corner.

Alex seized a broadsword from the wall and swung it, entangling the cat. Gant yanked the broadsword from his grip.

"Stop!" Imelda shouted, brandishing a dagger.

"Run!" Alex snatched a spear. "Get out of here!"

Imelda approached Gant from behind as he turned to look at her.

"Run!" repeated Alex, driving the spear into Gant's right arm. Before Gant could recover, Alex stepped forward with another powerful thrust.

Gant leaped back to dodge the blade, and his heel caught on the corner of the maiden. Agile for a big man, he pivoted in the air, but gravity overcame his balance. With bulging eyes and flailing arms, he tumbled backwards into the cabinet's gaping maw. Sharp spikes pierced his back, thighs, and calves. Gant discharged an incoherent howl. Triggered by his massive weight, the spring-operated lid slammed shut with a loud clang, further impaling a thrashing fury.

Alex and Imelda watched in horror as the maiden quaked and heaved from the violent death throes erupting from within. After a minute, the maiden stopped moving, and blood dripped on the granite floor. The dagger fell from Imelda's hand.

"Let's go." Alex retrieved the SIG and led her into the hallway, choked with smoke.

"How? . . Why? . . What brought you?" she said, as they ran down the hallway.

"This way."

They turned at the staircase Alex had passed earlier, and then up several steps to a narrow window.

Shouts and sounds of movement echoed from above. Alex stuck his head out; they were ten feet above the ground. "You first," he said, pointing at the opening.

She shook her head. "It's too small."

"You can do it," he insisted. "Try!"

He lifted her feet-first and slowly eased her legs outside. Her hips were too wide for the narrow width, but she could get through by rotating her body. Moving back, she grasped the windowsill with her hands and hung there, legs dangling below. She released her grip and landed feet first, tumbling backward when she hit. Sitting up, she waved and seemed okay.

A guard running down the stairs saw Alex hoisting himself into the window and called out to the others. Alex thrust his legs through, rotated his hips, and exhaled to compress his chest. Reaching back, he pulled himself into the narrow slot. Ragged stones tore the shirt and the skin from his chest and back. The holster snapped. The SIG clattered on the steps and the phone fell out of his pocket.

Guards yelled as Alex twisted and pushed, braving the pain in his back and chest, struggling to escape. Then, with one adrenaline-fueled shove, he broke free, falling backward into the void, and landed on his back, gasping for breath.

In an instant, a rifle appeared in the window, its sights fixed on Alex's head. Imelda quickly dragged him to the wall as bullets struck the spot where he had landed. She helped him up, and they ran for cover, holding close to the castle walls.

The fire quickly spread. Old, dry timbers and support beams in the upper floors flared like kindling, and wooden floors below ignited from the falling embers. Thick, black smoke billowed over the sea. A noxious plume of darkness rose and expanded into the early morning sky.

Fire engulfed the north tower as Enslein's men strove to save themselves. One trapped near the top of the tower jumped, screaming to his death. Falling beams claimed the lives of two more. The roof collapsed in a cloud of smoke, ash, and fire.

When the inferno mushroomed to the south tower, Enslein knew the castle was gone. The laboratory was bedlam when he arrived. Animals darting back and forth in cages, wailing and shrieking with fright as lethal gases filled the air. Like a stern, merciless taskmaster, Enslein stood over Chu, whose trembling hands downloaded gigabytes of data to storage devices.

Enslein seized his assistant by the neck and pointed a gun at his head. "Faster!" He cocked the weapon, his finger on the trigger.

Beaded in sweat, Chu raced to finish.

Enslein left him there and opened a wall panel. He punched six numbers on a keypad. The very thought of what he had done angered him, but there was no turning back.

forty-seven

MONOLITHOS, RHODES, GREECE

Alex and Imelda ran through the woods at a steady pace for about a mile, stopping once to look back at the thick, black smoke billowing into the morning sky. Enslein's men were nowhere to be seen.

"My car's in a village nearby," said Alex.

A loud explosion shook the ground, drowning out her brief response. They stared in amazement as the castle erupted in an orange fireball, discharging a torrent of stone, wood, and debris into the murky air.

"What the hell," Alex said. "Let's go!"

They ran and walked for two miles and hardly spoke, convinced that Enslein's men were close behind them.

The village was awake when they arrived and watched fishermen carrying nets, rods, and gear to their boats. Alex groaned when Spiros' cottage came into view. The rental car was gone.

He knocked on the door. "I don't think Spiros would take it." After a few more knocks, he tried the latch. The door swung open. "Spiros! Are you here!?"

They entered the kitchen, closed the door, and pulled down the shades.

"We could wait and see if he comes back," said Alex, "or leave now and try to hitch a ride."

She eyed his bloody shirt. "You're bleeding."

"It's risky if we stay. Enslein's men—"

"I know. But . . ." She motioned to his shirt. "Take that off or you'll get infected."

"I'm okay," he insisted.

She shook her head. "No, you're not." Opening the fridge, she found sausage, bread, water, and beer. "I'm starving and we need the strength. All I had was bread and water."

Dividing the meat and bread between them, she poured two glasses of water, sat back, and looked him in the eye. "What were you doing in there?"

"Looking for Enslein. Kartan hired me to find him."

"Martin Haley," she said.

"How'd you know?"

"I met him a week ago. He didn't tell me he hired a private eye, though." She ate some bread. "I thought he'd kill us. You saved us in there. How did you do that? How did you beat him?"

"I stayed in the moment."

She stared at him with a blank expression.

"In a battle—a life or death situation—you focus on the moment. Nothing else. Your attention is solely on the present. When you approached him from behind, for a split second, he lost his concentration, lost the moment. Then I knew we would win. And we did."

Alex drank some water. "Are you with the FBI?"

"Another agency. Enslein's a bioterrorist."

"Bioterrorist," Alex repeated.

"How'd you find him?" she said through a mouthful of sausage.

"I tracked his girlfriend to the castle."

"Girlfriend?"

"Majreen Kavi, owner of the Havasi Nightclub, the *Minotaur*, and what's left of the castle."

Her eyes swept the kitchen. "We have to find a phone."

They heard a car approaching. Alex went to the window and peered around the shade as a black limo stopped one house away and four armed men poured out. Alex recognized a guard from the castle.

"It's them." He rushed her into the bedroom—a small, monastic space, with an unmade cot, pole lamp, and a dresser. A green shade covered the solitary window facing the road.

Imelda opened the door to the closet—too small to hide in. Dropping to her knees, she looked under the bed and saw a tarnished metal ring.

"Alex." She shoved the bed to the side. "Look." And gave the ring a yank. The trapdoor creaked open, revealing an empty crawl space under the cottage.

He climbed down and looked around. It was five feet high and extended to the outer walls. She was gone when he returned.

"Imelda," he hissed.

Returning and carrying the bread, sausage, a bottle of water, and a jar of honey, she passed the food to him. He helped her down, then pulled the cot over the crawlspace and lifted it a few inches, allowing the trapdoor to close.

They sat on the dirt as their eyes adjusted to the darkness. Light filtered in from cracks in the stone foundation, enough to see by. Imelda crawled to a crack and peered out. "They're talking to a woman across the road. She's pointing in this direction."

A minute later, the front door opened, followed by the tread of heavy footsteps. Floorboards creaked above them and the closet door banged open. A man's voice called out. The window shade rolled up and spun before it stopped. Footsteps retreated. They heard what sounded like chairs sliding across the kitchen floor, followed by loud noises and Greek being spoken.

"*Býra*," she whispered.

Alex opened his mouth to speak.

"Shh. They're talking about women."

For almost an hour, they listened in the darkness, breathing the cool, musty air. The men's voices became louder and more boisterous, amidst laughing and stomping feet. A person shouted, and something heavy struck the floor. Then a bottle smashed, followed by a clunking noise. Thumps and thuds preceded heavy footsteps. The front door opened and slammed shut. Harsh voices faded to a welcomed silence.

Imelda crawled to the crack and peered out. "I think they're gone. No. Not yet. They're looking in other cottages."

"We'll wait until dark and make a run for it," he said. "What happened? How did you wind up in there?"

"I could ask you the same question."

"I climbed the cliff."

"That thug kidnapped me. I talked too much."

A long silence filled the air.

"Tell me about this terrorist thing," he said.

"I'm pretty sure Enslein is Vector, a terrorist threatening to release a deadly bioweapon in three American cities if we don't pay a ransom."

"That's insane."

"Yes."

"When did this happen?"

"Remember the flu breakout? He infected the three towns to prove what he could do."

"Do you know about his lab in Florida?"

She stared at him. "No. Where?"

"Palm Grove. The Talas Shrimp Plant. But it looks more like a meth lab."

"That must be Vector's base of operations, where he makes the stuff." She crawled to the wall and looked out. "Still there." She resumed her spot next to him and glanced at his abraded chest and back, oozing a pinkish liquid. She opened the jar of honey. "Take off your shirt."

He pulled it over his head and watched as she smeared honey on his wounds. "Kills germs."

He sniffed the honey. "As long as there are no bears around."

"What's this?" She pointed to the horseshoe on his shoulder.

"Street gang."

She tore the lining from her skirt and covered his wounds. "What's it like . . . in a gang?"

"Illegal and violent most of the time." He took a deep breath and examined her bandage. "Nice work, doc."

"You'll live."

He smiled. "How'd you get into this line of work?"

"After I graduated from med school, I got a call from this new government agency. When I learned what they did and how important they were, I joined them. I wasn't curing cancer, but saving lives just the same." She watched as he pulled on his shirt. "Did you go to private eye school?"

He smiled. "No. After the Army, I became a cop. Two years later, I quit the force and, with another ex-cop, started our own business."

She looked around disconcertedly. "I have to get to a phone."

"After dark. As soon as we get out of here." He lay back with his hands behind his head.

"We're on the run, unarmed, and without a phone, money or car," she said. "Let's make a plan."

"We wait until Enslein's thugs go and then head for Agios Isidoros."

"Where's that?"

"Not far."

"Okay. Let's try to get some rest." She snuggled next to him and in a short time didn't stir. The only sound was the quiet inhalation and exhalation of their breathing.

forty-eight

FISHING VILLAGE, RHODES, GREECE

"Alex," Imelda shook him. "Wake up. They're gone."

He blinked his eyes as she pushed up the trapdoor. Moonlight revealed her determined face as she slid the cot to one side and climbed out. "Hurry!"

He followed her out to the kitchen, cluttered with empty beer bottles and a broken chair. Cigarette butts, dirt, and ashes littered the floor. She found a leather wine pouch and filled it with water.

Alex opened the door and looked around. The black limo had gone. He walked outside and stood in the middle of the road, waiting and watching. The village was asleep, just the sound of cicadas crackling in the bushes and a breeze whispering through the cypress trees. She walked out, closed the door, and joined him.

He pointed the way. "We'll find a phone there."

Jogging for two miles, they hadn't seen a person, house, or vehicle, as the rising sun cast a rosy hue across the morning sky.

"Take deep breaths to calm your heartbeats," said Alex. "We think better when our hearts are pumping normally."

She stopped jogging when she heard a sound. "A car."

They stepped to the side of the road and waited as an old green compact approached. Alex waved his arms as it passed them in a cloud of dust.

"One of us has a better chance of getting a ride than the two of us together." About to take a drink, he spied the black limo coming over the ridge. "It's them."

They scrambled down a steep embankment and sprinted through an open area of foot-high grass and yellow flowers. At a small hollow about fifty yards from the road, they hid behind a stand of oak trees and spiny shrubs. Birds in the trees chirped and whistled at the intruders, crouching low to the ground.

Car doors slammed. They heard voices edging closer and a gunshot. The birds took to the sky, flapping and chirping loudly. Alex and Imelda lay motionless, listening, waiting, barely breathing. More voices, but fainter now. Doors opened and closed. The limo started and drove away.

They could be beggars, gypsies or desperadoes thumbing for a ride— ragged, sunburned, and wounded in torn, soiled, and bloody clothes, slogging along the narrow road to Agios Isidoros. A dead snake, empty beer bottle, and flattened pack of cigarettes were their only entertainment.

Imelda's sorry condition didn't reflect her state of mind, more determined than ever to capture Enslein and stop the attack. She glanced at the man walking beside her and wondered what it would be like with him. No time for that right now. Stay in the moment, she recalled.

The engine whined and wheezed as the old green Škoda climbed the hill behind them.

"Let me handle this." Imelda waved her thumb in the wind.

The driver, a young man in soiled work clothes, pulled over and rolled down the passenger side window. He had a weird-guy vibe that made her nervous. But beggars can't be choosers.

"Agios Isidoros," Imelda said.

The driver nodded.

As soon as Imelda got in, she smelled the weed.

The driver smiled when he saw her sniff. "I'm Theo."

Alex opened the back door and took the seat behind her. "I'm Alex and that's Imelda. Thanks for the ride."

Theo gave him a thumbs up and sped off, weaving back and forth along the road.

Of all the luck, thought Imelda, to get inside a hot-boxed car with a druggy who might crash before we get there. She felt high just sitting in the car, rolled down the window, and took a deep breath. "We're not in a hurry, Theo. Take your time."

The car swerved and bounced in a pothole. Alex hit the roof.

Theo tightly gripped the wheel. "They don't fix roads here like they do on Mykonos."

Imelda turned to Alex with a querulous expression, and Alex rubbed his head. Theo offered Imelda a joint. She refused. When he looked back at Alex, he didn't see the tractor up ahead.

"Watch it!" said Imelda.

Theo cut onto the right shoulder, just missing the tractor, and kicked up a cloud of dust. The tractor driver removed his hat and stared at them.

For the next two miles, Theo babbled on about the basketball player, Giannis Antetokounmpo, and how many three-point shots he had made. Alex and Imelda listened, grunted, and nodded affably, but hardly spoke. When they passed a sign for Agios Isidoros, Imelda pointed to a gas station up ahead. "Stop there."

"No problem." Theo pulled over and parked at the pumps.

Imelda opened the door and jumped out, happy to get out of there. Alex right behind her.

"Thanks," said Alex with a wave.

"Later." Theo floored the Škoda, as rear wheels whirled pebbles in the air, and quickly drove away.

A middle-aged man wearing oil-stained overalls and a white skullcap came out of the gas station and greeted them in Greek.

"American," said Alex. "American."

Imelda mimed talking on the phone. "Telephone. Telephone."

The man nodded and led them into a storage room filled with tires, batteries, and oil cans. The phone was under the desk. Imelda punched in her code and dialed Brockman. It rang three times before bouncing to Dunphy.

"Imelda!?" Joy flooded Dunphy's voice. "Is that you!?"

"Yeah."

"Are you—?"

"I found Enslein, Joe. I'm pretty sure he's Vector and—"

"What happened?" he blurted. "We were worried. Are you okay?"

"I'm fine. Fine. Listen, Enslein has a lab in Florida, in—."

"Where are you?"

"Not important. Listen, the lab is in a town called Palm Grove, near St. Petersburg." She glanced at Alex. "It's called Talas, T-A-L-A-S. A shrimp plant. It might be Enslein's base of operations. Brief Marv and notify the cops and FBI to raid the place."

"Okay. Got it."

"Joe, he's crazy. Kidnapped me and tried to kill me. We can't wait. Do it now. And run a search on Majreen Kavi." She spelled the name.

"Who is she?"

"Not sure. She works with Enslein." Imelda paused, mind racing. "What's today?"

"July 11th."

"If we work fast, we can stop him . . . Joe?"

"Yeah."

"Good to hear your voice. I gotta go."

"Imelda, wait—"

She disconnected and handed the phone to Alex.

Alex contacted Dimitri, who seemed uneasy and stressed about the dreadful events that were unsettling his peaceful island. After briefly explaining what had happened, Alex gave him the gas station address, and Dimitri said he was on his way.

Alex then called George and left a message: "Tell Kartan I found Enslein in a castle near Monolithos. He was there today but must have fled after a fire destroyed the castle. I'm traveling with a government agent and also looking for Enslein. I'll call later with details."

forty-nine

MEDITERRANEAN SEA

The *Minotaur* sailed southeast toward Alexandria in moderate swells. Captain Hassan reduced the speed to maintain a smooth ride, as Enslein had desired. The sun was shining and a cool breeze swept over the deck.

On the forecastle, Kavi undid her bikini top and lay face down on a towel, breathing in its lavender scent. She closed her eyes, lulled by the vibration and throaty drone of the engine.

Enslein admired her from a deck chair. Sensitive to the sun, he wore a white robe, dark sunglasses, and a safari hat pulled down over his eyes.

On the flybridge, Hassan stood beside two armed men as they scanned the horizon for any sign of trouble.

Marcos sat in the bow, an AK-47 resting on his knees.

Kavi raised her head and called out to her brother.

Marcos set his weapon against the hold, rose to his feet, and went to her.

"Be a good brother and get me a drink," she said.

He bent down, whispered something in her ear, and headed toward the bar.

Enslein smiled. "Secret tête-à-tête?"

Kavi spoke into the towel. "He loves me and would die for me."

"Such loyalty," he scoffed.

"Family, Gerfried, is all we can count on."

Enslein sneered.

"Professor?"

Enslein looked up at Hassan standing over him. "Tomorrow at 0900, we arrive in Alexandria as scheduled."

Enslein raised his hand in a gesture of acknowledgment.

"Madam," said Hassan, pointing to an island half hidden in the mist. "Cyprus."

Kavi glanced up at Enslein. "Why are we going to Alexandria, anyway?"

"A diversionary tactic, my dear."

She raised her head, looking for her brother. "Where's that dimwit with my drink?"

Enslein smirked. "Maybe he forgot about his sister."

She rose to her feet, went to the railing, and looked back at the twin feathers of foam fading in the distance.

Enslein's men ignored her presence there. She was out of bounds from any lewd glance, indecent gesture, or sign of recognition. Breaking the rules would risk a quick toss into the sea.

"I thought for a moment I saw smoke," Kavi said.

Enslein grunted. "Forget Monolithos. I will buy you a palace to replace it."

"Did they ever find the girl?"

"No." Enslein nervously covered his pale left instep exposed to the sun. Ever since he was a child and had fallen asleep on the beach, he avoided its burning rays and had the scars to prove it.

Kavi returned to her towel and squinted up at him. "Have you heard anything yet?"

"No."

She closed her eyes and rested her head on an arm. "What if they don't pay?"

"Don't worry. They will."

"And if they don't?"

"I will make them suffer."

She laughed. "With your deadly mouse?"

"Yes."

"And kill us all?"

He shrugged. "Humanity will survive."

He closed his eyes, his face serene. "In another life, I was a king. A great king. Men feared me, women desired me, and children cheered for me. I was famous for my legacy." He leaned forward and opened his eyes. "We will win, Kavi. Never doubt me."

Kavi stifled a yawn. "Yes, Gerfried."

fifty

HELLENIC PETROL STATION, RHODES, GREECE

Alex sat on the grass gazing at Imelda dozing under a fig tree. Her courage and determination impressed him. And there's no denying she was easy on the eyes. The sound of Dimitri's car snapped him back to reality. Dimitri got out, looking tired and unkempt. The fire and explosion and its uncertain aftermath upon the island's trade and tourism had taken a heavy toll on him.

He opened the trunk and removed a bag containing a first aid kit, bottled water, and sandwiches. Tucking the bag under his arm, he slammed the trunk. The loud thump awakened Imelda.

Dimitri frowned when he saw Alex. "You look like you have been through hell, my friend."

"We survived." Alex shook the captain's hand and nodded to Imelda. "Dr. Imelda Burke. The lady I told you about."

Imelda rose to her feet and shook Dimitri's hand. He gave her the impression of an older, thoughtful man in good physical shape.

Alex gestured to the road. "Enslein's thugs are after us. We have to get out of here."

"My men are stopping all cars," Dimitri assured. "You are safe." He turned to Imelda. "Are you all right?"

"Yes."

"We will find the people responsible for your kidnapping."

"It's more than kidnapping," she said. "Enslein and Kavi are terrorists. We have to stop them before they escape. You need to blockade the island now and search villages near the castle. They might still be there."

"We need sworn statements from you and Alex," Dimitri said.

"Statements?" Imelda's eyes widened. "This is more than kidnapping." Her voice took on an unfamiliar edge. "Thousands of lives may be at stake."

"We must follow international law," continued Dimitri. "Kavi is Turkish. Enslein is Swiss. It is important—"

"So are the lives of countless people," Imelda exclaimed. "We don't have time for that."

The captain continued in a calm voice, "If the right people get involved . . . It is the way we do things here."

"Excuse us, Dimitri." Imelda walked Alex out of earshot of the captain. "We can't let him handle this. I'll call my boss, get the State Department—"

"I know Dimitri," countered Alex. "He's a good man. He'll help us."

"I don't see it." She ran into the petrol station, dialed Dunphy, and left an urgent message: "Joe, the local police can't handle this. By the time they do their paperwork, Enslein will be long gone. Get the Greek government involved. Seal off Rhodes—airport and harbors—and find the *Minotaur*, Enslein's yacht. Use drones. The Navy. I'll leave as soon as I can. Call you later." Imelda hung up and joined Alex. "I asked them to blockade the island. But I'm afraid it may be too late."

"We can't ditch Dimitri," said Alex. "He'll help if we play this right."

She breathed a bitter laugh. "A terrorist plot to murder innocent people? I don't have time for him."

In an instant, Alex realized he couldn't fly home. He had to stay as long as necessary. "I'll help you get this guy if you want me to."

"Damn right I do!"

fifty-one

TALAS SHRIMP PLANT, PALM RIVER, FLORIDA

The Kid peered into Tomek's Firebird parked on the loading dock and was about to open the door.

"Don't even think about it." Tomek glared at him from behind a table in the driveway. "Get your ass over here."

The Kid patted the hood. "Man, that's *sweet*."

"Warnin' you . . ."

The Kid ambled over and joined Mario and Benson sitting on folding chairs in front of the table. Blue uniforms lay folded on their laps. "What's with these?" laughed the Kid, pointing to the uniforms. "Selling ice cream for Mister Softee?"

Mario and Benson laughed.

"Sit down and shut your mouth." Tomek held up a crescent wrench. "This opens the end cap on some feeder pipes. You can unscrew others with your hand." He set the wrench on the table and removed from a shipping container three pint-sized stainless-steel cylinders that had recently arrived from Rhodes. He placed them next to the wrench. "Open the feeder pipe, uncap the cylinder, and pour it into the tank. Simple. When you're done, cap the feeder pipe, and ditch the cylinder."

Mario looked confused. "What if somebody sees us?"

Tomek held up a fake work order containing the newspaper publisher's name and job assignment. "Looks real. Don't worry. You'll never have to use it."

Mario chewed his lip. "What happens if we can't make the drop?"

"Listen," said Tomek, getting testy. "I checked these plants myself. This isn't the mint or a bank. It's a newspaper plant. Security sucks. Fences falling apart. If there are guards, they're old or asleep most of the time. No dogs. Lousy lights or no lights at all. A schoolgirl could make this drop. No excuses."

Benson reached over and picked up a cylinder. "What's inside, Tomek?" He shook it like a cocktail shaker. "Is it gonna *explode?*" He laughed.

Tomek grabbed the cylinder out of his hand and returned it to the table. "Don't mess around . . . Benson, I-75 North toward Gainesville. Don't stop in Atlanta . . . Kid, I-10 West. No bar hopping in Houston and watch the speed limit . . . Mario follows Benson on I-75 to 24 toward Nashville."

Tomek paused and stared at them to make a point. "Only stop for gas, food, and motels. You'll have more than enough time to rest when you get there. No tickets. No cops. No fuckups. I reserved motel rooms under fake names on the licenses I gave you. Check in with those. Addresses are in your packets. Survey the plants, locate the ink tanks and fill pipes, lie low, and don't get into trouble. If you don't hear from me, make the drop Saturday, July 20th, before 11:00 p.m. and drive back to pick up your dough. Got it?" He waited for a response. "Got it!?"

"Yeah. Yeah. Yeah."

The drivers were raring to go, score the job, and get their dough. Mario leaned against the side of his van and glanced at Benson. "Ain't nobody like her." He stroked his beard. "It's why I wanted Chi-ca-go."

"We know. We know." Benson sighed. "Becky, right? Redhead."

"Did those wild, exotic dances." Mario did a little soft-shoe shuffle. "I'd hang out at the bar, have a beer or two and watch her flirt with the customers. But she'd always ask me to take her home. 'Don't wanna get mugged,' she'd say. 'You'll protect me, won't you, Mario?'" He reached into his pocket and showed Benson a crumpled postcard of the Sears Tower. "'Hope you're *this* happy to see me,' it says."

Benson laughed.

"My old man's from Chicago," said Mario. "He liked the Cubs and raved about Wrigley Field. I'm gonna see a game when I'm there."

"Think the Kid's in LA yet?" said Benson, walking to the van.

"He'll be lucky to get there the way he drives."

They climbed into their vans, and Mario followed Benson through the gate.

fifty-two

TALAS SHRIMP PLANT, PALM RIVER, FLORIDA

Michael Benson, Mario Cosenza, and Joseph Walsh, aka The Kid, would all die without the vaccine. Enslein planned it that way. Tomek would earn their shares: fewer witnesses and more incentive for the sole survivor.

One drop on their skin would infect them with a deadly strain of smallpox. If they were lucky enough to avoid it, they'd almost certainly die from contact with infected people who'd pass the virus to others.

Of those exposed, over two million would die, according to Enslein's calculations. Health facilities couldn't cope. Many of the infected would be without medical care and perish in their homes. Funeral parlors and hospitals would struggle to handle the number of bodies. America would have to resort to mass incineration and burial. It would take scientists at least a week to develop a vaccine for the virulent strain—too late to save most victims.

Enslein chose three big metropolitan dailies for the job: *The New York Globe* plant in Flushing, Queens; *The Daily Herald's* downtown Chicago facility; and *The Los Angeles World* Costa Mesa plant.

Timing was an issue. It would take Benson twenty hours to drive to Flushing, a two-day trip. Mario could get to downtown Chicago in nineteen hours, nonstop if he wanted. The Kid had the longest drive—over 2,500 miles to Costa Mesa. The way he drove, he could make the trip in three days.

Tomek planned on leaving last. He had already shipped the professor's lab equipment and supplies to storage in Tampa. Getting rid of the remaining chemicals and glassware was his responsibility.

He siphoned reagents from three fifty-five-gallon drums into the storm drain on the loading dock. A gray cloud of acrid fumes boiled out of the drain, burning his eyes and nose. He wiped the tears from his eyes and cursed Enslein for sticking him with this shit job.

A drum of broken glassware erupted into a flaming ball. Tomek loved burning things; he burned a barn when he was a kid and got away with it. Fire, he admitted, aroused him more than women. He waited until the fire died out and washed the floor, walls, and ceiling with a high-pressure hose.

The roar of the hose masked the throaty exhaust of a Palm Grove police boat docking behind the plant. Two plainclothes cops and an FBI agent jumped off and banged on the rear door of the building.

When Tomek heard shouting and glass shattering, he knew what was happening. He jumped into the Firebird and fishtailed out of the loading dock as three shots rang out.

Tomek sped down the access road in a cloud of dust and gravel and skidded onto Commercial Drive. The top was down and the wind whipped his hair like a mare's tail. He leaned forward, hunkering down for some serious driving and headed for Shore Road.

Two police cars from Palm Grove, with lights flashing and sirens blaring, raced directly towards the Firebird. Tomek roared right past them as they slammed on their brakes, reversed direction, and took up the chase.

Tomek downshifted on the Tamiami Trail and floored the Bird as the turbocharger kicked in, thrusting him back against the seat like on a carnival ride. "Catch me, motherfuckers." He checked the rearview: cops fading in the distance.

The road ahead looked clear. He pushed the Bird to ninety-five, gripped the wheel and smiled. Not a shimmy or a float. He figured to be in Adamsville in five minutes—a safe place to go to ground.

He pushed his lead to about a mile and saw a line of cars ahead, backed up by a stretch of construction work. He slowed to fifty-five as traffic squeezed from two lanes into one. Weaving in and out between cars, he checked behind him. The cruisers were a quarter mile away and closing.

Moving onto the grassy shoulder, he raced past the string of crawling cars and trucks. Angry drivers blew their horns at him for cheating. Fifty yards ahead at the Adamsville Road turnoff, he made a hard right, floored it, and checked the rearview to see if the cops had made the turn. When he looked back, he was thirty feet away from a Salty Sea refrigerator truck backing out of the Food Mart parking lot.

He braked hard, and the wheels locked. But the competition radials lost traction on the sandy road. The Firebird spun, slid sideways, and hit Salty Sea broadside with a crunching bang.

The truck's side panel burst open, dumping three hundred pounds of frozen Pompano and Red Snapper into the red convertible. The bird coughed, sputtered, and died a smelly death.

Buried in cold fish, Tomek could barely move and his door, wedged against the truck's axle shaft, wouldn't budge. But he kept his cool and tossed his cell phone into the back of the fish truck.

The bearded truck driver hung out the side window, cursing and waving his arms, as two cop cars pulled up with four officers and an FBI agent. A cop opened the Firebird's passenger door and stepped aside as a school of fish slid over his shoes. He pointed a gun at Tomek's head. "Hands where we can see them."

The FBI agent came around to the front of the car. "Step out of the car, please."

Immersed in fish, Tomek tried to move, but couldn't. "What's all this about?"

"FBI." The agent flashed an ID. "William Tomek. You're under arrest. You may remain silent. Anything you say can and will be used against you in a court of law."

fifty-three

KNIGHT'S HOTEL, RHODES, GREECE

A harsh ring shattered the dark stillness. Imelda's eyes snapped open. Reaching out, she silenced the alarm and eased out of bed. Her entire body ached as if someone had beaten her. She flicked on the bathroom light and rubbed her eyes, slowly adjusting to the glare. Setting the shower as hot as she could stand it, she stepped in and let the spray beat down on her sore and sunburned body. After drying off, she put on jeans, sneakers, and a sweatshirt. Comfort was more important than fashion for the long flight home.

It was almost 6:00 a.m. when she replayed Marv Brockman's voicemail. "Imelda. Thank God you're safe. Talked to Joe. Don't worry. Malone will twist some arms at State and we'll get things done in Rhodes. The FBI and local police made an arrest at Talas. Call when you have a chance and come home as fast as you can. We need you here."

Imelda quickly packed her belongings, checked out, and left a note under Alex's door.

Alex, Got a seat on the 8:45 flight to Athens. Sorry, I didn't have time to say goodbye. I want to see you again. Call when you get back to the states. Imelda.

She tried to rest on the short flight to Athens, but her mind was racing. She felt as if she was the only person on the planet who believed Enslein was Vector. And it was up to her to stop him before it was too late.

Rhodes deputies patrolled the airport and seaports and questioned workers at Monolithos. Interpol deployed an Incident Response Team to assist the local police. And three CIA officers were on their way to Rhodes.

But the Greek government refused to allow drones and planes to search for the *Minotaur*, last seen anchored in a cove near Retsina. Dimitri offered one thousand euros to anyone providing information on its whereabouts.

fifty-four

ALEXANDRIA, EGYPT

The *Minotaur* cruised into the west harbor of the Port of Alexandria, one of the oldest ports in the world, renowned for the lighthouse built by Ptolemy II Philadelphus in 247 BC.

While Hasan refueled the *Minotaur*, repaired a broken winch, and stocked up on food and water, Enslein and Kavi toured the Montaza Palace, famous for its royal gardens, beach and vistas of the sea. The size and beauty of the palace fascinated Kavi, while Enslein sat and stewed about his ultimatum and the U.S. government's reluctance to respond.

fifty-five

MONOLITHOS CASTLE, RHODES, GREECE

t was warm and cloudy as Alex drove his rental car to the castle. A gray mist hovered over the smoldering debris and a fetid stench soaked the air. He parked near the gatehouse and saw three boys from the village climbing the walls and searching the ruins for anything of value. There wasn't much left.

The towers had collapsed and the castle wall Alex climbed had disappeared into the sea. A few inner walls remained, and the drawbridge and gatehouse were also intact. The fire had spread rapidly and weakened the support beams, walls, and foundation. The explosion finished the job.

He crossed the drawbridge and climbed to the top of the outer wall. Charred beams, blackened furniture, singed tapestries, and unrecognizable items lay scattered in the open pit beneath him. He descended, careful of the splintered wood and jagged rocks, a few still warm from the fire.

The smoke was denser down there. He covered his mouth and nose with a handkerchief and slowly made his way around the perimeter, unsure of what he was looking for.

A sea shell remarkably unscathed from the explosion caught his eye. He placed it in his jacket pocket and was about to move

RICHARD ZANETTI

on when he spotted two reddish objects wedged under a beam. He climbed down to get a closer look. The beam was too heavy to lift, but he shifted it a few inches, uncovering two identical figurines of a woman lying on her side. They reminded him of similar paintings he had seen in a museum. He pocketed them as well.

The sun was setting when Alex returned to the city. Tourists packed the streets, heading for dinner, parties, or simply strolling, and excitement filled the air. Turning the corner near his hotel, he spotted the Archaeological Museum, remembering the figurines in his pocket. He parked and climbed the steps.

Curator Antigonus Gonatas stepped out of the museum and double locked the door. The gray-bearded man prided himself on knowing the history of every vase, statue, monument, and artifact inside. They would be his legacy. He shivered when a soft breeze fluttered his clothes, which hung loosely from his bony torso.

"Excuse me, sir."

The curator turned abruptly, glanced at Alex, and then continued down the stairs. "What is it?" he asked in a deep, resounding voice.

Alex grabbed his sleeve. "Excuse me, sir. Please. I have one quick question."

"Six o'clock!" He declared, pulling forward. "We close at six o'clock! Go to the aquarium!"

Alex reached into his pocket and produced the figurines. "I was wondering if you knew anything about them, where they came from."

Gonatas stopped, eyes widening, as he ogled the ancient relics. "I have seen similar figures before."

"Where?"

"Malta, from the ancient temples near Valletta. These are called the Sleeping Mother Goddess: a presentation of death and the eternal sleep. Where did you find them?"

"Monolithos."

"Of course, you cannot put a price on something like this. They are unique."

"Here." Alex handed the artifacts to the curator and hurried down the steps, returning to his rental.

"Wait," said Gonatas, nervously clutching the figurines.

Alex got in the car, waved, and drove off.

The old man sighed and gazed at the Sleeping Ladies. He'd call Malta in the morning and inquire if someone had stolen these irreplaceable relics.

At the hotel, Alex got a call from Dimitri. "Fishermen returning from the Sea of Crete saw the *Minotaur*, heading west."

"What's west?" said Alex.

"Malta."

fifty-six

VALLETTA, MALTA

From a distance, it appeared to be a featureless rock plateau. But up close one could make out terraces of olive trees, pines, and eucalyptus. The Republic was Enslein's second choice for a hideout after Rhodes—a perfect bridge between Europe and Africa, and home to the Hal Saflieni cult that celebrated women.

Hassan slowed the *Minotaur* to ten knots and weaved through the dozens of sailboats, yachts, and cruise ships in Grand Harbor. Gozo and Comino islands appeared in the northwest, their villages nestled on the flat-topped hills. Valletta, Malta's capital, loomed up ahead.

Enslein scanned the harbor for police boats as his men stood by, weapons concealed. Slowly, they cruised past the bastions of Fort St. Elmo and the imposing walls of St. Lazarus Curtain. At Fort St. Angelo, they bore left and docked at a slip in Dockyard Creek.

With a broad smile on his face, Enslein's handsome housekeeper stood waiting on the dock, holding a bouquet of long-stem white roses and a bottle of chilled champagne. Waving the flowers over his head, Stefano called out to Enslein, first to disembark.

"Welcome, Professor! Welcome!"

With barely a look at the flowers, Enslein tossed them into the sea, much to Stefano's dismay. He was about to do the same with the champagne, but after glancing at the label, tucked the bottle under his arm. "Everything ready?"

"Of course, sir." The housekeeper bowed and picked up Enslein's briefcase.

"Careful with that!"

Watching from the deck, Kavi ordered the men to remove her luggage, as brother Marcos looked on. Two cars were waiting to take them to the detached villa in the Floriana section of town.

After a short drive, the cars passed through an iron gate and proceeded fifty yards on the private drive through tall hedges and olive trees. They stopped in front of the entrance where luggage was unloaded and carried into the house. Two armed guards patrolled the grounds.

The villa on two and a half acres was no castle. But it had as many rooms, designed in an ornamental style and décor, with crystal chandeliers, frescos, sculptures, and marble throughout.

Kavi went straight to her room without uttering a word while thinking about Stefano and Enslein's reaction to the roses—purely driven by spite.

The house was immaculate, stocked with gourmet food and drink, fresh fruit, and flowers everywhere. Stefano dismissed the staff and retired to his room over the garage, where he'd wait for his master's call or something even better.

Enslein walked down the hall where age-darkened paintings of hunters and warriors bedecked the walls. He opened the door to the library, his favorite room, shelved with over a thousand volumes, including many first editions.

Four high-backed chairs bordered a Tabriz carpet in front of the marble fireplace. The carpet was thin as tissue paper and old as Methuselah.

He uncorked the champagne and poured a glass, downed it, and then another, and collapsed in a chair. He hadn't eaten for hours and the alcohol went right to his head. In a few minutes, his eyelids grew heavy, and he fell into a deep sleep. Except for the St. Georgen Grandfather Clock ticking in the foyer, the house was quiet as a tomb.

Bare feet descended the stairs, each step in time with the ticking of the clock. Kavi padded down the hall, stopped in front of the library door, and listened. The room was quiet. Slowly turning the doorknob, she eased the door open and looked in. Enslein's head was resting on his chest, eyes closed, lips parted, breathing deeply. Silently closing the door, she made her way to his office and opened the desk drawer. An index card contained Enslein's Swiss account number and password for the Zafar National Bank in Lebanon. She copied them on her hand, retraced her steps, slipped into sandals, and walked outside.

Purple shadows bathed the garden, and a light breeze was blowing. Thousands of tiny gnats flew in undulating waves over the goldfish pond. She walked across the white stone pebbles to a corner of the garden, out of sight of the house. Pausing, she looked around to be sure she was alone and then made the call. Speaking only for a minute, she hung up, and then quietly proceeded to the servant's quarters above the garage.

The afternoon sun cast flickering shadows on the wall above Stefano's bed. Long, dark hair partially covered his youthful face as he gazed at Kavi lying naked beside him. She took his palm and studied the lines.

"What do you see?" His voice was soft and romantic, unusual for a young man, albeit an experienced one.

"The lover you are."

He beamed with confidence. "The best."

She paused and smiled. "I've seen better."

He frowned. "Who?"

"An American I met recently."

His eyes grew introspective. "You are joking."

"Yes." She lifted a lock of his hair and kissed him on the mouth, her tongue barely touching his. Sliding her hand up his thigh, she was ready to help if need be.

Enslein stirred as the clock chimed, angry at himself for falling asleep. He felt clammy and beads of sweat dotted his forehead.

He picked up the phone and dialed Ahmad.

"Six-two-four-six," he declared.

"No deliveries today."

"They said they would pay!"

"Perhaps tomorrow will bring good news."

"*Perhaps*," said Enslein. He hung up and called Tomek. Tomek's phone rang and rang in the fish truck until the battery died.

fifty-seven

PALM RIVER, FLORIDA

Three cops and two FBI agents searched the Talas loading dock and grounds, while Joe Dunphy explored the shrimp plant, hoping to find a clue to what Enslein was doing there. So far, he came up empty.

Dunphy walked out when he heard the approaching Mobile Biological Research Center—BWG's esteemed weapon in the war on terror—and waited as Zack Wright drove through the gate and stopped a few feet in front of him.

Atkinson threw open the passenger door, jumped down, and shook hands with Dunphy, who had a worried look on his face.

"Hey, man," said Atkinson. "What's wrong?"

"They sanitized it."

Atkinson shook his head. "They must've missed something."

Wright climbed out of the cab, opened the rear panels, and unloaded empty Hazmat storage containers.

Atkinson gazed at the plant. "How'd the raid go?"

"We got Wiliam Tomek, the manager. But he's not talking." Dunphy handed Atkinson a respirator and gloves and nodded at the door. "Let's go. I'll show you around."

By nightfall, the men had tagged and bagged in storage containers whatever was left inside the plant. They loaded the containers into the MBRC.

Dunphy made a last inspection, checking the office and back rooms. He was about to leave the loading area when he noticed three keys on a chain hanging on a nail behind the door. He dropped the keys into his pocket.

fifty-eight

COUNTY JAIL, PALM GROVE, FLORIDA

Palm Grove Police Deputy Scott Moss showed up with Tomek's lunch: two hot dogs, pork & beans, sauerkraut, and a cup of water to wash it down. Moss opened the cell door and handed the cup and plate to Tomek, sitting on the edge of his cot, still reeking of fish. The dogs were tough, the rolls stale, and the water smelled like bleach. But Tomek was hungry and thirsty, and that was all he was going to get. He had almost finished eating when he heard a rap on the bars.

"How's the menu?" Lorenzo Gill, wearing a pale blue double-breasted suit, white shirt, and oxfords, flashed a perfect set of pearly white teeth, and held a white straw hat in a manicured hand.

"Worse than Durham," muttered Tomek, eyeing Gill with disdain.

"Take what you can get," the southern gentleman attorney drawled.

Tomek set his food aside, stood up and grasped the bars. "Where the hell were you?"

"At the club trying out my new nine iron. You should've called my cell." A mischievous grin spread over Gill's face. "I've known you a long time, William, and we've been through a lot together. But now you've got yourself into somethin' serious." He glanced at the arrest warrant. "Charged with seditious conspiracy. Know what that is?"

Tomek smirked.

Gill squinted as he slowly read the 10-point type. "Conspirin' to overthrow, put down, or to destroy by force the Government of the United States. Violatin' the Biological Weapons Antiterrorism Act, and conspirin' to conduct terrorist activities. I must tell you, sir, this is a first for me."

Tomek sneered. "Just get me the hell outta here."

"I'm surprised they allowed you a phone call. Anything you want to tell me?"

"No."

Tomek's stylish mouthpiece opened his notebook and unscrewed a gold ballpoint pen. At that moment, Tomek hated the pompous bastard.

"So tell me, William, what on earth did you get yourself into?"

"You know what I've been doin'."

Gill nodded. "Managin' some shrimp plant in Palm Grove."

"Cleanin' up. About to leave."

"Tearin' down the Tamiami like some NASCAR driver? Seems fishy to me. Pardon the pun, but you do smell, you know." Gill wrote something in his notebook, unbuttoned his jacket, and shuddered. "Terrorism makes my skin crawl." He stared Tomek in the eye. "You're no terrorist, are you, William?"

"No."

"Happy to hear that. Just a check forger—ole albatross 'round your neck." He closed the notebook and capped the pen.

Tomek made a smoking gesture with his hand. Gill withdrew a Cohiba from his pocket and passed it through the bars. "Chew it slowly, my friend."

Tomek unwrapped the "puro," bit off the tip, and spit it on the floor. Gill flipped a Satin Doll and held the flame through the bars till Tomek had a decent burn.

The ex-con took a drag and coughed, not used to this level of quality. "How can they hold me? They have no case. No proof. Nothin' to connect me to any of this terrorist shit."

"Then it's easy. We plead not guilty."

Tomek squinted as smoke curled up from his lips. "How about gettin' me the hell outta here?"

Gill shook his head. "Not possible. Judge Kelley made things difficult because of your prior, and the seriousness of the charges. Based on circumstantial evidence, he agrees the DA had probable cause. They won't set bail until after the arraignment."

"When is that?"

"Don't know. We have a meeting tomorrow at ten. If things go well, they may consider a lesser charge."

Tomek leaned over, his voice barely above a whisper. "You gotta do somethin' for me. Let my boss know. He always calls so he'll know something's wrong when nobody answers." He slipped a folded piece of paper to Gill. "Text him. Write 'cold and dry' in the subject box. He'll know what happened."

"Cold and dry." Gill opened the paper. Inside was an international phone number preceded by a private hash code that made the call impossible to trace. He placed the paper in his lapel pocket while squinting at Tomek. "You sure you don't want to tell me what this is all about?"

Tomek flicked some ashes on the floor. "Don't know, counselor."

fifty-nine

BIOLOGICAL WEAPONS GROUP HEADQUARTERS, ATLANTA, GEORGIA

Imelda parked in her designated spot, cleared security, and took the service elevator to level three. She glanced into the lab and saw Hazmat containers from Talas stacked floor to ceiling. Hunched over spectrophotometers, technicians analyzed samples as others moved containers into the storage room.

Dunphy knew she was coming home today, but never expected her at work, and almost fell off the stool when he saw her. "Imelda!" He rushed over and gave her a hug. Atkinson joined him, planting a kiss on Imelda's cheek.

Aware of the ruckus, Brockman came in and embraced her like a father who hadn't seen his daughter in a very long time. He brushed a tear from his cheek. "You scared the hell out of us, Burke. Sending you alone was a mistake."

"No, Marv. It was the right thing to do. We found Enslein, and I safely made it back, thanks to Alex West."

"You mentioned him before," said Brockman. "Get him down here. Maybe he can help."

"I'll try."

Imelda recounted her time on Rhodes, detailing her abduction, rescue, and escape, while admitting the foolish errors she made that nearly cost her life.

"Based on what I heard and saw, I knew we were right from the start," she said.

"The Talas raid proved it," said Brockman.

Atkinson showed her Tomek's mugshot. "Lawyered up and not talking."

"And not working alone," said Dunphy. "Somebody had to drive those vans."

"What vans?" she asked.

Atkinson piped up. "Joe found keys we traced to three Ford Econolines."

"All registered in Florida," Brockman said. "If we find the vans and drivers, maybe we can stop this."

"Prints?" asked Imelda.

"A few, but nothing on IAFIS." Atkinson sat back and slapped his thigh. "I just thought of something. Enslein must have immunized Tomek and the drivers against whatever pathogen he's using, right? Unless he wants to kill them, which is also possible."

"Worth a try," said Dunphy. "We sample Tomek's blood."

"I'll take care of it," said Brockman.

'What about soil samples?" Imelda said.

Dunphy drummed his pen on the table. "It might be anthrax. We found traces in the parking lot."

"There's not enough evidence to rule it out," said Atkinson.

Brockman nodded. "The CIA's been tracking an anthrax supplier out of the Balkans. It could've gone to Enslein."

"This just came in." Atkinson read a text. "The FBI found three bodies buried behind the shrimp plant. No heads or hands."

"How long were they there?" asked Imelda.

"A month or two," read Atkinson. "They're running the DNAs against CODIS profiles. It'll take a day or so before we know anything."

The meeting ended early, in deference to Imelda, who badly needed rest. Dunphy caught up to her in the parking lot.

She smiled when she saw him. "I thought you'd be pulling an all-nighter or something,"

"That was last night. Listen, I know you must be dead tired, but you want to grab a drink before you go home?"

"Sure." She got in her car and followed him to Smitty's, a tavern on Maple Street, where they sat at the bar and ordered beer.

When Imelda joined BWG, Joe was her buddy. He took her under his wing, familiarizing her with the job and with the covert practices of law enforcement agencies. He explained how personal or political motives often shaped information and how facts can be hidden or distorted. "It's almost impossible to get all the facts all the time," he had said. "Be skeptical and cautiously distrustful, and you'll do just fine."

They went out on a few dates, and it wasn't long before he asked her to move in with him. She said she'd think about it, but in the back of her mind, knew it wouldn't happen.

Like a tree girdled by vines, their yearlong relationship eventually wilted and died. It crushed him, and it was mostly her doing. After years of sacrificing social life for a career and then waiting until after graduation to get *involved*, she'd been eager for a fling. And she took the first one that came along until realizing her mistake and ended it, happy to be free.

"Welcome back." Dunphy clinked her glass and took a sip. "I just wanted to say that I missed you. Hey, we all missed you and were worried about you."

Imelda smiled. "Yeah. My fault. I should have planned it better. All the signs were there."

"Well, it worked out, didn't it? You IDed Enslein and came back safe and sound. If it wasn't for you . . ."

"It could've easily gone the other way. I was lucky, Joe." She sipped her beer and set the glass on the bar. "Chalk it up to experience. I'll know better next time."

He sat back and studied her. "Well, you look great."

She took a deep breath. "Joe, I'm exhausted and—"

"Look, I didn't want to talk about work tonight." He gazed into her eyes. "I've been thinking a lot about us. With you being away and all. And I've been thinking that, well, we had a good thing, and that's not so easy to find. What I'm saying is, what I'm asking is, if you want to try again? . . . I'd like to."

A wave of emotions swept over her and for a moment, she didn't know what to say. She had fallen out of love with Dunphy, but she couldn't tell him that, couldn't hurt him. She took his hand and held it for a moment. "I want you to understand that you are my dearest friend. I care about you. But I'm not ready, Joe. I'm sorry."

"I'm sorry, too, because I'll always love you."

sixty

COUNTY JAIL, PALM GROVE, FLORIDA

At the small conference table, Lorenzo Gill sat erect with an air of self-confidence and poise. On his right, William Tomek slumped down with scorning self-importance. Deputy Scott Moss and Brad Collins, FBI Special Agent in Charge, sat across from them behind a videorecorder aimed at Tomek.

Collins handed Gill a Strategic Framework folder from the Department of Homeland Security. "This explains Mr. Tomek's civil rights and civil liberties in these circumstances."

"I am mindful of my client's *Constitutional rights*." Gill's annoyance was obvious when someone tried to lecture him. He dropped the folder in his briefcase.

"You should read it," countered the SAC.

"And since when does the Constitution play second fiddle to anything?" replied Gill in an authoritarian tone. "These are outrageous charges. The facts will exonerate Mr. Tomek."

"Mr. Tomek," Collins said, turning on the videorecorder. "Do you understand what you say here may be used against you in court?"

Tomek nodded.

"State your full name for the record."

"William Randolph Tomek."

"You're accused of a serious crime, Mr. Tomek."

"Being a terrorist?" sneered Gill. "Conspirin' to overthrow the Government? Ridiculous!"

"We have evidence proving Mr. Tomek was producing anthrax at the Talas Shrimp Plant," replied Collins, "and planning to poison thousands of people in a terrorist extortion plot." He turned to Tomek. "If you help us and reveal your plan and those involved, we'll help you. If you refuse and are guilty as accused, the government will pursue the highest penalty allowed by law. Life imprisonment or death."

Tomek leaned over and whispered in Gill's ear.

"Mr. Tomek," continued Collins, "do you work for the Talas Shrimp Company?"

"Yeah."

"Do you know Gerfried Enslein?"

"Never heard of him."

"Records show you spent nine months at the Durham Correctional Center in North Carolina for forgery. Enslein was there at the time and overlapped six of your months. Guards said they often saw you together. Do you want to rethink your answer?"

"He may have been there, but I don't know the man."

"You're under oath, Mr. Tomek."

Gill cleared his throat. "My client answered the question."

Collins pressed on. "Mr. Tomek, are you a terrorist, a member of a terrorist organization, or any group seeking to harm the United States?"

"No."

"Are you involved in, or aware of, a plot to extort money from the U.S. government?"

"No."

"Have you heard of a terrorist group called Vector?"

"No."

"Were you aware of a terrorist attack on Memorial Day, May 27th in Springvale, Connecticut; Bay City, Texas; and Park Ridge, Pennsylvania?"

"No."

"Who do you report to at Talas?"

"I was in charge."

"Who is your boss?"

Tomek shrugged. "Never met him, never knew his name."

"How did you communicate?"

"By phone."

"Where's your phone?"

"Lost it."

"Where?"

"How do I know?"

"What's the number?"

Tomek didn't answer.

"Who's your phone provider?"

"A cheap burner."

"What did you do at Talas?"

"I was the manager."

"Does Talas sell shrimp?"

"Yeah."

Collins raised an eyebrow. "There's no evidence of that."

"We're remodeling."

"We found three male corpses buried behind the plant," said Collins. "They were missing heads and hands. Did you murder them?"

Tomek smirked.

"Who are they?" asked Collins.

"Anybody with a boat could've buried them there," said Tomek.

Collins sighed. "Did Enslein or anyone else order you to dump toxic chemicals into Hillsborough Bay?"

"I told you. I don't know this guy."

Collins checked his notes. "What did you flush into the bay?"

Tomek shrugged.

"According to the EPA, you released high concentrations of carcinogens, including chlorine, acetone, and benzene. Glucose and traces of anthrax were also in the effluent."

"What's effluent?"

"The stuff you washed down the drain," said the SAC.

Gill withdrew the handkerchief from his jacket pocket and mopped the perspiration from his brow. "Mr. Tomek admits to washing chemicals down the Talas storm drain."

"Do you know what this is?" Collins held up a small piece of glass. "We found several pieces like this at Talas."

Tomek shook his head, a bored expression on his face.

"It's a lens fragment from a gas chromatograph. Do you know what that is?"

"No."

"It's used to identify and separate chemicals. What's it doing in a shrimp plant?"

"My client has responded in good faith," sighed Gill. "I advise him not to answer any more questions."

Collins smirked and glared at Tomek. "You said you worked alone. Who drove the vans?"

Tomek looked away and didn't speak.

"The Ford vans, Tomek. Where are they? Who drove them?"

Tomek shifted in his seat. "I don't know what you're talkin' about."

"We have vehicle IDs for three Ford Econolines registered to Talas, Inc., Palm Grove. Where are they?"

"Don't know."

Collins checked his notes. "We need a sample of Mr. Tomek's blood."

Gill laughed. "Blood samples violate the 4th Amendment's protection against illegal searches, Mr. Collins. *You know that.*"

"The FBI has a right to get blood samples from prisoners and parolees."

"Let's see what the courts and ACLU have to say about that," rejoined Gill. "You're holdin' my client with no probable cause, and have no witness statements or viable records of what you claim he did."

"We're talking terrorism here," said Collins, turning to Moss. "I need to speak with Mr. Gill in private." He turned off the videorecorder.

"Use my office," said Moss, pointing down the hall.

When Collins and Gill departed, Moss addressed the prisoner. "You're not fooling anybody, Tomek. We'll prove you're involved."

"Screw you."

"What are you getting out of this? What did Enslein tell you at Durham?"

"I don't know what you're talkin' about."

"He's got anthrax, doesn't he? And you don't care. All those innocent lives. You're one sick son of a bitch."

sixty-one

INTELETECH, MANHATTAN, NEW YORK CITY

George phoned Martin Haley at Kartan and got Kevin Baines instead. The CFO said Haley was no longer with the company and George should direct all future calls to him.

George was upfront with Baines, explaining that Enslein was last seen on Rhodes but might not be there now because an explosion had destroyed his castle.

Baines was okay with that, explaining with Haley gone, the company would pursue the more practical route of insurance and payment instead of arrest and punishment.

He said the pharmaceutical giant would honor its commitment and wire Inteletech twenty-five grand, plus fees and expenses. The only catch: Inteletech could not refer to Kartan in its marketing campaign or suffer legal action.

A sense of elation overwhelmed George. He dialed Alex and left a message: "Good news, but you gotta call to hear it. Are you coming home or spending time with that blonde? Yeah, I guess you deserve a little fun."

George cracked the seal on a bottle of Black Label he'd been saving for a special occasion, then frowned and returned it to his desk drawer. The phone rang; Alex was calling back.

George gave him the news. His partner was happy, but then got serious.

"I'm flying to Malta," Alex said. "Enslein is a suspected terrorist and I'm helping to find him."

"Who says?"

"Dr. Burke."

George laughed. "Dr. Burke, the blonde? And you believe her? Why are you doing this? We're done. Time to celebrate."

"This is serious, George. Thousands of lives could be at stake."

"It's not our fight, man. Let the feds handle it."

"I can recognize Enslein and his men from Talas and the castle."

"This was supposed to be a few days, Alex. Now you're talking weeks."

"A few more days won't bankrupt us. I'll keep you posted." Alex disconnected.

sixty-two

BIOLOGICAL WEAPONS GROUP
HEADQUARTERS, ATLANTA, GEORGIA

Imelda turned on the lights in the forensic laboratory and stood there for a moment, overcome by the vast amount of work to be done and lack of time to do it. She liked to work late at night, accompanied by the whisper of the ventilators, freezers, and hoods, and the occasional beeping of the biosafety cabinets. No human or inhuman interruptions.

Primed and focused, she was determined to find the answer, the lost bit of evidence—the mystifying revelation of how Enslein would execute his plan. As always, she'd rely on her research to help.

She heated a flask of water over a Bunsen burner and poured herself a mug of green tea. A jolt of caffeine would keep her sharp tonight. She sat at her desk and scrolled through emails—hundreds had piled up since she had returned.

Reaching for the mug, she aimed too high and knocked it over. The steaming liquid spilled onto her files, Paul Stewart's three-ring binder, and *The Springvale Citizen* newspaper folded under the desk.

"Damn it!" She jumped up and quickly carried the dripping items to a nearby table. With paper towels, she blotted the files and binder and opened the newspaper to dry.

After pouring herself another cup of tea, she assigned Talas samples for forensic chemical analysis and cataloged photos for the Drug Enforcement Administration. She was filling out chain-of-custody cards when a text arrived from Alex.

Dimitri and I are heading to Malta. Minotaur spotted 600 km from there. Talk to you soon, Alex.

She quickly replied, updating him on the Talas raid and Tomek's arrest.

Hours passed, as she hunched over the computer, toiling relentlessly, drilling for the missing piece of evidence, the speck beneath the surface and the key to Enslein's scheme. An inkling of how he did it must be right under her nose . . . somewhere.

Stretching her arms and neck to relieve the soreness, she logged off, and resignedly collected her things. Her tired body had emphatically rebelled. It was 1:44 a.m. Time to go home.

As she rose from her chair, she caught an acrid odor in the air. Searching around, she traced the source to the tea stain on *The Springvale Citizen*. It smelled like vinegar.

The hairs on the back of her neck alerted her to something that wasn't quite right. Goosebumps flared along her arms and legs, as she again sniffed the newspaper to be sure. Yes, the odor was strongest there. She put on a respirator, and using tongs, carried it to the electron microscope, focusing on the dampened area.

She noticed nothing out of the ordinary until the image of a graft polymer in the ink caught her attention. Connected to the major chain of molecules was a homopolymer, as well as a double-bonded oxygen molecule and a single-bonded hydroxide molecule.

She tried to make sense of what she saw, recalling the methacrylic acid copolymer she had worked with years ago in organic chemistry class. She pulled up the college lab report on her computer. The copolymer in the ink was similar. But what was MAC doing in newspaper ink?

Increasing the magnification to 10,000,000x, she examined the copolymer again. Its toroidal shape resembled an inner tube, like something she had seen in Enslein's encapsulation patent. As she moved the beam, a chain of nucleotides—the basic structural unit of DNA and RNA—caught her by surprise, flooring her!

"Holy shit!" she shouted, her words reverberating off the laboratory walls.

There they were! Remnants of RNA genes of the Norwalk Agent, the degraded norovirus! Enslein had used methacrylic acid copolymer to encapsulate the flu virus in newspaper ink!

Ecstatic, she grabbed her phone and, with trembling hands, dialed Brockman. It rang six times until he finally picked up. She heard him fumbling in the dark and could barely contain herself. "Marv! It's in the newspapers! It's in the newspapers!"

He coughed, turned on a light, and cleared his throat. "Imelda? Is that you? What is it? What's wrong?"

"That's how he did it! The Norwalk Agent is in the ink!"

"Slow down, Imelda. Slow down."

"Enslein encapsulated the flu virus in newspaper ink."

"How?"

"MAC, methacrylic acid copolymer, Enslein's patent application at Pharmacap. The virus was inside the capsules. He increased the capsules' wall thickness and mechanical strength to protect the virus from heat and oxygen. I found traces of MAC and RNA in *The Springvale Citizen* newspaper. When the capsules hit the ink, they dissolve, freeing the virus."

"Anyone touching the newspaper is infected," said Brockman.

"Exactly! Oil on their skin absorbs the virus."

"But it won't work," he said. "Newspaper ink would kill it."

"You're right. That's why he used *The Springvale Citizen*. It's printed with water-based ink. Non-toxic. The virus is active for about a day or so before losing its effectiveness, enough time to infect everyone who touches it. I'd bet newspapers from Bay City and Park Ridge use water-based ink, too."

"Imelda, we never checked the newspaper printing plants. I bet they had a major flu outbreak at all three!"

sixty-three

EL PASO, TEXAS

The sun beat down on a flat, barren strip of I-10, as the Kid roared by at ninety miles per hour, singing along with Eminem's rap blasting through the speakers: ". . . blood, guts, guns, cuts, knives, lives . . . I'm gonna kill you. You don't wanna mess wit me . . . I'm gonna kill you . . ."

He closed on a young woman driving a late-model Chevy convertible in the right lane, hair blowing in the wind. He cut in front of her and slowed down. They rode like that for a minute until she got fed up and passed him in the left lane. As she drove by, she flipped him the finger. He laughed and resumed singing, " . . . you better kill me . . . you better kill me . . ."

She moved into the right lane as he sped up and pulled alongside her. She hit the brakes and let him by. He cut in front of her, eased up, and checked the rearview. She was right behind him. They rode like that for about a mile, barely over the speed limit.

"You don't wanna mess wit me," he sang. When he glanced behind him, she was gone, nothing but an empty road. From his blind spot, she suddenly zoomed by like he was standing still. When far ahead, she moved into the right lane.

He floored the van and closed the gap. "Nobody dusts the Kid!"

he yelled. "Eighty-five! Ninety-five! One-oh-two!" At one-twelve, the V-10 was redlining and burbling. "Eeeyow!" he screamed. "Ride 'em, cowboy!"

He was four car lengths behind the Chevy, which suddenly decelerated for a disabled car blocking the right lane. A 16-wheeler right next to him was slowing in the left lane.

Nowhere to go. The Kid jammed on the brakes. The van squealed and swerved. He had no choice except to turn right to avoid the Chevy. Skidding onto the shoulder, the top-heavy Econoline teetered on two wheels as the Kid fought to control it. But momentum won the fight. The van flipped on its side, screeching metal and glass, and rolled onto its roof before stopping on the grass.

The Kid hung upside down, an airbag scrunching his youthful face into an ugly grimace. "Fuck!" he shouted, as he unsnapped the seat belt and fell onto the roof. Crawling back, he opened the backpack and breathed a sigh of relief. The cylinder was undamaged. He pushed the backpack through the broken back window and climbed out.

Traffic moving on I-10 acted as if nothing had happened. No cops, no ambulances, no curious observers. Nobody stopped. Just another ho-hum rollover on your way to work.

Wasting no time, the Kid slung the backpack over his shoulder and walked toward the service road. He hiked for miles in the sweltering heat, took the phone out of his jacket pocket, hesitated, and then put it back. Nobody needed to know, especially Tomek.

A white cottage with an attached garage was up ahead. The Kid knocked on the door. "Anybody home!?" he shouted.

No answer.

He tried the door. Locked. And then the back door. Locked.

He made a fist and faced the window, then relaxed his hand and headed for the garage. Through a gritty, web-covered window, he could make out an old Honda Civic inside.

The hinged garage doors had a padlock on them. He found a rock nearby and with two well-placed strikes, broke the hasp and opened the doors.

"Yes!" he said, rewarded by the unlocked Civic. He searched for keys. No luck. Then he popped the trunk and found a toolbox containing a screwdriver, a hammer, and a wrench.

"Cool."

He carried the tools into the car and hammered the plastic ignition cover on the steering column, exposing the key cylinder inside. Unscrewing the cylinder revealed the switch.

He jammed the screwdriver into the switch and turned it. The car started, but the steering wheel wouldn't turn. Levering the wheel with the hammer on the dash, he pushed hard and heard a crack. The locking gear had snapped. He was in business and compensated with a full tank of gas.

He dropped his backpack in the rear, turned on the radio, and headed to the service road, figuring he could make it to LA in thirteen hours if he didn't stop. "Back in business!"

sixty-four

CHICAGO, ILLINOIS

Five Fire Hawks, wearing black and gold jackets, chilled out on the front stoop of a three-story walkup. Gustavo, a short, cocky youth with two gold chains around his neck and shoulder-length hair, hiked up his pants and slapped Pancho's arm. "Remember those Cobras talkin' shit? They won't be sayin' nothin' now."

Pancho stroked his goatee. "We shoulda taken 'em out."

"You get caught don't come cryin' to me," said Mrs. Loco, looking over.

Gustavo nodded at the white Econoline parking in the street in front of them. Mario got out, flipped his cigarette into the gutter, and locked the van. Gustavo wiped a hand across his chest in a sign of dismissal.

Pancho laughed and called out to Mario, "Wha' choo doin' man!? Can't park here!"

Mario paused and looked around. "Why not?"

"Because choo need a special sticker."

Mario walked around the van. "I don't see no sign."

Pancho stared at him, a faint smile in the corner of his mouth. "Gustavo don't like you, bro. Better watch it."

Mario crossed the sidewalk and climbed the surrounding steps.

RICHARD ZANETTI

Gustavo arched his eyebrows. "*Qué cojones.*"

Mario pushed open the lobby door, found Rebekka's name on 3A, and headed for the stairs.

Wrappers, butts, and paper bags littered the third-floor hallway, and the fixture had no lightbulb. Through a small window at the end of the hall, the darkening sky bore witness to a fast-approaching storm.

Mario paused at her door, pressed the doorbell, and knocked. Lightning flashed, followed by a loud clap of thunder. He knocked again, louder this time.

"Who is it?" Rebekka's tentative voice.

"Hey, Rebekka! It's me, Mario!"

"Mario?" Her voice sounded faint, nervous.

"Yeah. Remember me? From Florida? Molto Mario." He laughed.

The flap on the eyepiece opened, a chain fell, and two locks clicked. The door opened a crack and one eye was all he saw. "I'm busy. Come back later."

A man's voice, coarse and impatient, erupted from within.

"Gotta go," said Rebekka.

"You all right?"

She shut the door.

Mario stood there for a moment, then heard what sounded like a slap followed by a whimper. He tried the door. It opened into a long, dark hall, suddenly lit by lightning.

"Rebekka!"

A lean, bare-chested man in jeans stepped out from a side room and pulled a switchblade from his pocket. It sparkled in the dimness. "Take off, scumbag."

Mario took a step toward him. "Time to go."

Howling wind-driven rain rattled the windows.

Eyes locked on Mario's, the man bent forward, narrowing

the distance between them. Lightning flashed, revealing Rebekka standing nude in the hallway.

Mario glanced at her and didn't see the move. His left shoulder stung in pain. Sidestepping, he crouched and swung hard, hitting the knifer in the jaw. He heard a crack. The man gasped, leaned back, and dropped the knife. Mario stepped forward and hit him again, putting all his weight behind the punch. The man went down for good.

Rebekka ran to the knifer, moaning on the floor. She cradled his head in her lap. "You hurt him!"

Blood dripped from Mario's aching shoulder as he kicked the switchblade down the hall. He took one last look at Rebekka and headed for the door.

Pouring rain soaked Mario's bloody shirt as he stepped onto the street. The Hawks had vanished, leaving four flat tires on the van. Mario checked inside, relieved to find the backpack with the cylinder still there. He took the backpack, stopped an old man with an umbrella and asked for directions to the nearest hospital. The man pointed at the blue-and-white H on the telephone pole. An urgent care center was only two blocks away.

Except for two young women, the center was empty when Mario walked in. The nurse took one look at his blood-and-rain-soaked shirt and rushed him to a cubicle. Another nurse entered and examined him. "How'd this happen?"

"Fan belt slipped."

"Insurance?"

He nodded, but didn't have any.

The nurse cleaned and dressed the wound and applied a temporary bandage. She gestured to the waiting room. "Wait there for someone to call you. And keep pressure on it. You need stitches."

Fifteen minutes later, the desk nurse led Mario to a room where a young intern was waiting. He examined the wound.

"Fan belt, huh?" he said in a doubtful tone. "Looks like you got stabbed."

"Snapped right back at me," Mario said. "Like a whip."

The intern applied numbing gel, closed the wound with nine stitches, and bandaged it. Mario earned a tetanus shot and a packet of painkillers. The intern told him to see the receptionist about insurance and departed. Mario reset his bloody shirt and slipped unnoticed out the door. The rain had almost stopped, and the sky was brighter.

sixty-five

MALTA

Kavi drove south on Route 1 toward Albert Town, as she fired up a Gauloises filter, and glanced at Enslein, staring pensively out the side window. "What are you thinking?"

"I was wondering what made you change your mind and decide to come along?"

"I want to see the new cave, too," she said. "It's sixty feet below the ground."

He glimpsed the ash forming on her cigarette. "You are different today. You seem more . . ."

"Excited? Happy?" She opened the window a crack to let the smoke out and stopped at an intersection. "Maybe I am." The ash from her cigarette floated to the floor.

They drove on for several minutes past the Addolorata Cemetery on the right until he broke the silence. "I was thinking of letting Stefano go."

She stiffened slightly, but her tone remained serene. "He's been a loyal servant."

"He annoys me."

She shrugged, drove up the street, and parked in a lot behind the Hypogeum. Side-by-side, they proceeded to the entrance.

"Go on ahead," said Kavi when they reached the door. "I'll arrange for us to see the cave. It's closed to the public."

Hewn from limestone by the island's early settlers, the Hypogeum's network of temples and alcoves dated back to 3600 BC, when the last of the woolly mammoths roamed the earth. Objects in the museum suggested the islanders worshipped a Sleeping Mother Goddess and had a mystical cult.

Enslein had purchased what archeologists claimed to be authentic sleeping ladies for his castle library. He assumed the fire had destroyed them, and they'd be impossible to replace.

Kavi exchanged a glance with the guard, who departed without a word. She then joined Enslein, and they ventured through a long, descending tunnel lit by kerosene lamps, leading to the newly discovered cave.

Upon entering, the cave's stunning beauty overwhelmed them. Huge icicle-like stalactites hung from the ceiling, and smaller stalagmites jutted up from the rocky floor. Above, swirling dust refracted a pale blue light produced by phototropic bacteria and colonies of glow worms.

Enslein cupped his hands behind his ears. "Listen, Kavi. Listen to the cadence of dripping water and the high-pitched cries of bats lured by long-forgotten souls. Children of the night here to entertain us." He turned to her, but she was gone.

He sat cross-legged on the rocky floor beneath the swirling vortex, where a thousand years ago the Hal Saflieni Cult worshiped and died. He thought he heard somber voices murmuring to him. A strange vibration stirred his face. It came again in a coolness passing over him, swirling upward toward the ceiling. Footsteps broke the silence and echoed off the walls. Enslein's eyes flicked open. Valovitch stood before him, like a phantom in the eerie glow.

The professor's mind raced. "You? How?" He rose to his feet. "I . . . I have your money."

"Don't be a fool." The Russian leveled his Beretta at Enslein's chest. "You pathetic worm. Did you think I would not find you? Did you think you could walk away?"

Beads of sweat dotted Enslein's forehead; his clammy hands twitched. "Double. I will pay double."

As Valovitch moved closer, Enslein caught movement in the shadows. "Kavi?"

Valovitch smiled. "She knows."

Enslein's face whitened, his breathing labored. "You will get nothing if you kill me."

"But my satisfaction." A bat screeched. The Russian twitched as Enslein bolted across the floor. Valovitch fired at him and missed.

Enslein headed for a crypt. Valovitch fired again. The first bullet struck the professor's thigh, and the next two ricocheted off the wall. Valovitch continued firing wildly.

Rudely awakened from their inverted perches, hundreds of bats took to the air in a swirling cloud of ultrasonic shrieks that resonated from the ceiling and the walls.

Gunshots booming in the void and echolocating bat calls converged in a deafening roar. Ancient stalactites swayed side to side, quaking from the sonic rhythm of compressions.

Shaped from three thousand years of mineral drippings, a great stalactite shuddered. The crack in its foundation ruptured, setting free the eighty-pound travertine monolith. It plummeted straight down—a deadly, sharply pointed missile that split Valovitch's skull and plunged through his body.

It shattered on the cavern floor—a detonation of calcite, blood, and foul-smelling excreta. The Beretta clattered across the floor and came to rest near to where Enslein was hiding. Drawn by the body heat emanating from below, bats circled and then settled on the Russian's bloody carcass.

Enslein crawled out from behind the crypt, favoring his bleeding leg, and propped his back against a wall.

Kavi emerged from the shadows, a semiautomatic in her hand, as frenzied, screeching bats swooped over her. She stared down at Enslein, grimacing in pain.

"I never loved you, Gerfried. At least you'll die knowing the truth."

A fire burned in Enslein's eyes. "You will never be rich without me."

"It's over."

"You need me!" He shifted the weight off his aching leg and reached out to her. "Help me. Help me up."

She pointed the gun at his head and squeezed the trigger. Click. She tried again. Click, click, click.

"I removed the bullets." Enslein stretched for Valovitch's gun and aimed it at her. "Goodbye, my love." He pulled the trigger.

She glared at him as a bullet struck her chest. The blast dislodged another stalactite that fell between them and shattered in a heap of dirt and rock covering Kavi's body.

Blood ran down Enslein's leg. He removed his shirt, tore off a sleeve, and wrapped it tightly around the upper thigh. Rising to his feet, he hobbled for a few steps, stopped to rest against the tunnel wall, then limped slowly toward the entrance, a trail of bloody footprints in his wake.

sixty-six

NEW JERSEY

A former trucker, Michael Benson never lost his love of driving—the throaty power of the engine, moving isolation, and riding in the dark. He was heading north on the New Jersey Turnpike and would reach New York City in less than an hour. A mile south of Elizabeth, a high-pitched whine erupted from under the hood.

Benson slowed to sixty and listened. The keening noise persisted, but not as loud as before. He cut into the right lane and slowed to forty. He could barely hear it.

Battery? Water pump? Overheating? "It's a brand-new van!" He gave it some gas and stepped it up to sixty-five. The whine grew louder.

Ten minutes later, the dashboard lights faded and went out, and the engine died. The van coasted to a stop on the shoulder about five miles from the George Washington Bridge.

Benson put the van in park and tried to start it. After several attempts, he gave up and popped the hood. Everything looked fine. No leaks, no smoke. Oil level okay, water in the radiator, and half a tank of gas.

Swearing like a trooper, he grabbed his backpack, walked north for fifty feet, and stuck out his thumb. A few drivers slowed, but no one stopped for the muscular man resembling Hannibal Lecter . . . except for one good Samaritan.

Rick Roberts slowed to forty, passed the van, and pulled onto the shoulder. He lowered the passenger window and waited for the limping stranger to lean in.

"Goin' to the city," said Benson.

Roberts unlocked the door. "Throw your stuff in back."

Benson tossed his backpack onto the rear seat and got in.

"What's the problem?" asked Roberts in a friendly tone.

"No idea."

"Can't fix 'em like we used to," said Roberts. "Emergency phone is up ahead."

Benson unzipped his jacket and slumped down in the seat. "No thanks. Just the ride."

Roberts headed for the bridge and shot a glance at Benson. "I sell shoes."

"Shrimp," replied Benson.

"Hah! My wife could eat 'em for breakfast. I live near the ocean. Got seventy-five clams, last week. Littlenecks. But the ole girl made me throw them out. We had a big fight over it. She worries about hepatitis. A few cases down by us. Mayor said it was the clams. Politicians, right? What do they know? I was gonna boil 'em, but she didn't go for it. Worried we'd get sick." He shook his head. "I don't know. Maybe she's right. Never got sick from clams before. Must've eaten thousands. What're you gonna do?"

"You should've eaten them," said Benson, eyes on the road.

"Too late now." Roberts rolled through E-ZPass and crossed the bridge. On the right, majestic spires glistened in the morning sun. "Nice view, huh? I'm Rick." He held out his hand, but Benson didn't shake it.

"Jones."

"First name?"

"Mack."

"Pleased to meet you, Mack. I'm going to midtown. Where can I drop you?"

"Anyplace down there."

Roberts took the West Side Highway, got off on Eleventh Avenue, and headed east on 42nd Street in bumper-to-bumper traffic. He stopped at the corner of Eighth Avenue. "How's this?"

Benson grabbed his backpack, got out, and walked away.

sixty-seven

LOS ANGELES, CALIFORNIA

The Kid slowed down to watch guys and girls showcase their skills at the Hermosa Beach skatepark. He parked the Civic by a hydrant across the street, got out, and kicked the front tire. "Not bad for an old timer."

The beach was how he imagined it: white sand, blue sea, and a light breeze blowing off the water. He checked out two bikini-clad girls sitting on towels as he headed toward the water. The surf was up, the tide was in, and a few guys were surfboarding.

Sitting on the sand, he observed a pretty girl wearing a straw hat stand up and get ready to depart. She shut the cooler, rolled up the mat, and packed away a towel and suntan lotion. As she gathered her things and headed for the street, a purse fell out of her bag.

The Kid ran over and retrieved it. "Miss! Excuse me, miss!" he called out, catching up with her.

She stopped and turned with a wary expression.

He held out the purse. "You lost this."

"Oh!" She beamed and stuffed it in her tote bag. "Thank you! Thanks a lot!"

"No problem. Just headin' out myself." He walked beside her until they reached the sidewalk. "Come here a lot?"

She stopped walking and placed the cooler on the sidewalk. "After work. My friends like Manhattan Beach, but I think people are friendlier here. What about you?"

"First time. Just arrived."

"Really. Where from?"

"Florida. Near Tampa."

"Wow! Long trip."

He cocked his head. "Made it in three days. Burned up the road." He reached for her cooler. "I can help with this if you like."

"No, that's okay." She took it from his hand.

"What's your name?"

"Kimberly."

"Pleased to meet you, Kimberly. Friends call me Kid. Listen, I got my car nearby. Give you a lift?"

She shook her head. "I don't live far. It's okay."

"I'm right over there. Look." He pointed up the street.

"That's all right. Thanks again for my purse."

"Sure?"

She smiled and headed south on Beach Drive. The Kid stood there as he watched her walk away and checked the time. It was getting late, and he still had an hour's drive to the motel in Santa Ana.

A parking ticket was on the Honda's windshield when he got there. He tore it up, dropped it in the street, and then drove in Kimberly's direction. When he saw her turn left onto 17th Street, he coasted up next to her and rolled down the window. "Hey, Kimberly. Come on, get in." He stopped the car and opened the door.

She hesitated and then got in, placing her things on the floor in front of her. "What kind of car is this?"

"A classic. Got a great deal on it."

sixty-eight

VALLETTA, MALTA

The President of Rhodes, bolstered by the Nationalist Party, discouraged any attempt to discover what had really happened at the Hypogeum, fearing tourism would suffer. The Hotel Managers Association was in full accord with his decision.

A cursory investigation concluded that a falling stalactite had accidentally killed a Russian tourist. Observers suspected other people were in the cave, but authorities never confirmed it, effecting an unspoken government policy protecting "entitled residents," such as Gerfried Enslein. The President temporarily locked the new cave, fearing other stalactites could fall and injure others.

Enslein assumed the authorities didn't find Kavi's body beneath the rubble. "A perfect place for her," he uttered.

The Valletta mayor arranged for a quick, unmarked burial for Anton Valovitch in the Hellenistic Cemetery. An unknown donor rewarded the mayor and sexton for their discretion and quick and judicious work. Authorities believed tourists would forget about the incident in three or four days if they were lucky.

Dr. Maali clicked his tongue as he examined the X-ray of Enslein's left thigh. "A round-nose bullet with high-velocity and penetration," he said. "You need a nerve block." He injected the group of nerves and waited fifteen minutes. Then, using an awl, he expertly removed the bullet and cleaned the wound. "Roll up your sleeve, professor." He administered a shot of cephalosporin. "You were lucky." Maali presented the bullet for Enslein to see. "It didn't fragment and barely missed the femoral artery. One more inch and you would have died in there."

Enslein scoffed at Maali's statement.

Stefano drove Enslein to the *Minotaur*. The professor limped aboard, refusing any help. Captain Hassan greeted him on the flybridge. "Fully loaded and fueled, sir. I am happy you are up and about."

"Thank you, Hassan."

A disturbance drew Enslein's attention to the dock as Marcos charged up the gangplank, stopped on deck, and then headed to the flybridge, confronting Enslein. "My sister!" he yelled. "Where is she?!"

Hassan stepped between them. "Casting off, sir."

Marcos pushed Hassan away. "We don't go without her."

"Change of plans," said Enslein. "Call her."

"You lie!" shouted Marcos. "Something happened! We don't go without her!"

"Then you can stay here." Enslein pointed a gun in his face.

The engine roared to life, drowning out the gunshot. Marcos was dead before he hit the deck.

sixty-nine

VALLETTA, MALTA

"**M**alta is a perfect hideout," Alex said to Dimitri, as the Airbus circled for landing. "Exceptional security, wealthy lifestyle, and guaranteed anonymity to anyone with enough money to afford to live there. Enslein fits the bill."

Alex and Dimitri were among the first to deplane. A government official instructed the airport staff to expedite their customs process, which typically would have lasted nearly an hour. Twenty minutes later, they were in a taxi en route to the Naval Base on the coast of the Floriana section of Valletta. The road overlooked the Grand Harbor.

Dimitri frowned at the abundance of pleasure boats, trawlers, and cruise ships. "Finding the *Minotaur* will not be easy in that crowd."

Alex's face bore a look of concern. "Let's hope it's still here."

Dimitri acknowledged that with a nod. "According to the police, Enslein has a house on the island and a slip at Dockyard Creek. The commissioner referred me to Major Modina, the head of the country's maritime squadron. I have been in touch with him since yesterday. He has the team to help us."

The taxi stopped at the Hay Wharf Naval Base—a yellow,

three-story building next to a small dock at the foot of Valletta's defensive wall fortifications. The base oversaw training, border control, and staff accommodation for the squadron.

Dimitri greeted the lieutenant at the door and introduced themselves, and the lieutenant placed a call.

In five minutes, Major Modina, a tall, heavyset man with a slight paunch, emerged from his office and greeted them in English. When Modina saw Dimitri's badge, he shook his hand. "Sorry for the delay, gentlemen. I was informing the Vice Admiral about our situation." Modina introduced Alex.

They gathered around a table in the situation room, as Modina updated them on what he knew. "The judge refused a warrant to search Enslein's house because it lacked probable cause and violated Article 12 of the International Bill of Human Rights."

"Human rights?" asked Alex, wondering how that could be an issue.

"It grants foreigners certain privileges when they're here," explained Modina. "We tried to impound Enslein's yacht, but the judge stopped us again. We couldn't prove the *Minotaur* was involved in a crime." He sadly shook his head. "You should know the professor has Maltese friends in high places."

Alex was livid, speculating on what they needed to take someone into custody on this island. "Didn't you tell the judge what's involved? A suspected terrorist at large."

"Yes," replied Modina. "But our evidence was insufficient. The police posted two men at the entrance to Enslein's house and two at the marina at Dockyard Creek. At ten this morning, they stopped the houseboy running an errand. He said everyone but him departed at six. The cops said they never saw them leave."

"What about the *Minotaur*?" asked Alex.

"An hour before you arrived, someone reported that the *Minotaur* had left the dock."

"Do you have drones, air patrol?" asked Dimitri, with dismay.

"The helicopter is being repaired," said Modina. "And it will take two days for the administration to approve the use of drones. Tourists are frightened of them, but we have two patrol boats ready to go."

Modina gestured across the room at a man wearing a khaki shirt, matching pants, and combat boots. "That's Officer Kern. CIA."

"When did he arrive?" asked Alex.

"Today. He wanted a drone to blow up the *Minotaur* and wasn't happy when I told him we forbid it. He insists on accompanying us."

A lieutenant summoned Kern to their table, and Modina made the introductions.

Kern shook Dimitri's hand and said, "I called your office earlier, Captain, but you had already left. Three more officers will arrive tomorrow. We can handle this from here."

A frown appeared on Dimitri's face. "Enslein is wanted in Greece for kidnapping and suspected murder."

"He's a terrorist wanted in the United States," countered Kern. "Malta's prime minister approved our presence here."

"We tracked him here and know the *Minotaur*," Alex said, annoyed by Kern's obvious effort to dismiss them.

"Right," Kern said. "I didn't—"

"Excuse me, Mr. Kern," Modina interjected. "I have been in contact with the captain since yesterday. I insist he and Mr. West accompany us, or we will do the search ourselves."

Kern smirked, but didn't speak.

"Mr. Kern can join us," said Dimitri, glancing at his watch. "Shall we go?"

Alex, Dimitri, and Kern followed Modina to the dock where a 110-foot Island Class Patrol boat had just finished refueling.

The Navy armed the boat with two 22 mm machine guns and one .50-caliber machine gun, plus six lightweight assault rifles and several Berettas. The crew included a captain, executive officer, assistant navigator, two lance corporals, and two gunner mates. Alex and Dimitri armed themselves with Berettas.

When everyone had boarded, the gunner's mates cast off the lines. Captain Adami eased the boat out of the slip and into the pristine waters of the harbor.

Modina took a moment to address Dimitri, Alex, and Kern. "The *Minotaur* is white. It's a sleek, modern vessel about twenty-five meters long, with a cantilevered flybridge. Top speed is about thirty knots. The good news, we can outrun it. Our sister patrol boat is leaving Marsamxett Harbor as we speak and will work its way around the coast to meet us. We can cover the entire island that way."

Modina focused on Dimitri. "You take the starboard bow, Captain; Alex, port side. Officer Kern can move around. I'll be with Captain Adami on the bridge."

They proceeded to Dockyard Creek, and, as expected, the *Minotaur*'s slip was empty. Modina alerted the dockmaster to call him if the yacht returned. They cruised slowly up the channel, weaving in and out of heavy traffic as Dimitri, Alex, and Kern scanned the harbor for the *Minotaur*.

They passed Fort St. Angelo on their left, as a large Norwegian cruise ship was docking. Three girls leaned over the rail and waved. Dimitri peered up at them through binoculars, a big smile on his face.

"Maybe Enslein is up there," laughed Modina.

While the others were distracted, Alex caught sight of a white yacht moving north. It looked like the *Minotaur*. "There!" he yelled, pointing. "Is that it!?"

Modina raised his binoculars and confirmed it was the *Minotaur*. He signaled Adami and made a spinning motion with his hand. The captain reversed direction, opened the throttle, and turned on the siren.

Enslein grimaced at the howler's high-low wail and the sight of the approaching patrol boat. Hassan throttled forward and the engine sprang to life, pitching the *Minotaur* back into the water. Waves broke over the bow as it raced for the open sea.

Modina called for backup. The other patrol boat was on its way. The *Minotaur* rounded Ricasoli Point and capsized a small sailboat crossing the channel. Two boys hanging on to the gunwale were uninjured.

At St. Elmo Lighthouse, the patrol boat was way behind Enslein's yacht but gradually closing. Alex could see men on the *Minotaur*'s stern holding what looked like semiautomatic weapons. He released the safety on the Beretta and cocked it as if he were firing a weapon for the first time.

"Take cover!" shouted Modina when he saw someone on the *Minotaur* fire.

A bullet hit the patrol boat's side rail and ricocheted into the deck. Kern returned fire and called out to Modina while pointing to the unmanned .50-caliber machine gun.

Modina shook his head and gestured to the other boats within range of the gun. "Too dangerous to use!"

Another bullet twanged the deck.

Modina returned fire and got off three quick rounds.

Kern stood up to get a better shot.

"Get down!" Modina shouted, as a shot rang out.

Kern spun and hit the deck.

Three more bullets struck the hull.

Modina and Alex ran to Kern and dragged him out of the line of fire. The bullet had struck the right side of his head, and the exit hole revealed severe peripheral damage. Modina placed his hand on Kern's carotid artery and shook his head. He waved to two gunner mates who carried Kern below.

The patrol boat was now about thirty meters behind the *Minotaur* in choppy, open water.

"Close it up!" shouted Modina.

Adami increased speed and crossed the *Minotaur*'s wake to its starboard side, two boat lengths behind.

The *Minotaur* slowed abruptly, allowing the patrol boat to catch up. When it was almost adjacent, Hassan veered right, ramming the patrol boat. For several seconds, the two vessels rode side by side, separated by a few feet of roiling water.

Alex saw his chance. Leaping off the bow, he landed on the aft deck of the *Minotaur*. The combat training he endured kicked in as he rolled into a high crawl, aimed, and unloaded five rounds covering Dimitri, who hit the deck behind him. Bullets whizzed over their heads.

Enslein's gunmen fired from behind an access hatch. They raised their heads, fired, and then ducked for cover, effectively pinning down Alex and Dimitri.

Alex estimated a three-second interval between opposing shots. He waited for a gunman to duck down, counted to three, and fired at a spot above the access hatch. The gunman's head snapped back and disappeared.

When a bullet pinged the grating above Dimitri's head, he returned fire. A second gunman straightened up, staggered to the rail, and fell into the sea.

The cabin door flew open, and two men burst out, pistols in hand.

"Drop it!" shouted Dimitri.

The men fired and missed. Alex returned fire, striking a gunman in the shoulder, and the other gunman retreated to the cabin. Alex charged the wounded man and kicked his weapon overboard. When the wounded man resisted, Alex decked the guy with one punch, and Dimitri cuffed him unconscious to the rail.

The patrol boat slowed to twenty meters behind the *Minotaur* in rough water. The sister patrol boat was close by and nearing the *Minotaur*'s port side.

Alex and Dimitri climbed to the flybridge and threw open the door. Hassan, holding a handset, had his back to them.

"Police!" shouted Dimitri, pressing a gun against the captain's head. "Stop the boat!"

Hassan eased back the throttle, and the *Minotaur* settled into the choppy water.

"Enslein!" shouted Alex. "Where's Enslein!?"

Hassan pointed below. Dimitri locked the throttle and the wheel and cuffed the captain to the rail, out of reach of the controls.

Alex ran to deck level, Dimitri close behind him. The salon was locked. Alex fired two shots into the lock and kicked it open. "Cover me." He charged in, surprising a gunman who fired, striking Dimitri in the arm.

Alex ducked and fired twice. The gunman fell.

Dimitri remained outside, holding his left arm. "Okay!" he shouted. "Get Enslein!"

Modina's men boarded the Minotaur and engaged Enslein's men, as Alex ran through the salon to a rear door, kicked it open, and stood face to face with Enslein, aiming a pistol at Alex's head.

Enslein fired as the second patrol boat rammed the *Minotaur*, thrusting Alex against the wall. The bullet barely missed Alex's head, and the impact knocked the gun out of his hand. On hands and knees, Alex searched for the Beretta as Dimitri burst through the door.

"Where is he?" said Dimitri, swiveling his head.

Alex rose to his feet, holding the Beretta, and looked for Enslein. He couldn't find him. Gun drawn, he ran onto the balcony and stood at the rail, peering down at the sea; it was rough but crystal clear. No floater, swimmer, pool of blood or school of sharks.

Only one other door led out of the salon—the door Dimitri had entered. No other place for Enslein to go.

In disbelief, Alex shook his head. Did Enslein take his own life rather than suffer the humiliation of being caught? He returned to the salon and looked around again. Maybe they missed something—a trapdoor, a hidden recess, or a secret hiding place.

Modina rushed in and saw the blood on Dimitri's arm. "Are you all right?"

"Flesh wound."

"What about you, Alex?"

Alex nodded. "Enslein disappeared. Let's take this boat apart. If he isn't here, then he's either a wizard or down there swimming with the fishes."

Modina's men quickly took control of the *Minotaur* and headed back to the naval base, followed by the two patrol boats.

When they arrived, sailors searched the *Minotaur* from stem to stern, dismantling cabinets, engine room equipment, and galley assemblies. Enslein, they assumed, must have jumped or fallen into the sea and drowned.

"With all these boats and all these tourists, his body will turn up somewhere," opined Modina. Alex was less certain.

A sailor—at least that's what he seemed to be—was sitting on a bench in a public park, placing an important call. Stefano's phone rang. Only two people had this number: Madam Kavi and the professor.

"Yes?"

"I am in the park on the corner of Sant'Andrea and Sant'Anglu in Birzebugga," said Enslein. "Come alone and bring the black satchel from my bedroom. Do not tell anyone where you are going. Leave now."

"Two cops are at the gate," warned Stefano.

"Tell them you are shopping. Come now!"

Enslein hung up and took a moment to admire an attractive woman walking her dog.

Thirty minutes later, Stefano appeared, driving Kavi's car. Enslein opened the rear door and got in. "What took you so long?"

"I . . ."

"Where is the satchel?"

"In the trunk."

"Good." He shut the door. "Take Iz-Zaurrieq to the Blue Grotto view point. A boat will meet us there."

Stefano stared at Enslein in shock. "What happened?"

"The *Minotaur* is gone. I was lucky to escape."

"And Madam Kavi and the others?"

"Gone."

"Gone? Oh, how sad that is."

As they drove, Enslein explained how he had escaped. "I was brilliant, Stefano. I rushed out to the balcony and climbed onto the bridge. A dead sailor was lying there. I put on his shirt and hat and waited as the Marsamxett's patrol boat rafted up to the *Minotaur*. Then I boarded the patrol boat and carried the sailor to sick bay. I left him there, put on a mask, and found my way to the engine room and hid in the tool locker. As soon as the Marsamxett docked at the Naval Base, everyone disembarked to search for me on the *Minotaur*. In broad daylight, I walked off the boat and hitched a ride to Birzebugga."

seventy

WHITE HOUSE, WASHINGTON, DC

The President called an emergency meeting at the Oval Office. In attendance were DHS Secretary Jim Malone, Vice President Jennifer DiMarco, Clarence Galanis, Speaker of the House, and Bill Bossier, White House Chief of Staff.

As the President paced the room, he seemed anxious about something urgent on his mind. "Vector appears to be dead, but we haven't found the body yet. We have three days before the deadline. Once the gold is gone, it's gone. So, I'm debating not sending it."

"You're convinced he's dead?" said Galanis, with a doubtful expression.

"I'm not sure," said the President. "They searched his yacht and couldn't find him. The Vice Admiral of the Maltese Navy thinks he drowned himself . . . Jim, you've been on top of this. What's your opinion?"

"I'd pay the ransom," said Malone. "Why take the chance?"

"I agree," said DiMarco. "It's too big a risk."

The President shook his head. "Vector was on his boat a mile from shore. The water was rough, a challenge for even an excellent swimmer. The Maltese Navy searched for him. They think he's dead. What are the odds that he's alive?"

"I wouldn't bet on it," said Bossier.

"Let's put this to a vote," said the President. "All those who think we should hold off on the gold raise your hand."

Galanis, Bossier, and the President raised their hands.

seventy-one

JFK AIRPORT, QUEENS, NEW YORK

George leaned against the wall in Terminal One's arrival area, scouring the crowd for Alex. He'd been waiting for over an hour and was getting antsy. Limo drivers holding signs with passenger's names stood three deep in front of him. Among them, many uniformed cops and federal agents, responding to the latest orange security alert.

George waved when he spotted Alex in a sweatshirt, jeans, and sneakers coming through the door. Alex waved back and angled through the waiting drivers.

"Hey!" Alex shook his partner's hand and slapped him on the back. He missed his friend.

George gave him a one-armed hug. "After reading your report, I figured you were lucky not to come home in a box. Connie prayed for you."

Alex laughed. "I'm glad, I'm claustrophobic."

George swung Alex's travel bag onto his shoulder, and they headed for the parking area.

"How are you?" said George, eyeing the briefcase under Alex's arm.

"Good. Happy to be home." Alex lifted the briefcase. "Technical reports, lab notes, and flash drives for Imelda. It would've taken a week to ship them."

"She wants you to call her."

Alex nodded. "What's up?"

"Nothing, compared to chasing bad guys in patrol boats. I can't believe what happened there."

Alex smiled. "Good publicity for us, maybe. You held the fort, George. Saved the business."

"I did okay."

"One thing I gotta tell you. It felt good out there chasing Enslein, like my old cop self again."

George smiled. "Figured that."

"You do what you gotta do," said Alex.

"How'd you find him?"

"Long story. I'll tell you over lunch."

They walked across the parking lot, heading for the Trailblazer. George opened the rear door and dumped Alex's stuff in the back. "Do you think Enslein's dead?"

"Not sure. We never found his body."

George took the wheel and headed for the Van Wyck, as Alex called Imelda on his cell. The receptionist told him Dr. Burke was away from her desk, but she'd page her. The line went dead for a few seconds before Imelda answered.

"Alex? Are you home?"

"Yes."

"Listen, I'm up to my neck in this. And the country's in crisis."

"Code orange, I know."

"Maybe red. We're hoping Enslein's out of the picture now. Counting on it. But it makes our job a lot harder. There's no telling who else is involved. Tomek won't talk and . . . Alex?"

"Yeah."

"I need a big favor. Can you come to Atlanta today and help us out?"

Alex glanced at George. "I'm not sure I'd be that helpful."

"You said you saw three of Enslein's men when you were at Talas. You could help identify them. And the lab equipment was gone before we arrived. You might remember something you saw before they got rid of it. It'll help us know what Enslein was doing in there."

Alex glanced at George, staring at the road. "Give me a minute. I'll call you back." He disconnected.

George smiled and rolled his eyes.

"She wants me to go to Atlanta today," said Alex. "Thinks I might help."

"Today?"

"Yeah. I can catch the next flight out of La Guardia."

George moved into the passing lane and sped up. Then he cut into the middle lane in front of a pickup truck. The pickup driver leaned on her horn. "You got yourself into this, Alex. So, who am I to stop you?"

Alex was more disappointed than disturbed, expecting support from his partner. "Slow down, George. What's wrong?"

"I thought this was a partnership," George scoffed.

"It *is* a partnership."

"Well, if this is your definition, I'm not sure . . ."

"Look, the Kartan job turned into a terrorist attack. I saw the people and the lab. I can't walk away because our job is done. It's a national emergency."

"Whatever." George smiled and lifted his foot off the accelerator. "What's she like, this Imelda woman?"

Alex shrugged. "Down to earth. Academic type."

"Academic?"

"Smart and into her career."

"Pretty?"

"Sort of."

"Sexy?"

"Hardworking, gutsy, and cleans up pretty well."

"She's improving as we talk."

"It's business, George. Strictly business."

"Are you sleeping with her?"

"No."

"Too bad." George took the exit for La Guardia. "Delta's got an hourly shuttle. Call when you get there."

seventy-two

HARTSFIELD-JACKSON AIRPORT, ATLANTA, GEORGIA

melda double-parked outside the Delta terminal and slipped the guard twenty bucks to watch her car. "I won't be long."

The two o'clock shuttle from La Guardia had already landed. She hurried to arrivals, searching the crowd, and waved when she saw him. He looked tired, wrinkled, and unshaven, but very good to her.

"Hi." He hugged her and handed her the briefcase. "We found it on the *Minotaur*. Flash drives, lab notes, and other stuff."

"Great." Tucking it under her arm, she led him through the terminal and waved to the guard standing near her car. Alex opened the rear door, dropped his carryon onto the back seat, and sat in front. She turned off the emergency blinkers and headed east on the parkway toward BWG headquarters.

As they drove, she explained her discovery with a grim urgency in her voice. ". . . all the clues were there. We just never put them together. Springvale's health director mentioned the local newspaper didn't report the Norwalk Agent story because most of the staff had the flu. It didn't register then, but now makes perfect sense. Reporters, editors, and production people were the first to touch the paper and catch the virus. I just hope we have enough time to stop this."

"Helluva scientist," he said.

She pulled into the left lane and passed a line of trucks—a safe but aggressive driver. "Think he's dead?"

"Possible, but if I had to bet, I'd say he's hiding somewhere."

She pointed to a gray concrete monolith in the distance. "That's it."

Alex squinted into the sun and saw a dark gray cube, reminding him of a cremation urn in a funeral home. "No windows?"

She smiled. "One of the most secure buildings in America. They screen and control everything—light, air, food, and water. We deal with a lot of bad actors, even nuclear fallout. It's self-contained to protect the public. If something goes wrong, we're dispensable. They aren't."

"If you're trying to get me nervous, you are."

She smiled. "Don't worry. I wouldn't put you in danger. All five hundred of us have received vaccinations against thirteen deadly diseases."

"I'm feeling better already."

She stopped at the entrance and scanned her ID. The gate opened. She drove into the garage and parked in her designated spot. Upon entering the building, she gave Alex a visitor's badge.

The acoustical walls, ceilings, and floors glowed with a pale, phosphorescent light. Alex ran his hand along the smooth white wall. "Quiet in here."

"The walls trap the sound waves, turning acoustical energy into kinetic energy. They use it to heat water."

"Talk too much. You're in hot water."

She laughed. "It took me a while to get used to the silence. Like living alone in a spaceship."

"What's the benefit?"

"I don't know." She shrugged. "Self-reflection?"

"Nice."

"It stimulates the brain and increases awareness of what matters most, like stopping Vector."

"I hope it works."

He followed her to the Personal Qualification area, where they photographed and fingerprinted him and inserted his right hand into a box. He tossed her a quizzical look.

"Advanced biometrics: registers bone density, chemical composition, moisture, and palm print. The bad guys can get around retina scans. But they can't beat this. If they cut off your hand, they can't use it. Density, liquid content, and composition immediately change."

A buzzer sounded.

"You're cleared for level three," she said. "Air pressure increases as we go up. Nothing airborne from the lower, more-contaminated levels can enter the higher ones."

In the third-floor prep room, Imelda fitted Alex for a Hazmat suit, gloves, shoes, and a respirator. "You'll need this for later."

They made their way through the lab, packed with Talas containers, and entered the office area, where Dunphy and Atkinson were waiting.

"Alex West," said Imelda, nodding at Alex, "the guy I told you about."

Dunphy got up and stuck out his hand. "I'm Joe. A pleasure to meet you, Alex. Now we'll know if Imelda was telling the truth about Rhodes. Nobody here believes her."

Imelda growled.

Atkinson stepped forward. "I'm Roy, Alex. Welcome to BWG."

"I hope I can help." Alex shook his hand.

"I'm sure you can," said Brockman, walking in. "In fact, we're counting on it."

"Alex, this is Marv, our intrepid leader." She handed Marv the briefcase. "From Enslein's yacht."

Brockman passed it to Atkinson and then took Alex by the arm. "Nice work, Mr. West. Especially for Imelda. Let's talk."

He escorted Alex to his office and closed the door. "Have a seat."

Alex sat down while Brockman settled in the chair behind the desk and took a moment to compare the man to what he had heard about him. "Too bad about Officer Kern."

"He took a bullet to the head. Nothing we could do."

Brockman made a pyramid with his hands and pressed them to his lips. "What happened on Malta scared the hell out of us. Gold or no gold, dead or alive, we're worried Enslein will still go through with it. Doomsday is Sunday, July 21st. We got Tomek, who ran the place, but he's not talking. Three others are at large, determined to inject a bioweapon into newspaper ink. We don't know the weapon, cities, or the plants. But Imelda said you saw these guys."

Alex nodded. "Briefly. But I saw all three."

"A police artist will be here at ten. Help him sketch their mugshots. And you got a look inside the lab. The equipment may reveal what pathogen they're using."

"Sure. Whatever I can do."

Over the next hour, Brockman showed Alex hundreds of photos of lab equipment. Alex didn't recognize any of it until a skid-mounted fermenter appeared. "I remember that," he said.

Brockman stiffened. "It's used to make anthrax. We found traces of it on the loading dock. Did you see one of these?" It was a picture of a liquid chromatograph. "Removes impurities from protein solutions."

"Yeah," said Alex. "And the lighting in the lab was eerie. Greenish color."

Brockman nodded grimly. "Light alters proteins in certain receptors. Green is relatively harmless. That's why they use it. It implies Enslein was working with viruses. Anything else?"

"I don't think so."

Atkinson opened the door and leaned in. "Better have a look at this. One of the flash drives."

They entered Atkinson's office, where Imelda and Dunphy huddled over a monitor. Brockman studied the brick-like structure with a wary expression.

"Variola," said Dunphy. "A super strain. The Russians made tons of it during the Cold War. Nobody knows what happened to it."

Brockman stepped back and paced the room. "Smallpox."

"Here," said Atkinson, pointing to the screen. "Genetic sequencing. He may have mutated it."

"Make sure," said Brockman, stopping to stare at Dunphy. "When the police artist gets here, introduce him to Alex. I have a few calls to make."

Alex spent three hours with the artist. The sketches were as good as Alex could recall. They'd use them for most-wanted posters and distribute them to all the major media outlets.

After lunch, Alex and Dunphy changed into Hazmat suits to analyze material taken from the Talas plant. Dunphy placed a container next to the table and unloaded the contents from Tomek's office.

Item by item, they examined what was there: a tedious job since they didn't know what they were looking for. Hours passed.

seventy-three

ATLANTA, GEORGIA

Imelda drove slowly, despite the light traffic. Streetlights glowed yellow on dew-laden streets and the cicadas buzzed in the trees and bushes. "It's funny," she said. "I feel like I've known you for a long time."

He smiled. "What was it, like ten days?"

"Yes. But it seems like yesterday." She drove down the block and pulled up in front of the Marriott. "See you tomorrow morning. The boss starts early. Six, sharp. I'll be here waiting at five-thirty."

He got out, stood under the yellow cone of streetlight and watched her drive away.

seventy-four

Alex and Imelda joined Brockman and the team in the conference room to get their assignments for the day: Alex and Joe picking up where they had left off, going through the Talas stuff; Atkinson scanning and deciphering Enslein's flash drives; Imelda and Brockman coordinating emergency response plans with the Department of Health and Human Services and the CDC; and Martinez and Henchel, on level two, testing variola vaccines.

Alex secured his respirator and followed Dunphy into the lab, where they sorted through more containers. Like yesterday, he felt as if he were breathing his own exhaust. He turned to Dunphy and pointed to his respirator. "I don't know how you do this all day long."

"Anthrax spores escaped from one of our containment labs," said Dunphy, flipping through a stack of Talas sales receipts. "We still don't know how it happened, but two of our guys had taken off their respirators. Thankfully, the antibiotics proved effective. We had to decontaminate the entire area twice. That's what we deal with every day."

"How'd you get into this line of work?"

"Did forensic pathology work for the FBI in Quantico. Switched over to antiterrorism and came down here. Best decision I ever made. You were a cop, right?"

"Yeah." Alex smiled. It was a frequent question after he had quit the force. Everybody, it seemed, wanted to know more about cops.

"I always wanted to be a cop," said Dunphy. "But realized I didn't have the stomach for it."

That struck a chord with Alex. "Years ago, I was on my honeymoon on Maui. Divorced now. I took my wife to see a magic show. We sat up front because we were newlyweds. And the magician asked everyone sitting around the table what they did. When I told him I was a cop, he got serious. All during the show, he's telling jokes, zinging the crowd, big laughs. But just then, he gets serious. Looks at me and says, 'I used to be a cop. After one year, I quit. Couldn't take it. Seeing the worst of humanity day after day after day was destroying me.' Then he looks me in the eye. 'Don't do it, Alex. Get out before it's too late.' I got out," said Alex. "But it's in my blood. I don't think I'll ever lose the feeling."

After lunch, Alex got a text from Corrales with the names of the men who worked at Talas. They all lived in Palm Grove. Mario Cosenza on 28 Reid Street; Joseph Walsh, known as the Kid, on 22 Brookside Avenue; and Michael Benson, in a walkup at 651 Main Street.

All three had priors: the Kid spent six months at Hillsborough Correctional Institution in Riverview, Florida; Cosenza served a year at Tomoka Correctional in Daytona Beach, Florida; and Benson did nine months at a Brooklyn Detention Center.

"Great work," said Brockman. "Malone will go deep with this. Phone logs and cross files on everyone. In one hour, their mugshots will be in every police station, post office, airport, bus, and train station in America."

Atkinson had been quiet most of the day. That ended when he summoned everyone to his office. He had discovered in Tomek's emails references to potential newspaper plant targets in Chicago, Los Angeles, and New York City. Vector's plan was to carry out the attack on Saturday, July 20th when the Sunday editions are printed.

Imelda opened her laptop. "Let's start by getting addresses of all the big printing plants."

"Enslein would want a daily with a lot of circulation," said Dunphy, checking his phone. "*The Wall Street Journal's* circulation is almost three million daily, but it doesn't have a Sunday edition. *The New York Globe* prints about one million on Sunday. *The Daily Sentinel* has half a million. *The Post* and *News* about a quarter million.

"*The Globe* and *Sentinel* share a plant in Queens. *The Daily News* plant is in Jersey City. In Chicago, it could be the *News, Tribune, World Herald,* or *Sun-Times.* And in LA, who knows? *The World,* maybe."

"I'll run a merge-purge with those that use water-based ink," said Imelda. "That'll narrow it down."

Like most people, Alex had suffered through the COVID pandemic and was afraid of suffering through another. He recalled reading about the 1883 smallpox epidemic and a father struggling to hold back his tears as he carried his dead son's body upstairs to where his wife had also died. The desperate, heartbroken father set fire to his house with their bodies inside. Alex was terrified by the heart-wrenching tale.

He got up and studied a diagram of smallpox virus tacked on the wall. It resembled an ellipse with a green border and bright yellow edges. Inside the ellipse was a sea of yellow dots and a red and green wormlike object that looked like a sinister sea monster waiting to infect you. Alex wondered how a simple diagram could look so evil. It scared the hell out of him.

"How much would it take to contaminate the ink supply of a large newspaper?" he asked.

"We're working with microscopic stuff smaller than two-tenths of a micron, not quarts or gallons," said Atkinson. "I just got off the phone with a friend who works for *The Post*. He said most printing plants have a two-thousand-gallon ink tank."

Atkinson pointed at the diagram. "Let's assume Vector dumps a pint of encapsulated virus into an ink tank. That's trillions of biomolecules, more than enough to contaminate all the ink in that tank. Large mixers disperse the smallpox throughout the ink. How many papers will it contaminate? Every paper printed with ink from that tank, about one million for *The Globe*."

"Let's assume that three people touch every copy," added Dunphy. "That's three million potential victims."

seventy-five

THURSDAY, JULY 18TH
RED BANK, NEW JERSEY

Curled up on the couch, Sandy Roberts was half asleep as a TV news anchor reported a pending budget crisis in California. Slumped on the leather recliner, Rick wasn't paying attention until the anchor announced a national terrorist threat.

He sat up as photos of Mario Cosenza, Joseph Walsh, and Michael Benson flashed on the screen. When Rick saw Benson's mugshot, he raised the volume on the voiceover.

"The FBI is offering ten thousand dollars reward for information leading to the arrest and conviction of each of these suspects. Call the FBI hotline at 1-888-555-3434. We will hold all inquiries in strictest confidence."

Rick jumped up and pointed at the screen. "Remember that number, Sandy!"

She blinked open her eyes. "What?"

"Remember that number!" He turned and almost tripped over a scatter rug as he rushed into the kitchen to grab a pen and pad. "1-888-" he called out.

"555-3434," replied Sandy, sitting up. "What's wrong? What is it?"

"That guy I picked up two days ago!" shouted Rick. "Remember!?"

"What are you saying?"

"He's the guy! *He's* the terrorist!"

"A terrorist?" She hurried to the kitchen and stood in the doorway. "You're lucky you weren't robbed or—"

"His van broke down and I gave him a lift. How was I to know?" He lifted the phone and glanced at the number.

Sandy snatched the phone out of his hand before he could dial. "What are you doing?"

"Calling. I'm calling." He took back the phone.

"They'll find out it was you," she scowled. "You think they're stupid?"

"Who?"

"Them," she said with a blustery glance. "The terrorists. They could kill us."

He put his hand on her arm. "Relax, honey. Just relax, okay? I won't give them my name. Okay? Forget the reward. It's not about the money. I have to do this."

"Rick, stop! Remember the mugging? Remember what happened? We got all those calls, and they drove by all the time." She pointed out the window. "That went on for almost a year!"

"It's terrorism, for God's sake!"

Her face was grim, an expression she marshaled whenever they fought. "How do you know it's the same guy? You could be mistaken."

"Believe me, *I know.*"

"Somebody else will call." She peered into his eyes. "*Please,* let somebody else do it. Other people must've seen him."

"It's our civic responsibility."

"To put our lives in danger? Are you crazy?"

"I have to do this."

"Fine," she snarled. "Do what you want. You want to get involved?

Fine. You want to get us killed? *Fine*." She left the kitchen and raised the volume on the news to drown him out.

"I could never forgive myself!" He shut the door and dialed.

Sandy was on the couch, staring glumly at the TV, when Rick returned.

"They want me to go to New York," he said. "For a formal statement."

She exhaled and tossed her head. "What did I tell you? They got you now. You're involved. They know who you are and where we live." She dropped the remote on the table and climbed the stairs. "I'm going to bed."

seventy-six

THURSDAY, JULY 18TH
LOS ANGELES, CALIFORNIA

Hair still damp from showering, Kimberly pushed it away from her ears and made a face in the bathroom mirror. The doorbell rang. "That was fast." She ran to the door and unlocked it. "Hey, stranger," she said in a playful, flirty way.

The Kid handed her a sixpack of beer. "It's cold." He strode in, looked around, and plopped down on the couch, hands behind his head. "Nice place you got here."

"I was lucky." She offered him a can from the pack and got one for herself. "Friend of mine was living here. She married a chef and moved out. I didn't waste any time."

The Kid pulled the tab and took a swallow. "I got my place in Florida, you know. Right on the beach. Studio apartment."

"Sounds nice." Kimberly picked up the remote. "I thought we'd watch TV for a while." She clicked on Comedy Central, then opened her beer and took a swig.

The Kid patted the cushion next to him. She sat down, and he put his arm around her.

She snuggled next to him. "You never told me why you're in LA."

"Oh. Delivery job. One more day. After that, done—finito."

"Going back to Florida?"

He looked at her. "Depends. If I like it here, I might stick around for a while. Ever been to that Hollywood Bowl?"

Kim's eyes lit up. "Why?"

"Just askin' if you been, is all."

"Once. Dead Heat concert. Why?"

"Well, I was thinkin' of goin' next Friday."

"We need tickets."

He pulled two out of his shirt pocket.

She snatched them out of his hand and stared at them. "Awesome! I *love* these guys! This is *so cool*. I just met you . . ." She lowered the volume on the TV.

The Kid jacked his feet onto the coffee table. "So, you're an actress. How's it goin' with that?"

"Good, I guess. Got an agent. Now I just need more auditions. Tried out for a pilot once. Didn't get a callback. I think they wanted somebody taller." She took another swig of beer. "What's Florida like?"

He pointed outside. "Sort of like this, 'cept hotter." He got up. "Where's the john?"

She pointed behind her. He walked in and shut the door.

She clicked through some channels and paused on the news. About to click again, she stopped when she saw three mugshots flash on the screen and raised the volume. " . . . Mario Cosenza and Joseph Walsh, also known as The Kid. These men, suspected of terrorist activity, are armed and dangerous. If you know their whereabouts, call this number." An 800 number appeared on the screen. She gasped in fear as she memorized the number and nervously switched back to Comedy Central.

The Kid came out of the bathroom and looked around. "Kimberly?" No answer. He opened the fridge, helped himself to another beer, and slumped on the couch. "Hey, Kim!" He picked up the remote and switched to the Dodger game.

When he heard talking, he lowered the volume. It was Kim's voice, coming from the bedroom. He got up, walked to the door, and knocked. "Kim! Hey, you in there?"

She stopped talking and opened the door. "I was talking to my mother."

"Oh. Anything wrong?"

"No. I'm fine." She walked out and resumed her spot on the couch. "Do you wanna see the game?"

He sat next to her. "I don't care. Whatever you want." He put his arm around her.

She switched back to the comedy channel, and they watched the last fifteen minutes of a show. Her phone rang. She glanced at it. "I have to take this. It's my mom again." She got up, entered her bedroom, and closed the door.

The Kid watched TV for a few more minutes and was getting bored. He got up and knocked on the bedroom door. He could hear Kim's muffled voice. "Kim."

She didn't answer.

He tried the door. "Why'd you lock the door? Kim! Hey!" He knocked again. No answer. He pulled out his switchblade and jimmied the lock. It took him hardly a second to do it. The lock clicked, and the door opened. "Betcha didn't think . . ."

She had her back to him and turned when she heard him.

"What are you up to?" he asked, frowning.

"Nothing." Nervously, she brushed by him and out the bedroom door. "Another beer?"

He followed her into the living room. "Why'd you lock—? That wasn't your mother, was it? Callin' your boyfriend?"

"No. I don't have—"

"Ha!" He grabbed the phone out of her hand and pushed redial. "Maybe the freak wants to talk to me, too."

She tried to snatch the phone.

He jumped back, laughing.

"Give it back!" She anxiously reached out to him. "Give it to me!"

"I can play games, too, you know." He put the phone to his ear and heard a woman's voice.

"Who's this?" The Kid listened for a moment and glared at Kim. "Sneaky bitch." He threw the phone at her. It struck the wall and clattered on the floor.

She backed away. "Leave me alone."

"What'd you tell 'em? Huh? That I stole that piece of shit outside?" He stepped toward her.

She jumped back. "Go away!"

The Kid sneered. "I'm scared. Look how I'm shakin'."

She ran back to the bedroom and slammed the door.

"I don't give a rat's ass about the cops," he said, following her. "They won't catch me. I'll be outta here in no time."

He attempted to open the door. Locked. He banged it with his fist. "I'll bust this thing down, Kim. You don't want me to trash this dump, do you?"

"Go away!"

"I'm gonna count to three. If you don't open the door, I'm breaking it down . . . One. Two. Three." He took a step back and kicked the door. It held. He kicked it again and again. The frame splintered, and it flew open. He ran into her bedroom. The window was wide open and Kim was gone.

The Kid stuck his head out the window and saw her disappear

around the corner of an alley as two FBI agents appeared, guns drawn. "Freeze! Hands on your head!"

"Screw you, coppers!" The Kid ducked inside, grabbed the Suicide Special out of his backpack, and ran to the front door as two government agents burst in.

The Kid got off one shot before they gunned him down on the living room floor. He never regained consciousness and died the next day. The agents never located Walsh's car. Kim thought it was a Toyota.

seventy-seven

THURSDAY, JULY 18TH
CHICAGO, ILLINOIS

Wearing the cap pulled down over his eyes, Mario waited for the girl at the desk to check him in. She smiled when he presented his fake ID. "Paid in advance, Mr. Wilson. Do you want to give me a credit card for incidentals?"

"Nah. Just the room." He signed in and took an apple from the fruit bowl on the counter. "Save this for later." He dropped it in his pocket, thinking he might ask her out when the job was done. "How far is Wrigley Field from here?"

She pointed north. "About five blocks that way. Can't miss it."

"Thanks." He hoisted the backpack to his right shoulder and headed for Room 215 on the second floor across from the elevator.

Mario walked two blocks and crossed Cornelia Street. When turning to see if anyone was following him, he collided with an old man holding a fawn-colored mastiff on a leash. The mastiff lunged at Mario, tearing the leash out of the old man's hand.

The powerful guard dog seized Mario's left forearm in its jaws and got more jacket than flesh. Foaming at the mouth, he wouldn't let go, as Mario tried to shake him loose. A sharp pain shot through his left shoulder as the tenacious dog pulled him down onto the street. "Get this thing off me!" he shouted.

The animal growled fiercely, jerking its head from side to side, trying to wrench Mario's arm from its socket. The old man hollered at the dog while reaching for the leash. Mario's cap fell off as he struggled to get free.

Two cars and a delivery van stopped to avoid them, blocking the intersection. A police car on Seminary Avenue turned, bleeped its siren, and drove up on the sidewalk.

A cop got out and ran toward Mario, wrestling with the dog. The cop seized the mastiff by the tail and hit it with a baton. The dazed animal released its hold and sank to the pavement, whimpering. The cop pulled the dog to the sidewalk and tied it to a traffic sign. Rushing back, he lifted Mario to his feet and helped him to the sidewalk. "Are you okay?"

Mario pointed at the dog. "Fuckin' dog. Shoot that thing!"

"You okay?"

Mario's shoulder throbbed as he raised his left arm, dripping thick saliva. "Yeah."

"Wait here, sir." The cop handed Mario his cap and cleared the intersection.

While the cop was getting the old man's name and address, Mario quickly walked away. He walked one block and turned the corner. Glancing back, he saw the police car heading for him. He stopped and waited.

The cop pulled up and rolled down the passenger window. "Get in. I'll take you for a tetanus shot."

Mario shook his head. "No thanks. I'm good."

"You want to file a complaint?"

"Nah," he replied. "I don't wanna cause that old guy any trouble. Had a dog like that once."

"What's your name?"

"Wilson. Roger Wilson."

The cop pursed his lips. "All right, Mr. Wilson. But I'd get a tetanus shot just to be safe." He closed the window, made a U-turn, and drove away.

Mario took a right on Eddy Street and a left on Clark and saw a crowd outside Wrigley Field. His old man would turn over in his grave if he could see him now, he figured, as he winced at paying a hundred bucks for a seat behind home plate. He got his ticket and headed for Terrace 220. The ticket seller waited for Mario to walk away. Then he hung a closed sign on the booth and dialed the 800 number on the monitor.

When the game started, Mario noticed the ticket seller in the aisle looking up at him while talking to a man in a gray suit. Mario quickly slid out of his seat and followed the exit signs to the street. "Shit!" he said, while walking out the gate, as the crowd booed the Giants, scoring the first run.

When he crossed the street, he saw a blue Ford sedan approaching. Wheeling around, he took a right on Waveland and fast walked under the L train overpass. The sedan pursued him at a distance.

He started running when the car turned the corner. Another unmarked car skidded to a stop in front of him. Two men got out with guns drawn. "FBI! Stop or we'll shoot!"

Mario wasn't going back to Tomoka. No way! A sports bar on South Beach, jampacked with cool, happy people. That was the bouncer's dream!

Bullets flew. A 9mm slug hit him in the lower back. Another struck his head.

seventy-eight

THURSDAY, JULY 18TH
WHITE HOUSE, WASHINGTON, DC

The President praised his team, but grimly accepted the worst: they hadn't found Enslein's body and there was no sign he had called off the attack. The two dead drivers were intent on fulfilling their missions, and Michael Benson was still at large. Despite the President's efforts, the deaths of millions of innocent people were still hanging in the balance.

seventy-nine

THURSDAY, JULY 18TH
CIA HEADQUARTERS LANGLEY, VIRGINIA

The morning sun flickered through the window directly into Malone's eyes. The glare was remorseless, and Malone wondered if Sanford had planned it that way just to annoy him. He crossed his legs and squinted at Sanford's silhouette in front of him.

Sanford reached back from his chair and lowered the shade. "Walsh was a punk and Cosenza a career offender. We did very well."

"Too bad we didn't take them alive," said Malone.

Sanford smirked. "Too bad we didn't take Enslein alive. He might have given us some answers. I don't think Cosenza and Walsh knew anything. But what's done is done. Now we just have Benson to worry about." Sanford sat up—a small man, trying to look bigger. "It's just a matter of time."

"Brockman needs Cosenza's cylinder," said Malone. "Where is it?"

"Quantico at the lab's trace evidence unit. Once it goes through security, we'll ship it to him. They said it's smallpox."

"Why wasn't it sent directly to Atlanta?"

"Standard procedure."

Malone's eyes flared. "That isn't standard procedure! We need to check the efficacy of our vaccines! What if it's a mutated strain?"

"I'll talk to them."

"Do it now!" demanded Malone. "Overnight it to Brockman!"

"Don't worry. We'll get Benson and this will be over before you know it."

"There's a chance we won't," sighed Malone.

Sanford clicked his pen. "We'll get him."

"Still, if he's not in custody by Saturday, we should shut down all the major printing plants in and around New York City."

"What makes you think Enslein will use the same method or the same bioweapon, especially now that we're on to them? Have you thought about reservoirs, stadiums, and public transportation systems? What about Madison Square Garden, Penn Station, and La Guardia? They found Cosenza in Wrigley Field. Thirty thousand people were at that Cubs game. And Walsh had tickets to the Hollywood Bowl in his pocket. How many people does that hold?"

"We'd be foolish not to focus on printing plants."

Sanford clicked his pen again. "We're not convinced. We got the others. We'll get Benson, too, despite Brockman and his slackers. We'll cover airports, tunnels, bridges and the printing plants. There's no way Benson will get by without being seen."

Malone sat back and stared at Sanford. "I don't get it, Lou. Still pissed about Brockman for not processing your Ebola samples fast enough when you knew he was operating with a skeleton crew?"

"That's bullshit."

Malone pressed on. "Ignoring his recommendation to target Enslein until it was almost too late? Waiting to send an officer to Greece when Burke's life was in danger? Shipping the cylinder to Quantico, instead of directly to Atlanta, which has the technology to analyze the variants?"

"I follow agency procedures," said Sanford, glaring at Malone.

"Variola is the deadliest form of smallpox. Not some common flu virus. And anthrax . . ." Malone took a deep breath to calm himself. "You're spiteful, Lou, and gambling with national security."

eighty

FRIDAY, JULY 19TH
DEKALB-PEACHTREE AIRPORT, ATLANTA, GEORGIA

B rockman usually kept his cool. He was famous for that. But now, as the deadline approached, he was in danger of losing it. Nervously, he paced back and forth and glanced at the taxiway.

Alex and Imelda watched him as they waited for the private jet to take them to New York City. They had orders to report to the FBI's Critical Incidence Response Group, assigned with the overall management of "Operation Benson."

Reporting to the feds was a source of concern for Imelda. She had more than enough to do without talking to them. For the third time, she checked her bags, wondering if she forgot anything.

"Joe and Roy are already there," she said to Alex. "They got in yesterday to alert the local hospitals and clinics. They'll be the first to identify the bioagent and recognize an outbreak if one occurs."

Brockman stopped pacing and turned to her. "Make sure every facility has a committee chair in place and they're tied into DHS and FBI field offices, health departments, and the CDC."

"Got it," she said, making a mental note.

"Also review local emergency plans with the EMS, police, and fire departments."

"On my list."

"Good. I'll be at the Crisis Center in New York after I meet with the President."

"What about vaccinating everyone?" asked Alex.

"Risky," said Imelda. "People can die from the vaccines. And we're not sure what it is. I'd bet on smallpox, based on the FBI lab findings. But Quantico doesn't know if it's a mutated strain resistant to our vaccines. Only we and the CDC can determine that."

Brockman's face turned dark in anger. "Total screwup sending it to Quantico. I blame Sanford for that." He kicked a stone into the grass. "Smallpox killed three-hundred-million people over the past centuries. But there's no record of anybody getting it since 1977. *That's the problem.* Only a handful of people have natural immunity. Hopefully, we get the cylinder today, so we know what we're dealing with." His phone beeped. He checked his email and dismissed it. "A West African subtype resulted in an epidemic with the highest case-fatality ratio ever recorded. If it's that or something worse, it may be too late to prevent a pandemic. Mortality rates could reach thirty percent."

"What about evacuation?" asked Alex.

"In New York City?" Brockman smirked. "Think about it. Fear. Chaos. Traffic problems. Panic and dislocation. People with special needs. A horror show of disaster-management problems. The President is against it."

"Here it is," said Imelda, watching the approaching plane.

The Gulfstream jet taxied toward them and stopped as the groundcrew wheeled boarding stairs to the side door.

Charter pilot Ted Rush stepped out, wearing a light blue uniform with a gold MDO logo on the pocket. "Burke and West."

"That's us." Imelda and Alex approached the plane.

"Ted Rush." He shook their hands and grabbed their stuff.

"Safe flight," said Brockman, with a wave. "Talk to you tomorrow." They waved back and climbed onboard.

"Strap in," said Rush, as he locked the door and settled in. "Flight time to New York is about two hours and twenty minutes. I'll get you there on time." He double-checked the door, controls and gauges, then taxied to the runway and notified the tower. He was ready for departure.

After being cleared for takeoff, Imelda opened her laptop and started working. Alex took the seat across from Rush, who had been flying for fifteen years with the charter airline company.

Rush got the tower go ahead, released the brakes, and smoothly advanced the throttle to takeoff. The plane gained speed as he tapped the rudder to correct for a light crosswind and elevated the nose.

Rush checked the cabin pressure as they climbed to 45,000 feet. "Airlines fly at about 36,000. We go higher where there's less congestion."

"What's our weather like?"

"Unsettled. But in your case, it's an emergency, and I was told to get you there."

It was raining when they flew over the Jersey shore. Rush pointed out Atlantic City where Alex had lost his shirt playing Texas Hold'em ten years ago. Fifteen minutes later, they circled La Guardia.

Rush glanced back at them. "Air Traffic Control is rerouting commercial flights because of a few T-cells and hail nearby, but tower's allowing us to land."

The plane dropped suddenly, caught in a turbulent downdraft. The sudden weightlessness made Imelda anxious. She glanced at Alex, who seemed okay with it.

Rush gave them a casual wave. "I've been through a lot of these babies. We'll be fine."

His comment was the thing people say when they're in danger and are trying to calm the fears of others. Sure, it was a denial of the threatening weather, but Alex and Imelda were glad to hear him say it just the same.

Rush elevated the Gulfstream's nose and banked through wind shear into a broad holding pattern at ten thousand feet. He waited for another report from the tower. Through the window, they witnessed an impressive light show caused by a massive shelf cloud.

Rush estimated the anvil at fifteen thousand feet—a potential super cell. The cabin vibrated from thunder and the barrage of marble-size hailstones bouncing off the fuselage.

Imelda placed her hand on Alex's arm, a look of concern in her eyes. "What do you think?"

"No problem with Top Gun."

Rush got the go-ahead to land, circled twice, and started his approach. At five thousand feet, lightning struck the Gulfstream. The plane bounced, then shuddered, as Rush worked to stabilize it.

"That caused a burn-through on the starboard wing," he said. "Damaged our avionics. Hang tough. I'll get us in." He called air traffic control and reported the trouble. They offered to direct him out, but he declined. "I need to land these people. Health emergency."

La Guardia deployed emergency vehicles and firefighting trucks and tracked the Gulfstream as it circled.

The intensity of rain and hail and the updrafts and downdrafts wreaked havoc on the plane, its turbofans ingesting gouts of water. Rush slowed to cruise speed, enough to minimize the effect of turbulence, but fast enough to keep the plane responsive.

He had a strong tailwind and was high on slope as the New York skyline flickered through the clouds. He put down the wheels and held power to avoid a stall or spin, and brought that baby in. She bounced twice, skidded on the wet runway, and came to a stop a hundred fifty feet from Flushing Bay.

Alex congratulated Rush for getting them in safely. Rush said his friends called him "Crush" after he had taken out a bell tower when he was a test pilot.

A limo was waiting to take Imelda and Alex to FBI headquarters at Federal Plaza. The ride took almost an hour because of construction on the Belt Parkway. Imelda said little during the ride. Alex wasn't sure if it was the nerve-wracking landing or Benson on her mind.

Special Agent in Charge Brad Collins, who had taken part in the Tomek interrogation at Palm River, greeted Alex and Imelda in the lobby. FBI Director David Boyce had appointed Collins to head a special task force to apprehend Benson before he gained access to a target, using deadly force if necessary.

Collins appeared overdressed in the blue suit, white shirt, and red tie, like he was on a job interview, instead of directing the pursuit of a dangerous felon. He was courteous, but gave off a sense of urgency as he directed them to the third floor.

Collins grabbed a lobby chair and carried it into his office. "Conference rooms are busy. So we'll have to meet in here."

Before anyone sat down, the door opened, and a tall, middle-aged man in a gray suit walked in. Alex knew exactly who he was.

Collins gestured to the man. "Arnold Lindsay is assistant chief of New York City's Antiterrorism Squad. He'll be coordinating security with us. This is Dr. Burke from BWG and—"

"Alex West," said Lindsay, with mild contempt, "surprised to see *you* here."

"Hello, Arnold." Alex recalled Lindsay had been pushing to get out of Pinewood ever since becoming police chief and finally got his wish. Alex was unhappy with the timing, but decided he could live with it.

Everyone took a seat. Collins perched on the corner of his desk. "They appointed me head of the special task force to coordinate 156 federal agents, U.S. Marshals, and local police in a citywide manhunt for Benson. Chief Lindsay has 22 men on his team. Our job is to find Benson and secure the cylinder before he gains access to a target. We have phone taps on his ex-wife and relatives and are monitoring his credit cards and cell phone activity. We're also following up on several sightings. None of the alleged lookalikes turned out to be him."

Collins rubbed his chin and focused on Imelda. "Finding Benson is our job, Dr. Burke. With the addition of Chief Lindsay's antiterrorism squad, we have more than enough people to handle it."

Imelda bristled at his words. "We've been ordered to supervise the search for Benson. And we're best qualified to manage him, avoid a serious health emergency, and ensure the fewest number of fatalities."

"When we find Benson, there *won't be* a health emergency," said Collins.

She blankly stared at him. "I wish I could believe that."

"That's why we have hospitals and DHS."

Imelda clenched her teeth. "Agent Collins, as far as deadly contagious diseases go, smallpox is in a class by itself. Local hospitals aren't equipped to handle a disaster of this magnitude if it happens."

"We alerted all healthcare facilities. We're prepared."

"So are we!"

Lindsay leaned back with a smug expression. "Benson abandoned his van in New Jersey and hitched a ride to Manhattan. We're covering all the subways, buses, taxis, and Ubers, as well as the airports, train, and bus stations. We'll find him before he can do any damage."

Collins slid Benson's police photo across the desk. "It's plastered all over town. TV stations are airing it regularly."

"That's old," said Alex, glancing at the black and white mugshot. "You should tell your team he limps, is thinner now, and his hair's a lot darker and shorter."

"Noted," said Lindsay, in a dismissive tone.

Alex eyeballed his former boss. "What's your plan?"

"Protect and secure 21 potential targets, applying screening protocols, close circuit TV systems, and security bollards," blurted Collins.

"Including these?" Imelda handed him a list of metropolitan area printing plants.

Collins glanced at the list. "Of course. We're confident we can cover all these facilities and do it without causing a panic."

"It's safer if you shut them down," she said.

He smiled. "I disagree."

Lindsay cast a disdainful look at Alex. "I'm not sure of your involvement here, West."

"A company hired me to find Enslein. I tracked him to a plant in Palm River, Florida, where I ran into Benson."

"He can easily ID him," said Imelda, annoyed at having to defend Alex's presence there.

Collins turned to Alex, as a twisted grin appeared and then disappeared from his face. "You weren't much help to Officer Kern."

Lindsay raised an eyebrow and turned to Imelda. "Are you aware of Mr. West's past as a Pinewood cop, Dr. Burke?"

"Yes. I know he was a cop." Imelda's eyes shifted to Alex, who didn't react.

"He killed an innocent bystander during a robbery," said Lindsay. "A fifteen-year-old boy."

"An accident!" Alex protested. "A jury acquitted me of any wrongdoing. And that has nothing to do with this."

"We need people we can trust, especially under these circumstances," said Lindsay. "I'm aware of Mr. West's involvement in this case, but I seriously doubt his ability—"

"Alex has more than proven himself," Imelda interjected.

"Not to mention he's no longer a cop," said Lindsay.

Collins sat back and folded his hands. "I've dealt with PIs in the past. No place for them here. My orders are explicit. If there's a bio incident, of course . . ."

The door opened. A man stuck his head in and motioned to Collins. The SAC rose to his feet.

Imelda stood up and moved in front of Collins, eyes blazing. "Hold on a second."

Collins stopped short. "We'll involve—"

"Wait!"

"We don't have time for this now, Dr. Burke. Let my assistant know how to reach you." Collins took a step toward the door.

Imelda blocked his way and glared at him. "I don't think you appreciate the gravity of the situation here."

Collins sighed. "I'm well aware of the situation, *Dr. Burke*. But I also know our capabilities. We're trained for this."

"So am I!"

"Excuse me." He pushed past her and stepped into the hall. "My assistant will show you out."

In the lobby, Imelda could no longer restrain herself. "The level of pomposity and self-importance in that jackass is amazing! I don't know how he got to be in charge."

Alex opened the outer door for her. "We don't have to play by their rules."

She looked at him as they stepped outside. "What was he talking about in there? Why didn't you tell me about the shooting?" She waited, wondering what else he was hiding from her. Maybe she didn't know him as well as she thought she did.

"It never came up."

"So, what? It's a big deal! What happened?"

They descended the stairs and stopped on the sidewalk. "You heard him. I shot and killed a kid. A bystander during a holdup. They dropped the charges. I eventually quit the force because of Lindsay."

Imelda looked into his eyes. "If you had told me, I would've been ready to defend you."

"You're right. I should've told you."

eighty-one

FRIDAY, JULY 19ᵀᴴ
INTELETECH, MANHATTAN, NEW YORK CITY

Connie was vacuuming the foyer when Alex arrived, holding a small bouquet of wildflowers behind his back. She didn't hear the door open and gasped when she saw him as if he were a total stranger. "We didn't think we'd ever see you again." She shut off the vacuum.

"I wanted to make sure you'd get that raise." He handed her the flowers.

"Oh, Alex. You didn't . . . Thank you." She gave him a hug.

He dropped his backpack on a chair and poured himself a cup of coffee. "I got involved in something serious and had to see it through."

"You should have told us, Alex. We were worried." She filled a vase with water from the sink. "Things were neglected here. And George . . . " She put the flowers in the vase and waved at the surrounding mess. "I'm sorry it's such a wreck, but he told me to take off when you were gone."

"Don't worry. I'm back and we'll get things organized again." He entered his office and opened his laptop.

She came in carrying the mail. "You have a ton of messages, and the rent is due."

"I'll get to that later."

The outer door swung open, and George pushed through with a just-got-out-of-bed look. "Sorry, I'm late."

Alex smiled and sipped his coffee. "You look like hell, George. What's going on? Still pissed at me?"

"No. I'm all right."

"Get my email?"

"Yeah. Sure. I'll help."

"Good. Benson was last seen in Manhattan. The last guy standing. Cops and feds are spread thin. Imelda's convinced the target is one of the five big newspaper printing plants in the metro area. Could be any of them, not to mention a bunch of smaller papers serving the burbs and Long Island. Benson will try to dump a bioweapon into one of their ink tanks. People touching the newspapers will get sick and die. According to Imelda, it could kill millions."

George frowned and shook his head. "Disaster."

Alex described the ink tanks and where they might be. "I got a good look at Benson when I was in Palm Grove." He handed George his mugshot. "Muscular, about five-nine. His hair's darker and shorter now and he limps. He was last seen wearing a blue jacket and pants."

"I saw his picture on the morning news," said Connie, glancing over Alex's shoulder. "He doesn't look like a criminal."

"The cops and feds will focus on plants in the city," Alex said. "But I'm not sure they're covering the *Daily News* in Jersey City. Benson showing up there wouldn't surprise me. It's a short train ride from Penn Station."

"Sure," said George. "I can go."

"Arm yourself and be careful. Don't approach him. Benson's probably carrying. Call the FBI and local cops." He gave him Collins' number.

eighty-two

B enson lingered on the corner of 42nd Street and Broadway and then entered the corner deli jammed with people. Sandwich chefs in grease-soiled aprons hustled to keep up with the orders.

Benson elbowed his way to the counter for a pastrami on rye, dill pickle, and beer. The meat was pink, moist, steaming hot, and piled so high he had trouble getting it into his mouth. Wiping the mustard from his lips, he gulped some beer and looked around. An old man staring through the mirror got his attention. Not a casual look.

Benson turned away, took another bite, and checked again. Still there, watching him. He got up, dropped his unfinished lunch into the garbage, and walked out. Vanishing into the crowd, he moved east on the south side of 42nd Street, caught his reflection in a store window, and smiled.

Two cops across the street checked out the crowd. Benson walked behind a family of four, crossed Sixth Avenue on 42nd Street, and entered Bryant Park, where a thousand New Yorkers were talking, sunning, and lunching on the lawn.

A homeless man with yellow teeth hit him for spare change.

Benson gave him a buck and asked where he could get the Number 7 train to Queens. A nicotine-stained finger pointed northeast.

Benson crossed the park to 42nd Street and entered the subway station in the middle of the block. He descended the stairs to the platform for the Flushing Local and double-checked that nobody was trailing him. So far, so good.

When the train rumbled in, he took a seat in the last car and placed his backpack on the floor between his feet. It seemed heavier now than when he departed, containing the cylinder, wrench, Walther 9 mm, twenty hollow-point rounds, change of clothes, work order and a five-inch switchblade.

At the Flushing-Main Street station, he got off and walked to the Sands Motel on the corner of 37th Avenue and checked in. His second-floor room was at the end of the hall near the exit, a safer spot if things went south. He slid his card through the slot and opened the door to a gust of hot, stale air. Turning on the AC and TV, he flopped on the bed and shut his eyes.

eighty-three

SATURDAY, JULY 20TH
UNION OFFICE, QUEENS, NEW YORK

B obby Dresser was a powerful man and one of New York's top union chairs, holding sway over thousands of cardholders. Feared and disliked by publishers, the union boss paced his office, conveniently located three blocks from the *New York Globe* printing plant in Queens, his greatest corporate adversary. The phone rang. Dresser knew exactly who it was.

"Yeah."

"Bad news," said Benny Ross. "The drivers and machine operators rejected the offer. The vote was 89 to 66."

Dresser sighed. "Assholes. Stupid friggin' assholes. I told 'em *The Globe* won't negotiate. Once the pattern's established, management won't settle for less."

"Why not?" asked Ross.

"Pattern bargaining, Benny. One union's contract is the base for all the others. Midnight today is the deadline for an agreement with the local."

"It's wages," muttered Ross. "Cost-of-livin' keeps goin' up."

Dresser breathed out through a turned-down mouth. "I'm tryin' to keep this union together, Benny. This is the first time the drivers and machine operators ignored my advice. They're screwin' up my good standin.' You tell 'em what I said. *You hear?* You tell 'em what I said!"

"Yeah. Yeah. They know. Hold off till Christmas. They won't change their minds, boss. The local made signs and organized a picket line. Strike's set for today."

Dresser bit his lip and felt a burning sensation in his stomach. The stress had caused his peptic ulcer to act up. "It won't work. The paper won't back down. They'll draft editors and clerks to stuff ads and get independent contractors to drive the trucks. The paper *will* get out."

"Maybe not."

"Listen, Benny. Do me a favor. Go back in there. Tell 'em if the strike's defeated, they'll lose their jobs, and scabs will decertify us."

"Okay, boss. But don't be pissed if it don't work." The phone clicked dead.

An hour later, Dresser glanced out the window and moaned when he saw the enormous inflatable rat at the entrance of the Queens' printing plant. He shook his head. The deed was done.

Hundreds of workers gathered there. Some carried signs: GLOBE UNFAIR. STRONGER TOGETHER. LOCAL 174 DEMANDS A FAIR CONTRACT. JOIN US. Several strikers carried life-size cutouts of their managers. Lucy, a golden retriever, ran loose among the protestors, a STRIKE sign tied to her back. Behind the chain link, security guards and uniformed police paced while nervously eyeing the growing crowd of strikers.

Two hundred feet away, three FBI Agents and two U.S. Marshals huddled together, discussing how to deal with this unexpected turn of events. The agent in charge told his men to spread out.

eighty-four

SATURDAY, JULY 20TH
SANDS MOTEL, QUEENS, NEW YORK

Holed up in his room until dark, Benson checked his messages three times: nothing from Tomek. It was a go. He shrugged on the blue jacket and set the cap low over his eyes.

Nodding ironically to his reflection in the bathroom mirror, he slung the backpack over his shoulder, walked downstairs, and out the lobby door. No one paid him any notice.

It was a warm and humid night. After walking a block, the jacket and pants were already hot and uncomfortable.

Heading up Prince Street, he walked two blocks, waited for the light, and crossed Northern Boulevard. Proceeding three more blocks, he heard distant shouts and chants and banging that became louder as he walked. He stopped for a moment and then continued. On 35th Avenue he took a right and caught up with three men dressed in work clothes resembling his, heading toward the Whitestone Expressway. One carried a STOP THE PRESSES! sign.

At first, he avoided the strikers, and then sped up and joined them. They didn't seem to care who he was or why he was there, intent upon their mission. The more the merrier, as far as they were concerned. They walked under the Expressway and took a right.

The Globe plant was directly ahead, and surrounded by a growing cadre of strikers. When Benson got to the fence, a young woman offered him a TOGETHER WE RISE! sign. He hesitated, then hoisting the sign over his head, carried it into the crowd.

Strikers marched in a large, broken circle in front of the gate. Some vocal, others less so. They carried signs: GREED KILLS. MORE WORK, LESS PAY, NO WAY. SAFE WORK, FAIR WAGE. He joined the line, picking up a chant.

A young man slapped Benson on the back and thanked him for coming. Benson gave him a thumb's up and continued to circle with the others. Each time around, he scanned the fence perimeter, searching for the fill pipe that Tomek said was near the front gate and on the street.

The third time around, Benson spotted a man in a gray suit standing outside the fence, casually observing the strikers. His foot was resting on what appeared to be the protruding fill pipe.

eighty-five

Alex turned left onto 42nd Street and spotted Imelda pacing outside the Hyatt. At first, he didn't recognize her in black tactical pants, matching combat T-shirt, high-top sneakers, and hair tucked inside a military patrol cap. He pulled up and stopped next to her.

She opened the door and climbed in. "I called Collins a few minutes ago. They stationed cops and agents at every bridge and tunnel around Manhattan. He claims they'll cover the airports and train stations, as well as all the major printing plants. But my guess is *not well enough*."

He leaned back and looked at her. "Where to?"

"*The Globe.*"

"Queens, right?"

"Yeah."

He drove west on 42nd Street, took the West Side Highway uptown, and proceeded east onto the Cross-Bronx Expressway into traffic heavy for a Saturday night. The road got more congested as he approached the Whitestone Bridge, where he worked his way to the inside lane and crossed from the Bronx into Queens.

In ten minutes, *The Globe* plant loomed in the distance, a black rectangular building with a red, steep slope metal roof three blocks from the highway. He took the next exit and parked in the lot across from the building.

Hundreds of noisy, milling strikers handed out placards and posted signs on the perimeter fences of the plant. Inside, cops and security guards huddled in groups of three and four, observing the protestors.

"What the hell is this?" Alex said. "A strike? Tonight? You gotta be kidding me." A grimace crossed his face. "We can deal with it." He nodded at the corner. "You start here. I'll start down there," pointing down the street. "We'll meet in the middle by the front gate. Try to keep a line of sight between us. If you think you see Benson or anyone resembling him, call me. If I see him, I'll call you."

"I said I'd call Collins for backup," said Imelda.

"You can decide on that." Alex removed a loaded Glock 28 from the glove compartment. "He's probably armed." He released the safety and placed it in her hand. "Point and shoot."

She pocketed the weapon as if it were her keys or wallet. "I had sixty hours of firearms training, virtual and augmented reality."

He nodded. "It's never the same when it's real."

eighty-six

A woman tugged on Benson's sleeve and shouted above the din. "I work in the press room! What about you?"

"I'm new," said Benson.

She waved her arm at the printing plant. "This is long overdue."

A delivery truck drove in from the street and headed for the gate. Strikers locked arms and blocked the truck. "Scabs," said the woman.

Two men jumped out of the truck, yelling racial slurs, and threatened the strikers. A fight broke out. Two cops tried to break it up. Another cop shouted at them and banged his truncheon on the fence.

The two cops dragged a striker to a patrol car. A protester swore at them and gave them the finger. The crowd cheered and hooted. Another truck drove up, and three more strike breakers joined the fight. The picketers slashed the truck tires, jumped on the vehicles, and shattered the windshields.

The rally turned uglier as strikers stacked newspapers and wooden pallets in front of the gate and set them ablaze. Someone tossed in an old tire. In a few minutes, clouds of acrid, black smoke billowed over the street, resembling a battle zone.

Sirens wailed and two fire engines approached the plant. Militant strikers pushed back when police attempted to clear a path for the firefighters. Cops forcibly carried to a transport bus several strikers refusing to move.

Smoke engulfed the fence perimeter and the FBI agent standing by the fill pipe. He crossed the street and sat wheezing on the curb. A fire engine stopped in front of him, obstructing his view of the fill pipe.

Benson placed his sign against the fence and drifted toward the pipe, eyes tearing from the smoke engulfing him. He stopped twenty feet from his target as firefighters pulled hoses out of the pumper and dragged them toward the fire.

Strikers rebelled, pushing back the firefighters. More fights erupted. The peaceful protest rapidly deteriorated into a violent free-for-all.

Cops dragged enraged protesters fighting and screaming into nearby patrol cars, maddening the others. The punctured rat deflated on the street. Lucy, the strike dog, ran loose barking.

Benson headed for the safety of the crowd, and his distinctive limp alerted Alex from two-hundred feet away.

When Benson turned to look back, Alex knew for sure. He called Imelda and pointed at the striker in the blue cap and matching work clothes, fast walking toward the underpass.

Imelda called Collins for backup. When he didn't answer, she left an urgent message, hung up, and followed Benson.

Firefighters and police barricades hindered Alex as he fought his way through the crowd. He cut around the barricades, losing precious time, and when he searched for Benson, he couldn't find him.

Running as fast as she could, Imelda closed to within fifty yards of her target and looked back for Alex. He wasn't there. She thought about waiting, but decided against it. She was their only chance.

Benson hurried under the Whitestone Expressway, looked back, pegging Imelda as a cop, and ran. He headed for the subway station about two miles away. After running for two blocks, Benson stopped to rest, gasping for air, and soaked in sweat.

Cruising at a steady pace, Imelda called Alex. "He's going south," she panted. "What's there?"

"Subways and buses," said Alex, running toward the Trailblazer.

Benson hid behind a garage and reached for the Walther inside the backpack. He fingered it, then put it back.

Imelda stopped running when she couldn't find him. Angry with herself, she ran back to the last place she had seen him.

Benson peeked out from the garage. Not spotting her, he headed back the way he came, then jogged and walked, favoring his left leg, throbbing from the run.

Heavy traffic on Northern Boulevard stopped Benson as he looked back and glimpsed Imelda running toward him, a phone pressed to her ear. People eager to cross waited impatiently for the light to change.

Desperation consumed Benson. He couldn't wait and boldly stepped onto the busy boulevard to the warning shouts of those around him. Swerving to avoid him, a car struck a bus and then bounced into the car behind it. The swerving bus plowed into a delivery van which flew across the center median and crashed into a jeep going in the opposite direction. Traffic in both directions screeched to a halt.

Seizing the opportunity, Benson quickly crossed the boulevard and ran as fast as he could, the backpack banging painfully against his shoulder. He stopped on Main Street, looking for a place to ditch the cylinder.

Northern Boulevard was a madhouse when Imelda arrived there: people abandoning their cars, others trying to help the injured, and sirens wailing in the distance.

Imelda ran across the boulevard, avoiding people and disabled cars, as she glimpsed a figure that looked like Benson disappearing into the distance. She pursued him for several blocks and saw him enter the Flushing-Main Street subway station.

Benson bolted down the stairs and hurdled the turnstile. The Number 7 train sat idling in the station and the doors began to close. He wedged his left arm through the gap, allowing him to enter. The doors quickly shut, and the train pulled out. Benson dropped the backpack on the floor, sat down, and caught his breath.

Gun in hand, Imelda raced into the station, colliding with a young couple talking there.

"What's your problem?!" shouted the man, whose face dropped when he saw the Glock, and quickly raised his hands.

"Did you see a man run down here?" Imelda gasped.

The woman pointed at the stairs.

Imelda charged down, searched the empty platform, and ran back to the street. High beams flashed when she appeared, and the Trailblazer hopped the curb and stopped on the sidewalk in front of her. She threw open the passenger door and climbed in. "He's gone. The next station is Willets Point on Roosevelt."

Alex headed west, as Imelda called Collins on speaker phone.

"We found Benson at *The Globe* in Queens!" she said.

"No!" yelled Collins. "Lindsay's got him pinned down in the Bronx! Son of a bitch killed a cop! We're gonna take him down!"

"*We* got Benson!" Alex shouted.

The line went dead.

eighty-seven

SATURDAY, JULY 20TH
QUEENS, NEW YORK

Alex swerved around a garbage truck and clipped the side mirror off a parked car. "He was limping, and I saw his face."

Imelda took a breath and tightened her seat belt. "Collins—"

"He's a fool." Alex ran a red light, drove several blocks, and slowed in front of the deserted Willets Point Station. "This is wrong. Benson won't get off here. See where the 7 goes."

Imelda found the purple Number 7 line on her phone. "Last stop, West 34th Street Hudson Yards."

"There's no way out except for taxis, local buses, and the docks." Alex checked the GPS. "What's the stop before that?"

"Fifth Avenue."

"He'll get off there and go to Grand Central, the Bus Terminal, or Penn Station and get to almost anywhere. It's a crap shoot." Alex floored the Trailblazer and headed for the Queensboro Bridge. "He'll beat us there."

"Benson might have dumped the stuff," Imelda said, redialing Collins. "We should shut the plant down." She left an urgent message when Collins didn't answer.

Benson slowly worked his way to the front of the train and stared into the dark tunnel that seemed to go on forever. The engineer was singing. ". . . if we're in a garden or on a crowded avenue . . ."

The train slowed and stopped at Queensboro Plaza. Two men and a gray-haired woman carrying a shopping bag boarded the car. Benson studied their reflections in the window as the doors closed.

Sweat dripped down Benson's face, as he sat down, and read the sign across from him: "Victimas de Accidentes, Si Resulta . . . McCarthy and Stark, 1-555-Sonorro."

The train sped up, then slowed, and stopped on a curve. Red lights ahead. No announcement. Three long minutes passed as they sat in the shadows, waiting for something to happen.

Benson got up and nervously paced the car like a tiger in a cage. Other passengers seemed unconcerned with the delay and kept on talking or sleeping. He knocked on the engineer's door and heard a radio squawk. The train jolted forward and resumed speed.

The PA crackled, "Fifth Avenue."

Waiting impatiently by the door, Benson was first out and up the steps, two at a time. On the corner of 42nd Street, he stopped and searched for cops. Finding none, he checked his watch. 12:46 a.m.

A horse and carriage clopped by—an attractive couple snuggling in back. A garbage truck and an empty bus rumbled past. Across the street, a utility hole swallowed a Con Edison worker.

Benson headed west to 8th Avenue, then continued south to the Port Authority Bus Terminal. He sidestepped three men in front of the door, passing a bottle around, and entered the lower level, where the scent of pizzas and doughnuts filled the air. The Greyhound ticket window was straight ahead. Counting vouchers, the agent didn't bother to look up at the sweating, anxious face before him.

Benson rapped his knuckles on the glass. "Tampa! Next bus!"

The agent raised tired eyes and didn't speak.

"I don't got all night."

"One fifteen. Platform 22."

"One-way."

"$107.50," said the agent. "Better hurry or you'll miss it."

Benson slid five twenties and a ten under the window.

The agent gave him change and a ticket, while glancing at the "Wanted" poster under the counter.

"Where's the platform?"

"First escalator on your right."

When Benson split, the agent dialed the number on the poster. A woman answered. "I think I just sold him a ticket . . . Yeah . . . Yeah . . . He looks like your man." He gave her the location and platform number, and she told him to stay on the line.

The APB on Alex's police radio reported a "Person of Interest" at the Port Authority Bus Terminal, Platform 22.

"It's him," said Alex, as he weaved south on Eighth Avenue through light traffic, running three red lights. He took a right on 41st Street and another onto the bus terminal entrance ramp. "If he's going home, he'll be on the Tampa bus."

Two uniformed NYPD cops entered the terminal's Eighth Avenue entrance and ran up the stairs to the second level. They paused by the door, surveying the long line of platforms in the open air departure area. Several idling buses appeared ready to go. One, belching exhaust fumes, lumbered down the ramp toward the Lincoln Tunnel.

Passengers on Platform 22 waited impatiently for the Tampa-bound bus to arrive, suitcases, bags, and boxes stacked before them on the sidewalk. A hat obscured the face of someone reclining on a nearby bench.

The rookie cop shook the person by the shoulder. "Hey! Wake up!"

"Bug off!"

The cop flipped the hat, revealing the face of a young woman. "Sorry, ma'am. We thought you were somebody else."

Neither cop saw Benson peering at them from behind a pillar fifty feet away. A clamor at Platform 30 alerted Benson to the 167 bus in the process of boarding. He snuck away, clinging to the shadows.

Three buses blocked the Trailblazer on the entrance ramp.

"Now what?" said Imelda, twisting in her seat.

Alex cut left and sped up, while bouncing over the curb onto the walkway and around the buses. A bus driver honked at him.

The cops split up to screen the waiting passengers on Platforms 30 and 38. The rookie was first to spot the suspect, running toward the 167 bound for Hackensack. He called out to his partner as he sprinted for the bus.

Benson barely made it on the bus before the closing doors. The driver released the brake and started for the exit ramp on his last run of the night, unaware of the cop shouting and pounding on the back of the bus. The driver turned to Benson standing next to him.

Benson handed him a twenty and told him to keep the change.

"I need a ticket," said the driver.

"No time." Benson slid into a seat behind the driver, who pocketed the twenty and drove on.

Alex saw the cop pursuing the 167, but couldn't follow. They were stuck behind an Intercity bus that slowed and stopped.

Alex blew the horn, and the Intercity moved, but not enough. Alex blew the horn again while the bus inched forward, allowing barely enough room for them to pass.

Imelda leaned forward, straining her eyes. They were seven vehicles behind the 167 entering the Lincoln Tunnel. "I can make out the taillights."

"Call the Port Authority Police," said Alex.

She checked her cell. "No service."

Benson bent over and put his head between his hands. His leg and back were killing him.

"Hey, Nella." The driver addressed a middle-age woman sitting across from him. "Where're those brownies you promised?"

"Tomorrow, sugar," laughed Nella. "Didn't forget."

"Course you ain't doin' my diet no good."

"You only live once," she chuckled.

"Ain't it the truth?"

Benson sat up, peered through the driver's side-view mirror, and relaxed when he saw no blinking lights behind them.

Traffic thickened as the 167 began its long climb to Weehawken. Fifty yards from the mouth of the tunnel, the line of vehicles slowed to a snail's pace and eventually stalled.

Nella clapped her hands. "What's goin' on?"

The driver leaned forward, peering at the endless line of taillights. "Accident or somethin'."

The signature siren of a rescue truck wailed in the distance. Benson rose from his seat and approached the driver. "Hey! We're almost out. Go around."

The driver glanced at Benson. "That lane goes in the other direction."

Benson shook his head. "It's empty. Nobody's on it."

"Sit down, mister," Nella said. "You're not the only person who wants to get home."

The siren on the rescue truck alerted Alex and Imelda as they sat idling in the tunnel. Alex shut off the engine and opened the driver's door. "Let's go." They got out and ran toward the 167.

Four Port Authority cops from the New Jersey side of the tunnel approached the 167 on foot. Benson pulled the Walther out of his backpack and held the barrel to the driver's head.

Nella gasped, pointing a shaky finger at Benson. "He's got a gun! He's got a gun!"

Cries of fear and alarm erupted from the other passengers.

"Shut up!" snapped Benson, waving his weapon at them.

A frightened few ducked down behind their seats, shock and fear on the faces of others. A woman covered her face in her hands, and a man in the rear stood up and began to recite the Lord's Prayer. The terror-stricken driver crouched down in his chair.

Benson pointed to the left lane. "Do it! Now!"

The driver eased the bus forward, barely clearing the pickup truck in front.

"Move it! Faster!"

Alex and Imelda watched as the 167 moved out and sprinted towards it. A cop with a flashlight stepped in front of the bus and waved it down. The bus driver swerved to avoid him, striking the guardrail with a screeching sound as the cop leaped onto the hood of a nearby car.

Benson pressed the muzzle against the driver's temple. "Faster! Faster!"

The old man trembled and sped up to thirty miles per hour. Ahead, a heavy-duty wrecker blocked the lane.

"Gotta stop!" shouted the driver.

"Keep going!"

"No, you'll kill us!"

Benson smashed the gun against the driver's head, knocking him unconscious.

The bus sped up, plowed into the wrecker, and shuddered to a stop. Benson's head struck the windshield as he fell into the door well and dropped the gun. A discharged round struck the roof, and the door automatically opened, pinning Benson's left leg against the side panel. Stunned and disoriented, he tried unsuccessfully to stand.

Terrified, screaming passengers pushed down the stairs, trampling over him as they scrambled out the door. Diesel fuel from the wrecker's ruptured fuel tank poured onto the tunnel floor.

Benson grabbed the door with both hands, and after a few frantic attempts, freed himself, and staggered off the bus. They left the unconscious driver alone in there.

Alex and Imelda ran toward the bus as the pool of leaking fuel caught fire, and they barely made it out before the flames ignited the fuel tank on the 167.

Fire engines and emergency vehicles from Weehawken, Hoboken, and Union City rushed into the tunnel and spewed powder, foam and CO_2 onto the burning vehicles. In thirty minutes, the fire was out.

Port Authority police responded quickly, directing Jersey-bound traffic back to New York, while guiding ambulances and EMS workers from North Hudson and Christ Hospital to assist the injured and bring others to safety. Paramedics transported the severely burned bus driver to the North Hudson Burn Center for medical treatment. Benson, suffering bruises and a concussion, collapsed on the pavement outside the tunnel, head resting on his arms.

Imelda caught first sight of him, and shouting to Alex, they both ran toward him. Sergeant Cooley of the Port Authority Police raised his hand. "Stand back." He pointed to the yellow ribbon strung between police cars.

Imelda flashed her ID. "This is an emergency! We have to get through here."

Cooley shook his head.

Eyes flashing, Imelda pointed to Benson as a paramedic tended to a gash over his eye.

"That man's a suspected terrorist!"

Cooley folded his arms on his chest. "We've got it covered. Move behind the line, please."

Nella approached the sergeant and shook her finger at Benson. "He had a gun! Hijacked our bus! Hit the driver! Coulda got us all killed!"

Cooley called out to a patrolman and told him to guard Benson. "Wait here," he said to Alex and Imelda.

The Port Authority Police earlier had directed detective John McKenna to halt and inspect buses bound for Jersey and apprehend Michael Benson, an armed and dangerous terrorist suspect.

But after the deadly fire and explosion, a change order directed McKenna to get people safely out of the tunnel and enable access for emergency vehicles. The change order didn't mention Benson.

Cooley spoke briefly to McKenna, who waved Imelda and Alex over. She presented her ID and nodded at Benson. "That's Michael Benson, a suspected terrorist. We've been chasing him from Queens and need to quarantine him. He's carrying a deadly bioweapon." She looked around. "We need a respirator on him before he contaminates everybody here. And I need to speak with emergency services."

McKenna cast a doubtful eye at the prisoner. "If that's Benson, my orders are to apprehend him. I need proper authorization before I hand him over to anyone."

Imelda was livid. She dialed Collins and got him on the first ring. He sounded hoarse and out of breath.

"We have Benson at the Lincoln Tunnel toll plaza. The suspect in the Bronx isn't Benson."

"We know," said Collins. "Lindsay IDed him."

"We're not sure Benson accessed the ink tank," she said. "You need to close *The Globe* and allow me to bring Benson to Federal Plaza. Here's Detective McKenna, with the Port Authority Police." She thrust the phone at the detective.

Collins briefed McKenna, providing the FBI case number. The detective hung up and called headquarters to confirm what he had heard. Headquarters immediately sanctioned Imelda's request.

McKenna told Sergeant Cooley to quarantine passengers on Benson's bus and get their contact information. Then he summoned the lead paramedic and motioned to Benson. "That's Michael Benson, a suspected terrorist in police custody. Dr. Burke has the authority to manage him from here."

Imelda pulled the paramedic aside. "Benson is a terrorist carrying a deadly bioweapon. Mask and isolate him and everyone on the 167 bus. Notify area hospitals to prepare for a health emergency." Imelda gave the paramedic her card. "Call if you have any questions."

Two medics masked Benson, as Imelda kneeled in front of him. "Where's the cylinder?"

Benson rubbed his head and looked away.

Imelda turned to McKenna. "We need a car to take him to Federal Plaza."

McKenna pointed to two plainclothes detectives. "Rinaldi and Werner will take you."

"I need to search that bus before we go," she said.

McKenna scowled. "I wouldn't go near it if I were you."

"There could be evidence inside."

"Your call."

Alex's eyes teared as he pushed the 167's battered door aside, allowing them to enter the scorched metal shell. Plastic seats, panels, and the steering wheel had melted into amorphous forms like in a Dali painting, and the air inside was barely breathable.

Imelda found Benson's charred knapsack on the floor and dumped out the contents. "The cylinder's gone," she said. "Check in back."

Alex searched the rear, as Imelda called Collins, and left a message explaining that the cylinder was missing.

Collins was on the phone with FBI Director Boyce informing him that Benson was in custody, and they had successfully apprehended all three of Vector's carriers. Boyce immediately informed the President, Malone, and Sanford.

Alex and Imelda hurried back in time to see Benson rip the respirator from his face and drop it on the ground. Imelda ordered Rinaldi and Werner to mask up, cuff Benson, and reapply the respirator.

Werner then pushed Benson into the back seat of an unmarked car and climbed in next to him. Alex and Imelda sat up front with Rinaldi who was driving, all wearing respirators. Slowly maneuvering around emergency personnel and towing equipment, Rinaldi headed towards Manhattan.

Imelda looked back at Benson. "Where's the cylinder?"

When Benson didn't answer, Werner elbowed him in the ribs. He didn't talk.

"Stop here," said Alex, when they reached the Trailblazer. "We'll follow you."

Alex and Imelda switched cars, and Alex made a K-turn, flashed his lights, and tailed Rinaldi to Manhattan.

Imelda focused on the back of Benson's head. "I've got a bad feeling about this."

"I don't think he had time to dump it," said Alex. "He wasn't near the fill pipe when I saw him."

Imelda took a deep breath. "There was so much confusion with the strike . . . We can't take the chance."

As they emerged from the tunnel, Imelda contacted *The Globe* and strained to hear a woman speaking on the phone.

"FBI," Imelda said. "Emergency. I need to speak with someone at the Queen's plant."

"Char . . . Holman. Super . . . there now."

"Louder! I can barely hear you! It's important I speak with someone at the plant!"

". . . don't know . . . transfer . . . security."

A machine answered and beeped, as Imelda impatiently detailed her reasons for shutting down the plant and left instructions to call her back as soon as possible. Disconnecting, she turned to Alex. "We've gotta seal off that plant."

She dialed Collins, got his voicemail, and hung up. "Where the hell is he!?" Desperation in her eyes. "What time do they deliver newspapers!?"

"Early." Alex checked the time. "I'll drop you off and head back to the plant. Maybe they can stop the presses."

He maneuvered around a truck and followed Rinaldi onto the West Side Highway behind flashing red and blue lights, and a siren wailing. They made it to FBI headquarters in fifteen minutes.

Special Agent in Charge Collins was in front of the building drinking coffee. Alex remained behind the wheel with the engine running, as Imelda jumped out and confronted Collins.

"We can't find the cylinder," she said anxiously. "We have to shut down *The Globe*."

"Hold on." Collins dialed Boyce and got him. "I'm with Dr. Burke at headquarters. She thinks Benson dumped the cylinder at *The Globe* plant and wants to shut it down."

Collins stopped talking as he paced back and forth, nodding

repeatedly. Imelda waited and checked her watch impatiently. She gave Collins another thirty seconds and then snatched the phone from his hand. "This is Dr. Imelda Burke with BWG. Who's this?"

"David Boyce, Dr. Burke. What can I do for you?"

"Benson won't talk and we can't find the cylinder. He might have dumped it at *The Globe*. We can't take the chance he didn't. Close the Queens plant. Do it now!"

"Three agents and the NYPD covered that plant," said the FBI Director. "There was no report of anyone near the feed pipe."

"So what? The risk is there."

"I need proof. Or there's no reason to shut it down."

"Proof? You're insane!"

The line went dead.

Fuming, Imelda turned to Collins and jammed the phone into his hand. "You do it! Shut the plant down!"

Collins' expression was incredulous. "You still think they're trying to poison the newspapers?"

"Yes. Dammit!"

"The other drivers weren't anywhere near a newspaper plant. Cool it!"

Imelda ran back to Alex. "They won't do it. Go back to the plant. Tell the manager to stop all deliveries until we can examine the newspapers. Give them my number. Hurry!"

Imelda returned to Collins. "Benson was at *The Globe* when we saw him. No question that was his target. Help me break this guy and we'll know for sure."

"He's your baby, Dr. Burke. You handle it." Collins walked away.

eighty-eight

The copy editor's hands were black with ink as he followed the production manager's instructions on how to do an ink fountain washup. It wasn't easy.

"If you're covered in ink, you're doing your job," said the manager with a smile.

The strike delayed production by almost three hours, but the mandate from management was clear: publish the paper!

The copy editor rushed to get the press online again. Behind him, the oscillating resonance of other presses unleashing the newspapers were music to his ears.

The manager gave the editor a thumbs up and marched around the pressroom, checking gauges and inspecting the sheets as they flew off press number 61. In defiance of the workers' strike, the ragtag team of editors, secretaries, and managers he assembled would run the presses, stuff ads, and load papers into U-Hauls.

eighty-nine

In a holding room on the third floor, Benson closed his eyes and laid his head on the conference table, still gasping from the respirator. Head and leg throbbing, he looked up as Imelda and a police officer walked in, wearing respirators and gloves. The cop stood at the door as Imelda circled the table. "Make this easy and tell me what you did with the cylinder."

"I know my rights," the ex-con muttered. "I don't talk without a lawyer."

"Benson, look at me," said Imelda, standing off to the side.

He sat up and looked at her.

"Think about what you're doing: how dangerous it is. You don't want to be responsible for this."

"My head hurts."

"Where's the cylinder!? Did you dump it!?"

Benson coughed into the respirator.

"You don't look so good," she said. "Are you sick? Wanna vomit? You have all the classic symptoms: bloodshot eyes, sweaty, greenish color." She sat on the edge of the table and looked down at him. "You must've known the risk." She tapped his respirator. "Did you wear one of these at Talas?"

He stared at the table. "Why would I?"

"To protect yourself. Unless . . . Unless you were vaccinated."

Benson sniffed the foul air and pointed at the respirator. "This is fuckin' killin' me."

Imelda turned to the cop with a mystified expression. "He doesn't know, officer. Do you believe that? *He doesn't know.* You're no fool, are you, Benson? You must have known what was going on: all the risks, the danger."

"I don't talk without a lawyer."

Imelda examined her gloves. "Bioterrorism is a serious crime." She turned her back on him. "Ever heard of smallpox?"

Benson sucked a breath of air.

"Terrible killer." She walked to the window, studying his reflection in the glass. He was staring at her. "We're all vulnerable. High fever, rashes, and bloody sores all over the body."

"What's that gotta do with me?"

She turned to the cop. "Don't let him take off the respirator, officer. This man could infect both of us. Kill us, too." She paced the room. "Smallpox attacks the nervous and circulatory systems. Internal hemorrhaging, terrible pain, and seizures." She stopped and faced Benson. "Most people die. New strains can kill you quickly if you don't get treatment. How do you feel?" she asked in a casual tone. "Head hurt? Nauseous?"

Benson didn't move, staring at the wall.

Imelda sighed. "Those few that survive are disfigured for life, as their bodies develop large sores filled with blood and pus that never heal. They leave deep craters on your face, chest, and hands." She let the words sink in. The only sound was Benson's labored breathing. "They exposed you—"

"Bullshit."

Imelda leaned across the table and stared into his eyes. "Don't you see? You were a sacrificial pawn. Tomek used you, Cosenza and Walsh to make millions from what you did."

Benson's jaw muscles tensed. A drop of sweat found its way to the end of his respirator, hung there, and dropped, forming a dark spot on the table. He shut his eyes.

"I don't know what Tomek told you," said Imelda, "but he sent you on a job knowing you wouldn't come back alive. He was vaccinated, by the way."

Benson squirmed in his chair and glanced up at her.

"What are you getting out of this?" She waved her arm. "Doesn't matter. Whatever it is, you won't be able to spend it."

ninety

SUNDAY, JULY 21ST
NEW YORK GLOBE, QUEENS, NEW YORK

Sanitation workers shoveled charred wood and paper, broken signs, and waterlogged trash into the back of garbage trucks, as others power washed graffiti from the walls and pavement. The noxious smell of burned rubber still polluted the air.

Alex parked as close as he could get to the plant and headed toward the gate. He stopped and looked down at the three strikers sitting on the curb.

"What happened?"

"Who're you?" snapped a woman, holding a bloody rag to her forehead.

"A friend."

"They hired scabs."

The man beside her got up and removed the sports pages he was sitting on.

"Don't touch that," Alex said before noticing it was yesterday's paper.

"Why not?"

"Nothing." Alex headed for the gate.

A cop approached him, holding a baton. "What's up?"

"Health emergency," said Alex. "I need to see the plant manager. Open the gate."

The cop stared hard at Alex. "Nobody comes in."

"Call the FBI." Alex presented Collins' number. "They'll explain what happened."

A truck horn blew.

Alex turned and saw a line of U-Haul trucks moving out the gate. "Delivery trucks?"

"Get lost!" The cop turned and walked away.

ninety-one

There was a sense of unease in the interrogation room, like the calm before a storm. Benson studied the sweat spots on the table, while Imelda looked out the window, fearing time was running out.

"Mario and Walsh are dead," she said. "And Tomek's behind bars."

"Liar!" Benson erupted.

Imelda turned to face him. "Do you know what was in that cylinder you were carrying?"

"I'm not sayin' nothin'! I wanna see a lawyer!"

"You dumped smallpox in the ink," said Imelda. "A deadly strain."

"I don't know what you're talkin' about."

She slammed her hand on the table. "Damn it, Benson! We'd be more than happy to let you die from this thing! But don't let innocent people die, too! The virus will kill you. One drop on your hands or face is fatal. You have little time left unless you're vaccinated."

Benson's eyes shifted nervously, and he wiped his hands on his shirt. "You can't let me die. There are laws . . ."

"You're involved in the mass murder of millions of people. Weighed against that, you're as dispensable as a housefly."

"We were supposed to screw up the presses. That was it."

"That's what Tomek told you," said Imelda. "Big lie. Where's the cylinder?"

Benson ground his teeth and stared at the table.

Imelda seized him by the hair and ripped out a handful by the roots. Benson squealed in pain.

"Where's the cylinder, you piece of shit? Where is it!"

"A mailbox."

"Where?"

"Northern Boulevard, somewhere." He moaned and shook his head. "I don't know. I don't know."

Imelda rushed out of the room and called Alex.

"Too late," Alex said. "The paper just went out."

Her heart skipped a beat. "Benson said he dropped the cylinder in a mailbox near Northern Boulevard. He could be lying. I don't think it can fit. But there's a chance. Look for one. If we're lucky, the cylinder's inside and it's full."

"On my way," he said.

"Don't forget your gloves and respirator." She disconnected and then called Brockman with the news. He said all hospitals and clinics were on high alert. Dunphy and Atkinson were at Roosevelt Hospital analyzing newspapers as soon as they came out. Thus far, they had tested the *New York Post* and *Daily News*. Both were clean. Meanwhile, more vaccine was being flown in from the National Strategic Stockpile. In the event of an attack, the President was ready to quarantine the entire metropolitan area and bring in the Army and National Guard to cope with widespread fear and panic.

ninety-two

SUNDAY, JULY 21ST
QUEENS, NEW YORK

Alex drove slowly as he retraced Benson's escape route, wondering if this was a fool's errand, a waste of time. The paper had already hit the streets, and people were touching it. What difference did it make? A knot tightened inside his stomach, and he took a deep breath to calm himself.

An old-style pull down mailbox was under a streetlight on a road, a block from Northern Boulevard. Benson must have run right by it.

Alex parked nearby, put on a respirator and gloves, and got the tire iron from the back of the Trailblazer. He knew he was committing a federal offense, with penalties of up to a quarter million dollars and five years in jail. But he had to open that box.

Two cops in a cruiser from the 12th Precinct slowed down when they saw him and Sergeant Steele glanced at Officer Ginsberg. "What's this joker up to?"

Intent on his mission, Alex didn't notice the approaching cruiser as he jammed the tire iron into the front panel of the mailbox. The panel bent but didn't pop. He slid the iron lower to get better leverage and tried again.

The siren and lights startled him, but he didn't stop until Ginsberg stepped out of the cruiser with his gun drawn and ordered him to drop the tire iron. It fell on the sidewalk with a loud clang.

Alex raised his arms. "I'm a private detective, working with the FBI. ID's in my hip pocket."

Ginsberg pushed him against the squad car as Steele circled behind. "Hands on the roof."

Steele removed Alex's wallet and flipped through it. "Used to be a cop, West? You should know better."

"Call the FBI. I'll give you the number."

Ginsberg pulled off Alex's respirator and gloves and cuffed him.

"It's about the terrorist APB," said Alex. "I'm looking for a metal cylinder."

Steele shook his head. "Not even the feds can go around busting up mailboxes." He frisked Alex, discovered the Glock, and reset the safety. "Licensed for this?"

Alex looked the sergeant in the eye. "You're wasting valuable time. This is a matter of life and death."

Steele slipped the Glock under his belt. "What's the number?"

Alex gave Steele Collins' number and watched as he returned to the cruiser and placed the call. Steele managed a few words and then grew silent. Two minutes later he hung up, got out of the car, and addressed his partner. "Terrorist APB, like he said. If the cylinder's inside, he can take it with him. We have to secure the mailbox."

Ginsberg removed Alex's cuffs. "Pretty damn important, if you ask me."

Alex noticed a U-Haul truck with store-stacks of newspapers turn left at the corner.

Steele gestured to the mailbox. "Be my guest."

Alex reapplied the respirator and gloves, retrieved the tire iron, and picked up where he had left off. Using all his weight, he bent the panel back far enough to see inside.

The cylinder was lying on a stack of envelopes with the cap on. He took it out and shook it. *It was empty.*

Alex stood there in a stupor, tore off the respirator, and buried his face in his hands.

Steele stared at Alex. "What? What is it?"

Alex shook his head. "Nothing. Nothing."

Ginsberg notified the Forest Hill Post Office about the break-in, as Alex collected the cylinder, the tire iron, and his gun from Steele, and drove off.

Nausea and dizziness overwhelmed him. Afraid to lose control, he stopped in a parking lot, unfastened the seatbelt, opened the door, and vomited on the pavement until he was heaving nothing but air. He waited for his stomach to settle, then phoned Imelda and left a message to call him. He closed the door and passed out in the driver's seat.

ninety-three

SUNDAY, JULY 21ST
MANHATTAN, NEW YORK CITY

Nintin Chowdhury arrived at his newsstand on Madison Avenue at 5:00 a.m., as usual. The carrier had piled multiple bundles of newspapers in front of Chowdhury's stand. *The New York Globe's* bundles looked small for a Sunday, and Chowdhury could tell the news section was missing.

He checked to see if the carrier had misplaced the bundle somewhere. Not finding it, he unlocked the stand, turned on the lights, and hauled the papers inside. With a pocketknife, he cut plastic bands on the *News* and *Post* and placed them in their metal racks.

The Globe was popular on Sundays, usually selling out before eleven. Chowdhury stood to lose sixty bucks if the paper wasn't complete. He walked outside, searching the street for the delivery truck. This had never happened before.

Returning, he unlocked the register and filled the candy rack when the jogger from 57th Street approached. She always stopped to buy the morning paper. "No *Globe* today?"

Chowdhury shrugged. "The news section is missing. Check back later. I will hold one for you."

As they spoke, a U-Haul truck stopped in front. A young man in a Harley Davidson T-shirt dropped the missing news section on the curb. Chowdhury stepped out the door ready to complain, but the U-Haul was already pulling away. The jogger waited impatiently.

Chowdhury carried the bundle inside, opened it, and quickly assembled a complete paper. He handed it to her with ink-blackened fingers.

ninety-four

SUNDAY, JULY 21ST
GLENWOOD, NEW YORK

Willy Gortz peered over the shoulder of the passenger sitting in front of him on the train bound for New York City. The man was reading *The Globe* Sports Section, and a headline proposing a new basketball stadium in Brooklyn caught Gortz's eye.

When they arrived at the Grand Central Terminal, the man dropped the paper under the seat in front of him and, using a tissue, wiped ink stains from his hands. Gortz picked up the paper as soon as the man walked out.

ninety-five

SUNDAY, JULY 21ST
SCARSDALE, NEW YORK

I t was a Sunday ritual for Karen Shelley and her husband, Bert, spending the morning in the sunroom reading *The Globe*, one section at a time. Today, she rubbed her mother's embroidered tablecloth with a wet paper towel. "The ink isn't coming out," she said dejectedly.

Bert shook his head. "They must be saving money on the ink."

ninety-six

SUNDAY, JULY 21ST
QUEENS, NEW YORK

Alex felt a burning sensation as a red sphere infused his vision, like the afterimage from a bright light or flare. Opening his eyes, he turned away from the morning sun blazing through the Trailblazer's windshield.

Pulling down the visor to block the rays, he looked into the mirror and saw a sad and anguished face. After a deep breath, he wondered how long it would take before the first person got sick. Nothing for a day or so during the incubation period. Then pandemonium would occur. Flicking on the radio, he heard the mention of a fire at the Lincoln Tunnel, turned it off, and set out for Manhattan.

In a daze, he cruised through light traffic and parked in the lot on East 41st Street. The city appeared gray and motionless to him, as if frozen by Vector's heinous crime.

Instinctively, he walked toward the Chrysler Building and was about to enter when a U-Haul truck pulled up to the curb. A stack of *The New York Globe* landed on the pavement in front of him.

Shuddering, he turned and headed toward the Hyatt. On the corner of 42nd Street, he stopped, not sure which way to go. Everything felt different now, in slow motion, and the traffic thrum was gone. Two people passed him, their voices strange and unintelligible. A mother kissed a baby in her arms and remained in that position.

He kept walking and stopped at a newsstand where a man was reading *The New York Post.* "TERRORIST PLOT AVERTED!" proclaimed the frontpage headline. Under it was a mugshot of Michael Benson staring out with those glassy eyes.

"Excuse me," said Alex, pulling the paper out of the man's hand. "Can I see that?"

"No," said the man, reclaiming it. "Get your own."

Alex saw a woman reach for *The Globe.* "Hey! Don't buy that! Don't buy any of these!"

"What are you talking about?" shouted the owner of the newsstand, thrusting his head out over the papers.

Alex pushed *The Globe* stack onto the sidewalk.

The owner shook his fist at Alex. "Get out of here, you nut! I'll call the cops!"

Alex kicked the papers into the gutter. "Don't touch them! There's poison in the ink! You'll die!"

He turned and ran toward the Hyatt, fleeing hopelessness and a sense of no tomorrow. He couldn't feel the pavement beneath his feet, and a high-pitched wail pulsed in his ears.

Crossing Fifth Avenue, he tripped and collided with two men heading in the other direction. They shouted and glared at him.

Anxiously, he ran into the hotel lobby, stepped into the elevator, and ascended to the fifteenth floor, his stress and fear intensifying with every stop.

Heart racing, he rang the doorbell to Imelda's room. No answer. Then he pounded on the door and waited. Nothing. With trembling hands and a profound sense of despair, he sank to the floor, his back against the door.

It felt like hours before the elevator door opened and she appeared and read the sorrow in his eyes.

He rose to his feet, relieved that she was there. They embraced.

"Alex," she said. "Oh, Alex." Tears rolled down her cheeks. "It's okay. It's okay."

"What do you mean?"

"The city is safe."

ninety-seven

MONDAY, JULY 22ND
MANHATTAN, NEW YORK CITY

It was a quiet evening at Thompson's Steak House. Alex had a table in the rear and sat with his back to the wall so he could spot Imelda when she arrived.

He felt anxious, uncertain of what had happened. But he believed they had miraculously avoided the pandemic. All he could remember from last night was speaking to Imelda briefly before he passed out on the couch in her hotel room. She was gone when he awoke. Her note said she'd be in meetings all day and would meet him at Thompson's at seven for dinner.

"Hey, Alex." Vickie set a glass of ice water in front of him and lit the candle on the table. "Where's your partner tonight?"

"George isn't coming."

She handed him a menu. "Can't hold court without an audience."

"I'm expecting someone."

She gave him a coy smile. "Big date?"

"Strictly business."

"Wanna drink?"

"I'll wait."

"Whenever you're ready." She headed for the kitchen.

He took a sip of water, opened the menu, and then closed it. Three people sang "Happy Birthday" to a woman with a daisy in her hair. She forcefully blew out eight candles on the cake. Cheers and claps for her 80th birthday.

The door opened, and Imelda appeared, looking radiant in a sleeveless white cocktail dress and matching heels. Blonde hair fell in waves on her shoulders. She smiled when she saw him and joined him at the table.

He got up and hugged her. "Hi."

"Hi." She sat across from him and unfolded the napkin on her lap. "You okay?"

"Yeah."

Vickie returned and handed her a menu. "Something to drink?"

"White wine," said Imelda.

"Bourbon on the rocks." Alex waited until Vickie walked away. "It's still a blur."

"We were too late," she said. "The papers were already on the streets. Hospitals were on high alert. The President was ready to quarantine the entire metropolitan area and bring in the National Guard. Smallpox turned up in *The Globe* and *Sentinel*. But . . ."

". . . the virus was harmless," said Alex.

"Yes. The genetic material degraded."

He shook his head. "I still don't get it."

"It's the ink," she said. "The regular ink company honored the picket lines and wouldn't deliver. So, to get the paper out, *The Globe* used a backup supply of *oil-based* ink. At 9:20 last night, the fill pipe automatically switched to the backup tank. Benson dumped the virus at 10:47 into the oil-based ink tank."

"Destroying the virus."

Imelda nodded. "Volatile organic compounds degraded the viral genome." She took a breath. "We were lucky. Benson successfully completed his mission. If it weren't for the strike . . ."

"A miracle."

"Yes, and our vaccine wouldn't have worked. Enslein used a deadlier strain. And it would've taken several days to produce a new vaccine, too late to stop a pandemic. Millions would've died."

For a moment, he didn't speak while staring at the table. "It's too horrible to imagine."

Vickie served their drinks and removed a pad from her pocket. "Tonight's special is shrimp scampi. Fresh from Florida."

"I'll pass," said Alex, with a fleeting thought of Talas.

"Me, too," said Imelda.

Vickie took their steak orders and headed to the kitchen.

Alex raised his glass. "Good health for everyone!"

"Right on!" She clinked his glass.

They sipped their drinks and sat for a moment until Imelda broke the silence. "Years ago, Enslein was one of the brightest virologists in the world. I studied his unpublished papers on genetics in med school. He discovered key mediators of cell-to-cell interactions before anyone else and never received credit. But his colleagues and coworkers knew he was deeply disturbed."

"Yeah, with an evil desire to victimize others while feeding his own depravity." Alex sat back, introspectively. "What happened to the gold?"

"He never got it."

"What?"

"The President stopped delivery when Enslein disappeared," she said. "He assumed Vector was dead, and the nation was safe."

Alex smirked. "The President got lucky, too."

"They never found Enslein's body, did they?"

"No."

"And Kavi? What happened to her?"

Alex shook his head. "Enslein's houseboy told the police she had gone to some tomb and never came back."

Imelda sipped her drink. "You met her, didn't you?"

He nodded.

"What did you think?"

"Dimitri called her a siren."

"Was she?"

Alex chuckled. "Maybe you could call her that. Good dancer."

"Was she attractive?"

"Not bad for a homicidal terrorist."

Imelda grinned and looked up as Vickie served their steaks. "You think there are other members of Vector we don't know about?"

"Dimitri said Interpol had evidence linking Valovitch to Enslein. It might help them break up a drug operation in the Balkans. Other than that, I wouldn't know."

"I'm glad we helped." She tasted the steak. "Good."

Alex took a bite and nodded.

"I'm heading back to the lab tomorrow."

He gave her an appraising glance. "You handle yourself pretty well *outside* the lab."

"Thanks."

Once their meals were done and plates cleared, Alex retrieved from under his chair a white box with a red ribbon and handed it to her.

Her green eyes sparkled in the candlelight. "What's this?"

He shrugged. "A little something from Rhodes."

She untied the ribbon and opened the box. Inside was an Argonauta shell, just like the one she had seen in the marketplace.

"How did you know?"

ninety-eight

J im Malone walked into Lou Sanford's office and closed the door.
"This is a surprise," said Sanford, looking up from his desk. "I figured you wouldn't be bothering me now that Vector is history."

Malone sat down and looked Sanford in the eye. "Some things never change, Lou. It's the nature of the job . . . I just came from a Cabinet meeting. I wanted to tell you that the President appreciates all you and your team have done."

"Well," Sanford said sarcastically, "that's nice of him. I attribute that to our dedicated staff. Magruder did an outstanding job."

"Yes, but the President also mentioned some issues he wanted me to discuss with you."

The CIA Director raised a disapproving brow. "Issues?"

"He's recommending a congressional investigation into your team's work procedures and intelligence gathering."

Sanford smirked. "Given the time constraints, I think we did a damn good job. I should remind him he waited to involve us."

"The President believes you made mistakes."

Sanford nodded. "They come with the job."

"He believes if you had listened to Brockman from the start and focused on Enslein, we would've avoided risking lives."

"Really? Did you tell him at the time there was no reason to believe Enslein was Vector? Why should I commit assets to someone's hypothetical opinion?"

"That *someone* was Marv Brockman," stated Malone. "His opinion carries weight."

"Yeah, sure." Sanford blew out some air. "We were busy. Serious work. We've dealt with known terrorist cells. Did the President forget we nabbed the brains behind al Qaeda's global terror network? We know how terrorists operate, Jim. Had a lot of suspects. I couldn't believe we'd trace this back to one individual, let alone a former professor and military scientist. Who could have predicted—"

"It's not our job to predict, Lou, but it *is* our job to follow the evidence, trust our colleagues, and go where the trail leads us. Remember, they have to be right just once."

"I still say there was no clear sign—"

"At the June 19th meeting, you said Enslein *wasn't on your list.*"

Sanford pushed back his chair. "He wasn't at the time!"

"Lou, the President knows your history with Brockman."

Sanford grimaced. "If I let petty squabbles affect my work . . ."

"I read Brockman's report yesterday. It mentions a call asking you to send your Athens officer to Rhodes to help locate Dr. Burke. You refused."

"I didn't *refuse*. McAuley was alone in Athens, on assignment. I told Brockman I'd look into it."

"But nothing happened. You never followed up. If it weren't for Alex West, Dr. Burke may have been killed."

"As I recall," said Sanford, "all Brockman said was that she hadn't called in."

Malone sat back and cocked his head. "You told me we'd be

better off without BWG. You also advised Boyce and Collins not to depend on them, that 'they were unreliable.' I believe those were your exact words. But this is the most critical issue, Lou. You dismissed BWG's report on the newspaper ink and persuaded Boyce not to close down *The Globe*, putting millions of lives in danger."

Sanford flushed. "No one thought the ink theory held water. We had to protect dozens of potential targets all over the city."

Malone stiffened. "I'm afraid to think about what might've happened. We were lucky, is all I can say."

Sanford's eyes narrowed as if he were staring at a bright light. He folded his arms and didn't speak.

"But it's not about that, Lou. There may be a next time. We can't afford . . ." Malone got up and glanced at the pictures on Sanford's wall. "You've got a long history with the agency."

"Twenty-eight years. I've given my life to this place, with a lot of good years ahead of me."

Malone turned and faced him. "The President thinks it's best if you retire."

ninety-nine

D unphy caught up with Alex in the cafeteria and shook his hand. "So, what's next for Inteletech?"

"No idea," said Alex.

"Come down here and work with us," Dunphy said. "We need a guy like you onboard. And Marv really likes you and wants to offer you a job."

Alex felt flattered by the compliment, recalling that a few months ago, he couldn't get people to return his calls. "I'd have to talk to my partner first. He's the business manager."

"Hey," said Imelda, approaching them with a big smile. "Did you hear? The President asked the House Finance Committee to follow through with more funding."

Dunphy gave her a high five. "I bet Marv is happy. He'll sleep well tonight."

Imelda took Alex's arm. "Excuse us, Joe. I have to talk to this guy." She looked up at Alex. "Let's get some air."

It was a warm summer night, and a light breeze blew in from the west as they strolled down Peachtree Road together. A piano concerto played faintly in a distant apartment.

On the corner of Buckhead Avenue, they waited for the light to change. A car whizzed by, blowing a scrap of newspaper against Imelda's skirt.

When she reached down to remove it, Alex held her arm. "I wouldn't touch that if I were you." Sharing a smile, they watched the paper flutter down the street and then continued their walk.

"Dunphy said Marv might offer me a job down here," said Alex.

Imelda laughed. "I told him to forget it. That you were too independent to report to someone."

"Yeah. But you and I worked together, didn't we? We were a team."

"Yes. To win and put first things first."

"Does this mean we're cool?"

"I don't know." She frowned. "I'd have to think about it."

The city grew silent as he took her in his arms.

one hundred

ONE YEAR LATER
ZURICH, SWITZERLAND

Albert Brunner, aka Gerfried Enslein, wearing a silk robe and matching slippers, checked the locks on the front door of his house on Neptunestrasse. He had little reason for concern. The Zurich neighborhood was safe and people minded their own business there.

Since arriving in Zurich, Brunner had grown a beard and bleached his dark hair white. And a facial reconstructive surgeon had straightened his nose and rebalanced his face. Brunner looked and felt like a new man.

He always watched the news on German-language TV before retiring for the night. The lead story from New York City was riveting. It covered the anniversary of Michael Benson's arrest and the U.S. government's success in thwarting Vector's sinister extortion scheme.

Gerfried Enslein's mugshot flashed on the screen. The commentator mentioned his name three times during the story and said the authorities believed him to be dead.

Brunner smiled. He felt secure living under the alias he had established years ago, and optimistic about his plans for the future—more sinister and devastating than anyone could imagine. They all deserved his vengeance.

The doorbell rang. Brunner heard Stefano get up to see who it was. He waited for a minute and then called out to him. "Who is it?"

Stefano walked into the living room, followed by Kavi, wielding a Beretta with a silencer.

A mixture of fear and anger overcame Brunner, as he blanched in shock.

"Miss me?" Kavi said, leveling the gun at his head.

"You, too, Stefano?" sputtered Brunner, glancing at his loyal friend and confidant.

Kavi fired one 9 mm round into Brunner's forehead and watched as he crumpled to the floor.

"What now?" asked Stefano, staring at his boss.

"You have his files, encryption codes, and passwords."

"He believed in me."

"As do I," said Kavi with a snickering laugh. "And we have countless worlds to conquer."

* * *